REDEMPTION OF A RAKEHELL

The Rakehells of Mayfair
Book 1

April Moran

Dragonblade Publishing, Inc. is an imprint of Kathryn Le Veque Novels, Inc.
P.O. Box 23
Moreno Valley, CA 92556
ceo@dragonbladepublishing.com

Produced in the United States of America

First Edition August 2025
Trade Paperback Edition

Dearest Reader;

Thank you for your support of a small press. At Dragonblade Publishing, we strive to bring you the highest quality Historical Romance from some of the best authors in the business. Without your support, there is no 'us', so we sincerely hope you adore these stories and find some new favorite authors along the way.

Happy Reading!

CEO, Dragonblade Publishing

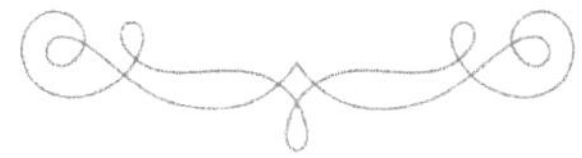

PROLOGUE

Lucien Ashcroft Westley,
Earl of Ashcroft and too many other titles to humbly list.

Mayfair, England
Spring, 1819

"HE WILL NOT budge on this, gentlemen. My father has decreed that I am to find a suitable bride, and should I fail, I will most certainly be disowned." Lucien swore, tossing back his brandy and pouring another healthy splash into the glass. His jaw clenched at the thought of his father, known to have sown quite a few of his own wild oats back in his day, decreeing anything with such permanence.

It was four o'clock on a glorious spring day in the heart of London. While most polite society gathered in the drawing rooms of Grosvenor Square's extravagant homes and townhomes for afternoon tea, the three gentlemen occupying Lucien's study imbibed far more potent libations.

"Bloody hell." Simon Blackthorne, Earl of Camden, threw a riding crop onto a chair, rubbing a hand over his furrowed brow. He'd only just arrived, cutting short a jaunt around Hyde Park during the hour when it was not so crowded. "It seems our fathers have been conspiring together. Having been issued my own edict last week, I knew it was simply a matter of time before you received yours."

"It's true," Wylder St. Clair grumbled. "The royal decree was delivered this morning when I stumbled in at daybreak." He plopped down in a chair near the fireplace and leaned over, cradling his head. "My head is still pounding from the full-throated lecture my father gave me."

"That is also caused by overindulgence, Wylder. The spirits served at The Scarlett Petticoat are known for their potency." Simon laughed softly.

The Earl of Wyldewood grinned, grabbing his glass and clinking it with Simon's. "But not so potent that it prevented me from satisfying the lovely Miss Beatrice." Tossing back the liquor, he swallowed the grimace at the taste of the brandy. "She was quite persistent, and I endeavored to prove myself worthy of the reputation the other girls touted of me. Indeed, I endeavored mightily the entire night."

"How many skirts did you bed?" Lucien inquired, his green eyes shrewd as he studied his friend.

"Just the one. But, lads, let me tell you, she possessed the stamina of ten women." Wylder closed his eyes in remembrance. "I feared I might not leave there alive, if you must know the truth. She positively wrung me dry. Which could partly explain my lackluster response to Father's declaration."

The three young earls, each no older than twenty-eight years of age, were not blood related. Having grown up together, they had formed close friendships and considered themselves even closer than true brothers would have been. With striking similarities in build, handsome looks, and charming arrogance, they cut quite a path through the *ton* as prime husband material.

Due to their unapologetic antics, they'd also earned the somewhat notorious moniker of the Mayfair Rakehells. Tall and athletic, with thick, dark hair, broad, muscular shoulders, and mesmerizing eyes, their physical attributes were complemented by sharp wit and piercing intelligence. Those attributes alone were enough to have women of all ages swooning. Still, their undeniable appeal swelled to even greater proportions when one also noted each man's abundant fortunes.

"I, for one, refuse to bow down to the senseless, archaic command that one must marry to carry on the family name," Lucien declared, his jaw clenching with determination. "I've no desire to tie myself to one woman when the world is filled with such a lovely assortment of willing bed partners. There are untold delights to be found in the gaming hells, private clubs, and brothels around this fair city… marriage would put a definite damper on the enjoyment of such things."

"On that, we are all in agreement," Wylder said, a note of something that might have been worry in his tone. Twirling his glass of brandy, his silvery gaze narrowed on Lucien. "What are we to do about it? If our fathers follow through on the threat of disinheritance, it won't matter that we choose to disobey. Not one of us will have a shilling to our name once we are cut off. Bloody hell, my family is determined to run us into the poorhouse as it stands now."

"You should invest your money more wisely, Wylder," Simon laughed. "I've been doing just that once we graduated, having seen this day coming since our days at Eton. I never relished having my funds dictated by my father, so I took steps to resolve that problem. Of course, it is impossible to enjoy a grand life on those simple funds alone, but it does put more than a bit in my pocket during those months when the allowance runs dry."

"You've always had a better head for finances than the rest of us, Simon," Lucien mused. "Perhaps we should follow your advice on such matters."

"Happy to share my secrets," Simon replied, tilting his glass in a half-mocking toast.

Lucien sighed heavily. "However, it will not change the fact I am being banished from town for the next few months."

"What?" Simon exclaimed, his blue eyes round with surprise.

"The devil you say." Wylder scowled. "It's the height of the season. Realistically, it would be impossible to find a bride if you were nowhere near the cream of the marriage mart. What can the old duke be thinking?"

"He's thinking it will sober me up and focus my attention. He is demanding I become more responsible and labors under the notion that this is the way it can be done. I've also been given a task. Ashcroft has been neglected of late, and Father says I must bring it all up to snuff. Not only that, but he has settled upon me the enormous responsibility of deciding on a new vicar. The previous one passed away a year ago and was never replaced."

"Now, that is astonishing," Simon chuckled. "If there's one thing upon which we have no personal expertise, it is in matters of the clergy."

"I don't agree with that assessment at all," Wylder drawled, lips quirking in a rare smile. "Dear, sweet Miss Beatrice called me 'God' several times during our delightful evening together."

"Regardless, I will depart in three days." Lucien ignored Wylder's irreverent observation, drained his glass of brandy, and poured yet another. "I should like to propose something I believe we each have considered recently. We all enjoy our freedoms and the amusements that come with it. Our titles provide those amusements, but it is unfair that the responsibilities associated with those same titles should bring our merriment to a crashing end. I suggest the swearing of a pact here and now. To remain bachelors forever, or at least until we grow bored with gambling, horseracing, and bedding a different chit whenever we please. We won't allow our fathers to dictate how our lives ensue. But, gentlemen, our actions must conform to what is expected of us, or all will be lost. We shall give all indications of taking our fathers' threats seriously and undertake the necessary steps of appearing to hunt for suitable brides, but only at arm's length and never seriously. They will not know this is simply a delay and diversion tactic."

"An excellent proposal, Lucien!" Simon nodded enthusiastically. "Bloody clever of you. A true military strategist, you are."

"Yes, let us raise a glass to seal the pact, my friends," Wylder said, coming to his feet and reaching for the snifter of brandy on the gleaming oak desk. He quickly refilled Simon's glass and his own.

"To our continued bachelorhood and the survival of the Mayfair Rakehells. Long may we reign," Lucien intoned, raising his glass to clink with those of his two friends. "And may no one break the bond we've sworn here today. No matter the demands of our fathers, the pleas of meddling mothers, or whatever enticements arise from a pretty bit of skirt."

A rousing cheer went up, after which Wylder grimaced and rubbed his aching temples. "Perhaps it's best we celebrate our commitment a bit less enthusiastically."

CHAPTER ONE

Lucien Westley,
Earl of Ashcroft

On the road to Ashcroft Manor in Lincolnshire

THE DEVIL HIMSELF undoubtedly crafted this coach. Lucien swore silently, gritting his teeth as the bone-jarring journey continued along the road. It appeared the driver was purposefully seeking out every bump and rut, and Lucien could not recall a more unpleasant trip than this one.

His head pounded with every jolt, his stomach revolting at the nausea-inducing sway of the vehicle. Of course, his father, the Duke of Westley, was to blame for his current state of discomfort. Had it not been for the man's banishing him to the countryside, Lucien would not have been forced to stop at the Dewdrop Inn when the ducal coach broke a wheel axle. He would not have been forced to hire this inferior coach and inattentive driver to take him to Ashcroft. And he certainly would not have drunk more than his share of the noxious brew the inn's barkeep passed off as some sort of ale.

The beverage smelled as bad as it tasted, yet Lucien overindulged anyway. There wasn't much choice in the matter, as the only other offering was gin, and he refused to drink that. Gin was the preferred drink for the poor, so even a couple of glasses were out of the question for someone of his social standing.

The pretty barmaid, eager to spend the night with an expensive toff, had flounced out of his room sometime after midnight in an angry huff. Her opinion of Lucien's inability to stand upright, much less being able to toss her skirts for an hour or two of pleasurable enjoyment, was loudly expressed while slamming the door during her exit.

Just the thought of drinking made Lucien's stomach turn over. He groaned, banging a fist on the roof of the coach.

"Damn you, man! Are you intentionally seeking out every rut and hole on this cursed road?"

"Wot, my lord?" the driver yelled back over the coach's creaks and rattles and the rhythmic pounding of the horses' hooves.

Lucien did not respond to the infernal coachman. Instead, he flopped back against the threadbare cushion of the seat, praying either the nausea would pass, or the journey would end. Neither seemed imminent. He was dying. He was sure of it. And he would expire in this dilapidated coach traveling along a pig trail of a road on the way to an estate he cared nothing about.

He was still unsure why his father banished him to the barren wilderness of Lincolnshire, other than the sole purpose of removing him from London's temptations. He knew nothing about running an estate or managing the accounts, and he surely knew nothing about hiring a new vicar to oversee the spiritual needs of Ashcroft Manor and the surrounding village.

With a heavy sigh, Lucien contemplated how long he would be forced to stay in Lincolnshire. Mr. Phillips, Ashcroft's steward, was aware of his imminent arrival, and a list of vicars seeking positions had already been assembled for perusal. Interviewing candidates would be Lucien's sole responsibility, but he'd already vowed to select the first one who showed up at Ashcroft. A couple of weeks of pretending to look over the books should be enough to satisfy his father. He would then return to London and pick up where he'd left off.

Do not forget the ruse of searching for a bride once I return to London. It must be convincing enough that Father is appeased for the time being. Eventually, he will forget the crazy notion that I must marry.

Just the thought of marriage sent a fresh jolt of nausea through Lucien. Sitting upright, he banged on the roof again, swallowing hard against the bile that swelled in his throat.

"Pull the coach over!"

"Wot's that, my lord?"

"Pull over! Now, for God's sake! Now!" Somehow, Lucien shouted loud enough that the man understood the directive. The coach squeaked in protest, the driver cursing at the horses as they pulled at the bit and slowed their pace.

Lucien waited in desperate impatience, one hand on the coach door handle, the other clamped over his mouth. He was ready to leap from the moving vehicle. Everything from the night before sloshed around his stomach until it felt like the inside of the coach was one big pint of stale beer.

Before the coach rolled to a complete stop, Lucien flung open the door, leaping from the vehicle before the folding steps could be extracted for a more dignified exit.

"We're near Ashcroft, my lord," the driver called out, watching from his perch as Lucien stumbled to the side of the road. "Can't wait that long?"

The road was bordered on one side by a wide, rolling meadow and a forest on the other. The foliage was thick on that side of the lane, and Lucien wrapped one arm around a slender oak for support. He took several deep breaths. He had it all under control… until his stomach roiled, and everything came up in one violent upheaval.

As the coachman called out sympathetic encouragement, he embarrassed himself by expelling the contents of the night.

If only the man would be silent, Lucien was confident this unpleasant business would soon be over. But it was hard to concentrate with all that infernal blathering going on.

Then, Lucien heard a female voice so annoyingly cheerful that it made him retch all the more.

Good God. The indignity of this situation is entirely unacceptable.

"Hello there!"

The horses snorted, their harness jingling as they impatiently stomped their hooves.

"Good day to you, miss," the coachman replied in a tone just as cheerful and carefree as hers.

"As I was coming across the meadow here, I could not help but... um... overhear the sounds of someone in distress," the woman asked in a voice ripe with concerned curiosity. "And I thought perhaps I could lend assistance."

"His lordship has taken ill, miss. I'm sure we will be moving along shortly."

Glancing back over his shoulder, Lucien realized he could not see her as she stood on the opposite side of the coach. Since she was only visible from the knees down, the one thing he knew for certain was that her walking boots were dusty and worn. The boot leather appeared extremely thin. Not only that, but the hem of her dress was so unfashionably short that it exposed her stockinged ankles.

Trim, delicate ankles, if Lucien cared enough to catalog their characteristics. Which, damnit, he did.

"I've no wish to intrude, of course, but I have something that might help. It is a tincture made from cardamon. Quite helpful in alleviating the symptoms your lordship seems to be experiencing. I will gladly administer it. That is if the gentleman allows me to approach."

"Don't you dare let her come over here," Lucien croaked, pointing a finger at the coachman. The older man had twisted around on his perch to gauge his passenger's reaction, a crooked smile revealing two missing teeth. "I don't require assistance." Another round of retching punctuated his rejection of the woman's offer and made the driver's grin spread wider.

"Oh," the woman tsked in a lilting, musical voice. "The poor thing. Sir?" She called out louder, although obviously, Lucien had no problem hearing her in the first place. "I promise it will make you feel a thousand times better than you do at the moment. If only you will—"

"Stay away," he growled, beyond caring if his rudeness was offensive.

"Might better listen to him, miss," the coachman interjected sheepishly. "He's not the friendliest of fellows."

Lucien glared at the man but clamped his mouth shut, afraid another wave of nausea would unman him.

"He'll be in a much better mood if he just lets me help him," the woman said cheerfully and stubbornly.

"He's being right contrary," the burly coachman added. "Do you think your concoction might work, miss?"

"I don't need your bloody help." Lucien swallowed back a moan of distress that was most unmanly even to his ears. What the devil had he done to deserve this? First, the addle-minded coachman, and now this harridan who seemed hell-bent on lending assistance he did not want.

"Sir." Her voice contained all the righteous indignation one should expect. "There is certainly no need for such profane language. I'm simply extending a bit of Christian charity—"

"Hang your Christian charity!" Lucien roared, finally reaching the far end of his patience.

There was a moment of stunned silence in the direction of the coach. The birds twittered in the trees, the wind rustling through the leaves, while the horses stomped their hooves on the rutted road until the harness jingled a merry tune. Lucien nearly held his breath as the earth seemed to pause in its rotation in recognition of his outburst.

"This is quite ridiculous." The woman sighed heavily. A moment later, she rounded the coach and the team of horses and marched with dogged determination toward the slender oak holding Lucien upright.

Lucien knew his mouth was agape. Because the woman advancing on him, her jaw set in a stubborn tilt, might have been an angel dropped straight from heaven. And somehow, although she looked hardly tall enough to reach his mid-chest, she nonetheless managed to steal the air from his lungs.

A bit of silk ribbon, inadequate for the job, tried capturing hair the color of sunshine at the nape of her neck, and a bonnet hung by its strings down her back. The golden waves streaming over her shoulders starkly contrasted with the coiffed and coiled hairstyles the ladies of his acquaintance sported. A heart-shaped face with full, pink lips pursed in exasperation was a study of heart-stopping beauty, accented by large, startlingly blue eyes fringed with thick, dark brown eyelashes. She couldn't have been much older than eighteen years of age, and while her body was slender, her curves were readily apparent. In fact, she was delightfully plump in all the places a woman should be.

She halted just out of arm's reach and pointedly averted her eyes from the evidence of Lucien's indiscretions from the previous night. Ignoring his lack of response, she dug into the oversized basket hooked in the bend of her arm and pulled out a tiny glass bottle.

"Sir, I insist you take this tincture."

Thrusting it toward him, she avoided eye contact, for which Lucien was strangely grateful. It was certainly dehumanizing that a beauty like her should witness his deplorable condition. His frustrated rage fizzled and seeped away, leaving him chagrined by his own behavior.

Slowly, taking the bottle from her gloveless fingers, he noted that her moss-green walking dress was indeed threadbare and at least three or four seasons out of date. Despite the apparent lack of wealth, she wore the garment as though it were made of the finest gossamer rather than sturdy cotton.

"Now, you must take only a drop or two at first. If the symptoms persist, you may take two more drops in four hours." She dusted her hands off, wiping them on her skirts while shooting him a quick glance to determine if he was paying attention to the instructions.

A sizzling lightning bolt of something passed between them when their eyes locked. The girl, visibly shaken, inhaled a deep breath of awareness and quickly looked away.

Lucien was equally affected. His hand tightened around the glass bottle, and his eyes narrowed in consternation as a grumbled "Thank you" slipped from his throat. He wished he had a glass of water to rinse the sour taste from his mouth, but the thought was cut short when the girl twirled away from him. In a flurry of skirts, she quickly walked toward the coach.

"May we offer you a ride to your destination, miss?" the coachman asked.

"Unnecessary, but thank you for the offer, sir." Flashing a smile at the man, she cut across the road to a section of the woods where a small trail led off into the dense trees. "That wouldn't be proper. Besides," she called over her shoulder before disappearing into the foliage, "I prefer my own company to that of rude gentlemen incapable of appreciating the kindness of others."

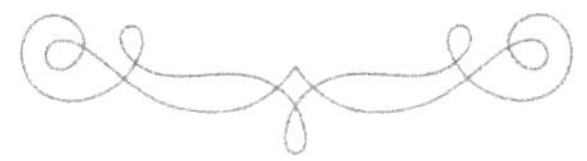

CHAPTER TWO

Charlotte Kathleen Windsor
Current resident of Hollyhock Cottage in the village of Ashcroft

CHARLOTTE STOMPED DOWN the well-worn trail, her heart pounding with something she could not identify. It left her feeling unsettled and jittery. She'd never experienced such strange emotions before.

"What a thoroughly unpleasant man!" she muttered beneath her breath. "An ungrateful, uncouth, uncommonly rude man."

A tree branch snagged the bonnet still hanging down her back, snatching her backward and nearly causing her to drop her basket. With a squeal of frustration, Charlotte untangled the bonnet from the limbs, smashed it down on her head, and continued walking. By the time the woods thinned out and the meadow surrounding Hollyhock Cottage came into view, she had calmed herself.

Although still unnerved by the encounter, she smiled upon seeing her home of the past ten years. The charming cottage, constructed of stone in warm brown and cream colors, was surrounded by a rickety, white wooden fence covered in climbing roses, hollyhocks, and fragrant jasmine. It was a whimsical little house resembling something straight out of a fairy tale. Charlotte loved it dearly and had since the day her father opened the front door with her infant sister in his arms and ushered her inside.

Her soul softened, thinking back to that sunshine-filled day. She'd cried all the way from Bristol. And as if in commiseration, her two-month-old baby sister screamed nearly the whole way as well. Charlotte's poor, frazzled father, grieving the recent loss of his wife during childbirth and now solely responsible for the care of two young daughters, was at the end of his rope. The trip to Ashcroft was brutal, but walking through the front door of the pretty little cottage instantly soothed something inside each one of them.

That day, Charlotte felt instantly at home. Even little Faith felt the peacefulness of the cottage, her screams dying away into soft hiccups as Vicar William Windsor sighed heavily and squeezed Charlotte's hand.

"Your dear mother would have loved this place," he had said quietly and with a sad smile. "It's what she wanted most for her girls: fresh air, room to run and explore, a place of our own for as long as we like. We shall visit her grave often to tell her of our adventures though, won't we?" Despite the exorbitant cost, her father had arranged for Charlotte's mother to be buried in the village's small cemetery alongside the church. It made Charlotte feel better knowing her mother was still close to the family, rather than interment in a lonely grave in the village where they last lived.

And it was an idyllic upbringing. Charlotte and Faith thrived in the village of Ashcroft, and all was well until a little more than a year ago. While walking home from the Widow Merriweather's, her father was caught in an unexpected thunderstorm. Suffering from a severe cold, he passed away two weeks later. Charlotte and Faith had been on their own ever since.

Charlotte pushed the gate open, wincing when the slightly warped wood scraped noisily against the stone pathway. The hinges were sagging again and would need repair soon.

"Is that you, Charlotte?" Faith called out from the inside of the cottage. "Are you finally home?" A second later, her sister skipped out the front door, two golden braids swinging down her back. "Did you get the eggs?"

Charlotte smiled as Faith ran to her. Her sister took the basket and slid it into the crook of her own elbow. "Did you finish your lessons?"

Faith impatiently waved her hand. "Yes, yes. All done. Did Mrs. Merriweather give us enough eggs to make tea cakes?"

Charlotte laughed. "I think so. However, I do believe my waist grows exponentially every time you bake something."

Faith scoffed, her blue eyes twinkling. "That's not true, Charlotte. You are the perfect size."

"Hmmm." Charlotte pushed the gate shut and followed Faith as she headed toward the cottage. "I'm sure I lost a pound or two in Mrs. Merriweather's chicken coop. That awful rooster of hers chased me all around it as I cleaned it and gathered up eggs."

"She hasn't made that beast into a stew yet?" Faith asked, setting the basket on the round table in the tiny kitchen. She began removing the eggs from it and placing them in a crockery bowl.

Charlotte removed her bonnet and hung it on a hook by the door. "No. But when she does, I will gladly take a bowl if she offers it." She quickly washed her hands in the washbasin and carefully returned the sliver of soap to the small dish beside it.

Faith ducked her head. "I should have gone with you to help clean the coop. At the very least, I could have kept Old Scratch at bay."

Charlotte shook her head. "No, your lessons are far more important. I managed on my own well enough." Plopping down in a chair, she smoothed her hair with one hand. "My adventures in Mrs. Merriweather's coop pale in comparison to what I encountered on the way home; I came across the most disagreeable, degenerate man I've ever had the misfortune of encountering."

Faith's eyes lit with interest. "Really? You must tell me all about it while I make you a cup of tea."

Charlotte's lips pursed. "There's not much to tell. A hired coach, obviously just passing through, had pulled over. The passenger had apparently taken ill. But when I offered my assistance, I was rudely rebuffed."

"What did he look like?" Faith set the kettle on the small potbellied stove and gathered up the items for tea. "Was he handsome or ugly as a toad?"

"His manners were certainly toadish," Charlotte grumbled.

"Ah, then that means he was not hard to look at."

Faith's smug smile had Charlotte grinding her teeth. "He smelled like a goat and was ridding himself of a night of debauchery. The stench was unmistakable."

Faith frowned. "Well, that's certainly disappointing. But it must be pointed out that you are a bit... ah... fragrant yourself at the moment."

Charlotte scoffed at her sister's reminder she'd been stomping about a chicken coop that afternoon. "I offered him the extra bottle of tincture I made for Mrs. Merriweather. The blasted man was not appreciative in the least." Charlotte could not bear to admit that the man she'd helped was indeed a fine specimen of manhood. Even hunched over and ill, his presence had been most overwhelming. With his scruffy, unshaven face and rumpled clothing, he'd given the impression of a rough and dangerous scoundrel. And Charlotte found herself intrigued despite his apparent shortcomings.

"Did you get his name?" Faith's eyes were round and guileless. "Perhaps he will need more of the medicine in the future. He could pay for the next bottle."

Charlotte shook her head. "I did not get his name, nor did I wish to. As for his illness, I suspect that if he refrained from strong drink, he would find himself miraculously healed. I don't want to talk about it anymore. It is ruining my afternoon."

"Nothing exciting ever happens around Ashcroft, and now you won't share your encounter with a handsome stranger." Faith frowned. "Do you think he's visiting Ashcroft Manor?

Perhaps he's a friend of the earl." Faith's pretty face lit up with concern. "What if he is the new vicar? Mister Phillips said Father's position would be filled the moment a suitable replacement was found."

"Mister Phillips said that a year ago. It hasn't happened yet. My hope is we still have some time before that day comes to pass." Charlotte clucked her tongue. "And Lord help the good people of Ashcroft if that man was the new vicar. A drunkard is far from a fitting replacement. Father would never approve of such a man."

Faith's apprehension about their future was on full display as she nibbled her bottom lip. "This gentleman could be in Ashcroft to apply for the position. Was he a young man, Charlotte?"

The tea kettle began to sing its ear-piercing tune. Charlotte jumped up, removing it from the stove's surface. It gave her something to focus on rather than the memory of the stranger's dark gray eyes and the funny feeling in the pit of her stomach when he stared back at her.

More importantly, she had no wish to worry her younger sister with her own concerns for their future. Once a new vicar was chosen, Charlotte and Faith would be forced to find new accommodations and a way to survive in the world. Thankfully, their father left behind a small nest egg, which Charlotte carefully doled out for their expenses. And she supplemented that with various services to the village's inhabitants. In addition to concocting tinctures for various ailments, she also tutored the blacksmith's two daughters and occasionally cleaned the Widow Merriweather's chicken coop in exchange for a few eggs. The kind, elderly woman also shared vegetables from her garden with Charlotte and Faith.

The unwelcome thought of someday leaving Ashcroft and Hollyhock Cottage brought tears to Charlotte's eyes. She could not imagine living anywhere else, although it would certainly occur at some point. To that end, she'd already started planning for employment as a governess. Mrs. Merriweather had promised to ask a friend living in London to send advertisements she could peruse for available positions.

Putting on a bright smile, she poured the hot water over the tea leaves Faith had already measured into the china cups.

"Yes, the gentleman was young. Older than myself, but a young man, nonetheless." Charlotte purposefully spoke in a cheerful voice that did not convey her secret fears. "But that is of no consequence when it comes to us, Faith, and I'm sure I'll never set eyes on him again. Now, let us speak no more of it. Let's have our tea and begin making that batch of teacakes."

CHAPTER THREE

Lucien

Ashcroft Manor's steward placed several letters on Lucien's desk.

"There are a total of nine applicants, my lord. Much better than anticipated, to be truthful. We had hoped for at least five inquiries for the position, so this is a veritable bounty of interest. Your father informed me that you will enjoy sole discretion in choosing a replacement, but I wonder if you might welcome a bit of guidance in the matter." The elderly man's smile was faint as he waited for Lucien's response. "After all, it's not every day that one must choose a new vicar who will be charged with the spiritual well-being of an entire village. It is a tremendous responsibility."

Lucien nearly groaned aloud. Obviously, the steward doubted his ability to select a suitable person for the position. As Lucien freely admitted his lack of expertise in such matters, the man's lack of faith was indeed warranted.

"Are you offering assistance with the task at hand, Phillips?" Taking a sip of tea, he grimaced. It had gone cold in the cup while he sorted the correspondence that had accrued. More than half were invitations to attend social functions at the homes of Ashcroft's neighbors or thinly veiled requests to call upon Lucien while he was in residence. News of his trip to the country estate had circulated before he even made it to the outskirts of London. His lips tightened with annoyance. He had little interest in lingering in the country long enough to socialize with the local gentry. He planned on choosing the first vicar on the list who was even remotely qualified, seeing to the man's establishment, and returning to London as quickly as possible once this ridiculous task was accomplished.

"Of course not, my lord." Phillips chuckled. "However, there is someone who might prove invaluable when considering the qualifications of each applicant."

"And who, pray tell, is this expert on hiring vicars?" Lucien asked, distracted as he studied an invitation to a soiree at Lord Edmund Nichols's home. The baron lived just a few miles from Ashcroft and preferred the country to life in town. Lucien knew this because the man's daughter mentioned it numerous times during a party they'd both attended a month ago. Joanna Nichols made no secret of her search for a husband, and Lucien endeavored to avoid the flighty brunette at all costs as a result.

"Miss Charlotte Windsor." Mister Phillips tsked, taking it upon himself to freshen Lucien's cup with hot tea, even though such duties were beneath his position. "She and her younger sister currently occupy Hollyhock Cottage."

"What," Lucien cleared his throat and took a gulp of tea, "is a Hollyhock Cottage?"

"The vicar's residence, my lord."

Lucien rubbed a hand over his jaw, feeling wholly inadequate for such in-depth conversations so early in the morning. "Am I to understand that this Miss Windsor leases the cottage?"

"Not precisely, my lord. You see, Miss Windsor is the daughter of Mister William Windsor, the previous vicar. When he passed away, she and her sister simply remained in the home. Lord Ashcroft gave no indication of desiring to evict them before a new vicar was selected. It has been advantageous for the good of the estate and the young ladies. They manage the cottage's upkeep, so it does not fall into disrepair, and in return, they live there."

Lucien scowled. Not only was he tasked with finding a vicar, but now he would also have to evict two orphans. "How long have the Windsors called the cottage home?"

"Ten years, my lord."

"And these two have lived there without paying a shilling for the past year?"

Mister Phillips' smile melted at Lucien's tone. "Well, yes. But, as I said, my lord, it has been a mutually beneficial arrangement all around."

Lucien leaned back in his chair, fixing the elderly steward with what he hoped was a disapproving stare. "I can hardly believe my father has allowed someone to occupy this cottage without receiving compensation. Please notify this… ah… Miss Windsor… that I require her presence here at two o'clock this afternoon. We shall discuss the matter and work out a repayment plan."

Damn his father for throwing this tangle into his lap without even a whisper of warning. The earl expected him to take over management of the estate? Well, he would begin with the obvious problem at hand.

"Of course, my lord. I shall have the message relayed at once." Mister Phillips's demeanor was coolly professional as he bowed at the waist. "I'm sure you will have much to discuss."

"I'm sure we will," Lucien muttered beneath his breath, dreading the moment already. There would surely be tears and begging for mercy once the lady realized she could no longer take advantage of his family's lack of attention for Ashcroft.

Smoothing a hand over his hair, Lucien stalked down the corridor, his long strides carrying him toward the east parlor. After spending the afternoon reviewing the accounts, he had discovered that even with years of inattention, the estate turned an annual tidy profit. While it was a pleasant surprise, he still had no desire to invest more energy or interest into Ashcroft than was necessary. There was a plan, and he needed to adhere to it.

Evict this woman. Select a vicar and return to London as soon as possible. Oh, and also feign interest in any suitable woman with the singular intent of deceiving Father. *But that's a task that must wait until I am back amongst the civilized members of society.*

With his hand on the doorknob, he paused outside the parlor as the tinkling laughter of a woman reached his ears. It was most likely one of the downstairs maids. A moment later, his speculation was confirmed when he recognized a second female voice as belonging to Ashcroft's plump, jovial housekeeper and wife of the estate's steward. The two women were probably preparing the parlor for the hastily arranged afternoon meeting.

Before he could turn the knob to enter the room, the door swung open, revealing Mrs. Phillips.

The elderly woman laughed upon seeing him, her blue eyes bright and friendly. "Oh, your lordship, you gave me such a fright just now! I was hardly expecting to see you standing there."

Lucien's mouth curved into a charming smile. He liked the housekeeper. She seemed to do a very fine job running the house alongside her husband. Such dedication to duty was invaluable, and Lucien certainly appreciated her efforts as the entire manor was spotless and gleaming.

"Mrs. Phillips, do forgive me for startling you. My guest should not arrive for another twenty minutes, and I'd like one of the maids to have some tea and cakes brought in."

"Already taken care of, your lordship. I also added a few small sandwiches to the tray in case you desired something more substantial. And Miss Windsor is here, my lord. A very prompt young lady, she is. Certainly not one given to arriving late for an engagement. In fact, Miss Windsor is usually early for most things."

Mrs. Phillips grinned, stepping aside so Lucien could enter the room. "I'll return in a bit and freshen the tea for you, my lord."

Lucien nearly laughed aloud when he saw that the house-keeper deliberately left the door open. It was apparent that the elderly woman believed in heading off any hint of impropriety regarding his meeting alone with Miss Windsor, as ridiculous as that seemed. But he remained silent as Mrs. Phillips hurried down the corridor.

At first, Lucien did not see her in the large room, but a slight movement by the floor-to-ceiling windows overlooking the east rose garden caught his eye. Stalking closer, the male portion of his brain noted how lovely the woman's figure was... even if only her backside was visible. She was of slender build, although the flare of her hips was apparent beneath the straight lines of her gown. Blonde hair was pulled into a low bun, and she held a bonnet by the strings in one hand. Something about her stance was vaguely familiar.

He cleared his throat. "Good afternoon, Miss Windsor. I'm so pleased you came today, as I realize it was very short notice."

She slowly turned at his voice, her blue eyes wide as their gazes clashed. "You!" she exclaimed, her mouth tight with disapproval.

"You!" Lucien growled simultaneously, recognizing the girl as the very same who witnessed his ignoble moment just the day before.

For a moment, the two did little more than glare at one another before the girl broke the silence.

"I'm relieved to see you are not the replacement for my father."

Her words were a cutting indictment, reminding Lucien of his previous indiscretion. Her statement also confused him.

"What do you mean?" Lucien frowned. What the devil was she talking about?

"Never mind." Miss Windsor pursed her annoyingly plump, pink lips and gave a tiny shake of her head. "Ignore what I just said."

"I'm afraid that's impossible," Lucien said, moving closer.

"Please... elaborate on your statement, Miss Windsor."

She shifted her feet, an expression of discomfort crossing her delicate features as she smoothed the front of her dress with one hand. Lucien noticed her garments were far more attractive than the day before. Even her shoes were in better shape. He found himself wondering why she'd dressed so shabbily before.

At her continued silence, Lucien's eyebrow arched. That resulted in Miss Windsor letting out an exasperated sigh.

"After we... ah... met yesterday, I related our encounter to my sister. She thought you might have been the new vicar, which I had to admit secretly was a possibility. I was disturbed that a man like yourself could replace our father as Ashcroft's spiritual leader." Her gaze, clear and direct, lifted to meet his.

"Instead, I find you are the man charged with selecting the new vicar. And honestly, Your Lordship, I am just as concerned about that reality as I was horrified by the former."

Lucien was momentarily stunned by the girl's bluntness. She did not bother to spare his feelings. Irritation prickled him as he realized he did not like that she had so quickly formed an unflattering opinion of his character. And the fact that bothered him at all was itself bothersome. "Miss Windsor, what you witnessed yesterday was an unfortunate event. I assure you; I am not in the habit of such public displays."

Her pretty lips twitched with what might be a smile. "I should hope you are not in the habit of private displays, either. However, Your Lordship, as lord of the manor, you have the right and wherewithal to behave however you please."

Lucien inclined slightly at the waist, fighting to keep from scowling. "I beg forgiveness for my boorish behavior."

Miss Windsor regarded him for a long moment, then sighed again. "I'm afraid I must apologize as well, Lord Ashcroft. One of my regrettable traits is being too quick to judgment and not holding my tongue when it is prudent to do so. Of course, I am not privy to the circumstances behind your illness, but I immediately thought the worst of you. And for that, I am sincerely sorry. Truly, I am."

Lucien's gaze drifted over the young woman standing in his parlor. She had such an air of innocence that he couldn't help but feel like the worst of lechers. Now that he stood closer, he saw her complexion was as smooth as cream, her slightly upturned nose dusted with a spray of golden freckles. Those wide, dark-blue eyes returned his perusal, and when she realized he'd caught her staring, her gaze dropped to the bonnet gripped tightly in her hand. She twirled the ribbons of the headpiece around long, elegant fingers as silence fell between them.

Even with her youthful appearance, Lucien quickly noted the tiredness in her features. The worry that flitted about the sparkling depths of her eyes. She carried the weight of responsibility on her narrow shoulders, and a pang of guilt struck Lucien. He had no inkling what that sort of weight felt like, but this young lady, orphaned and alone in the world, practically penniless, no doubt, and caring for herself and her sister, knew it all too well.

"I failed to properly thank you for your assistance yesterday. The… ah… medicine worked very well to alleviate my symptoms."

Taking Miss Windsor by the elbow, Lucien guided her to the settee and waited until she was settled on the green velvet seat. He ignored the tingle in his fingertips when he took the bonnet from her hand.

"Oh, I am very glad to hear it," she responded in a more breathy tone than before. Her cheeks flushed slightly pink as Lucien sank into a Chippendale chair upholstered in a pale yellow chinoiserie. The chair's frame was too delicate for his tall, muscular form, but damned if he would sit beside Miss Windsor on the narrow settee.

"Would you like some tea before discussing the matter for which I summoned you here?" Lucien reached for the teapot on the low table situated between them. He almost missed Miss Windsor's frown as he poured the first cup.

"Yes, thank you."

Taking the offered beverage, she took a sip and watched him over the china cup's rim as he prepared his own. "I will admit to being slightly mystified as to why you called me here today."

"The reasons are twofold, Miss Windsor. I believe in getting the unpleasant portion of things out of the way first, so we shall begin with that."

"I am not one for putting off bad news either, Lord Ashcroft. But what unpleasant business can we possibly have to conduct?"

"We must discuss the matter of your residency in a cottage for which the estate is owed recompense. The books indicate the last payment for the rent was a little more than a year ago." Lucien wished he had brought the ledger sheet. It would have been easier to settle the matter with the irrefutable evidence at his fingertips.

Miss Windsor's mouth parted, her face paling with Lucien's statement.

"There was an understanding—"

"Whatever was allowed in the past will not be allowed to continue now, Miss Windsor. Surely, you see the need for the estate to be reimbursed for the time you have occupied the cottage," Lucien said, taking a sip of tea. His chest inexplicably tightened at the dismay darkening Miss Windsor's lovely features, but he steeled himself before continuing. "Now, I am not without some sympathy for your plight. I know your father's passing most certainly had an impact on your income, and I wish there were another solution to this problem, but regrettably, there is not. And while the sum is not terribly substantial, it must be repaid. One way or another."

Lucien gave her a smile that he hoped would ease the sting of his harsh words.

"What exactly are you saying, Lord Ashcroft?" Miss Windsor's fingers gripped the curved handle of her teacup with such force that Lucien absently wondered if it might crack under the pressure.

"I'm saying I will collect the debt on behalf of the estate, Miss Windsor. I am lord here, after all. As I am responsible for overseeing all aspects of the estate, I have a proposal for you. It will repay the debt while fulfilling a need simultaneously."

CHAPTER FOUR

Charlotte

CHARLOTTE JUMPED TO her feet, the teacup rattling upon its saucer when she slammed it onto the table.

She could not believe what spewed from this awful man's mouth. It was of no consequence that he was beyond handsome, graced with beautiful, deep-green eyes framed with dark, thick eyelashes, and possessed a voice crafted of the smoothest honey; he was little more than a scoundrel. A rakehell above all rakehells. A bounder preying on the misfortune of those beneath him in both social standing and wealth.

Did he honestly believe she would agree to whatever illicit arrangement he'd dreamed up?

She quivered with outrage. Fear of the future. Fury that she was in a position to be so easily taken advantage of.

And regret that her dear father left behind only a small inheritance to assist his two daughters in navigating a cruel, harsh world.

Charlotte's chin tilted high.

No matter what, not even if forced to work as a scullery maid until her hands were bloody and raw, would she ever become a man's mistress to pay a debt, especially when said debt existed only in this pompous man's mind.

"Lord Ashcroft, I do not know what manner of woman you

take me for, but I will have you know I am not in the habit of taking things that I have not paid for. My sister and I have indeed occupied the cottage following our father's passing. And it is true we've not paid a traditional lease, but only because we've seen to its upkeep using our own funds while also helping the people of this village. Consider this, Your Lordship. I have cooked and cleaned for those unable to do so. I've scrubbed chicken coops and mucked stalls. I've painted, weeded gardens, and repaired gates and fences to the best of my ability. I also tutor children who require it and concoct tinctures and medicinal salves for those in need. It goes without saying, but I will say it nonetheless..." Charlotte snatched up her bonnet from the end of the settee, "I will not engage in the type of sordid arrangement men such as yourself expect from a woman in my particular situation. I am alone in this world and lacking in wealth, but thankfully, I am in full possession of high morals. I would never dishonor myself or my family in this manner, and if you had any semblance of honor and decency, you would be ashamed of yourself." Charlotte paused, her glare withering. "But I suppose one can expect no less from a rakehell of Mayfair."

His Lordship sat silent and still, his mouth slightly agape as though her impulsive and impassioned outburst dumbfounded him.

A full ten seconds ticked, the time marked by the tall case clock standing in the parlor corner. The air in the room grew stagnant even as the atmosphere seemed to electrify itself with the energy of an impending lightning storm.

Ashcroft's brow furrowed in annoyance. "What the devil are you talking about, Miss Windsor?"

"Ha!" Charlotte crowed, wagging an accusing index finger in his direction. "Don't bluster about as though you are the innocent party in this matter, Lord Ashcroft. I am the one being propositioned."

"Propo—" Ashcroft breathed incredulously, raking a hand through thick, dark hair that gleamed like black silk. He unfolded himself from the chair, rising to his full height until he towered over her. When he gripped her elbow this time, it was far from conciliatory. In fact, he held it so tightly that Charlotte squeaked in alarm as he furiously hissed through clenched teeth, "Have you gone mad? Do you honestly think I am offering to take you as my damned mistress?"

Charlotte gasped, shocked by the bluntness of the earl's question. He seemed as outraged by the insinuation of her becoming a mistress as she was. That made little sense as he was the one putting forth the proposition. The man was undoubtedly arrogant enough not to be shamed by his outrageous actions.

"Aren't you?" she shot back, her eyebrows soaring in disbelief that he was denying his intentions.

Lord Ashcroft leaned closer… and closer still until their noses nearly touched. It was entirely improper, but Charlotte could not help but notice how his eyes flashed like emerald flames. Nor could she ignore the warmth of his breath as it feathered her cheek. To an outside observer, it would appear that the earl was on the verge of sweeping her into his arms so he could kiss her. Thus, proving her accusations regarding his lack of character to be correct.

Would that be so terrible? a tiny voice deep inside her asked.

"Miss Windsor, as attractive as you are, I've no inclination to take a vicar's daughter as a mistress. I prefer my women unattached, fully experienced, and cheerfully willing to indulge my somewhat exotic desires. Whatever scenario you have concocted in that pretty head of yours is crafted from your own imagination. Maybe even a secret wish to escape the mundane existence of your uneventful life. I have other ways of seeking repayment for the year you've lived on my family's property. And they hardly involve taking you, an innocent, silly girl, into my bed." Squeezing her elbow a bit tighter, Ashcroft jerked her even closer, a slow grin spreading across his sculpted features. "However, if you are hellbent on following through with your outrageous suggestion, I will certainly entertain you. Understanding, of course, that this was your idea and not mine. I'll not stand for messy entanglements once we've both gotten what we want from our arrangement."

"Sir!" Charlotte cried out, finally coming to her senses and pushing him away with her free hand. "The last thing on my mind is forming any sort of entanglement with you."

Ashcroft released her, that wicked grin teasing her until Charlotte's knees felt weak and her cheeks flushed hot pink. "Good. Then we are in accord, at least on that point. Now, let us move on to the business of your repayment."

"There is nothing to repay, Lord Ashcroft," Charlotte gritted between clenched teeth. "I can't imagine any other way of clarifying this fact for you."

The earl's eyes narrowed slightly. "Do you have a written agreement between yourself and my father that sets forth the terms of your living in the cottage for free?"

"No," Charlotte grudgingly admitted. "But as I already explained—"

"Do you have anything giving you the legal right to remain in the cottage?" Ashcroft prodded, a look settling upon his features that indicated he was enjoying her comeuppance far too much.

"You know I do not. Why do you persist in this interrogation?"

"Because your admission is all I need to continue with my proposal, and as my father set me on this path of taking responsibility for this estate, you have become the first matter of business I will attend to. Although no money will exchange hands, and I am not entirely unsympathetic to your current plight, I will consider the matter settled if you agree to my terms." Ashcroft sat back down, indicating with a wave of his hand that Charlotte should do the same. With one leg crossed over the other, he leaned back in his chair, looking extremely pleased with this turn of events.

Charlotte frowned, intrigued despite herself. If he was not asking her to be his mistress, then what the blazes did the man expect from her?

As if commanded by a silent, higher power, she sank onto the settee with her hands folded in her lap and her bonnet clutched between her fingers. Her stomach roiled with nerves as the reality of her situation crept in. This scoundrel was attempting to trick her into some lascivious arrangement that would undoubtedly leave her compromised and eager to slink off into the shadows to conceal the shame.

Faith and I will be forced to seek other housing arrangements immediately once Lord Ashcroft gets his way. Maybe I can work out suitable arrangements in a month or two, but it would be a catastrophe right now.

"What could you possibly want from an innocent, silly girl like myself, Lord Ashcroft?" she asked primly. The fact she mocked his earlier words did not go unnoticed. The earl's mouth tightened with ill-concealed annoyance.

"Much," he replied in a husky murmur.

Before Charlotte could reply to that cryptic statement, Mrs. Phillips bustled into the room. She carried a tray containing a fresh pot of tea and more tiny sandwiches. Her pleasantly round face revealed her disappointment when she saw the tea cakes and other treats she'd set out before had gone untouched.

"My goodness, have you two talked the entire time I've been gone? You've not even touched the cakes, and Cook worked so very hard getting the batter's consistency just right."

"We've been consumed with other matters, Mrs. Phillips. I promise we shall dive right in once our business has been settled," Ashcroft drawled.

The smile he flashed at Charlotte all but dared her to reveal the nature of that conversation. She pressed her lips together, ignoring the earl's obvious amusement when she stubbornly remained silent.

"Well, I'll just freshen up the tea and make myself scarce. Ring the bell if you should need me for anything else, my lord. And Miss Charlotte, Cook made up a little package of teacakes to carry home."

"Thank you, Mrs. Phillips. You are always too kind to us," Charlotte replied with a grateful smile for the elderly woman. "Should you or Cook need more of that tincture, please let me know. I'm working on a new batch as I gave the last of it to the Widow Merriweather. Her back has been bothering her something terrible the last few days."

"Good Lord, Mrs. Merriweather is still alive and breathing?" Lord Ashcroft chuckled, eyebrows raised high in disbelief.

"Yes, and she's doing quite well for your information, Lord Ashcroft," Charlotte said with a frown. "Your concern is touching."

"That old dragon. I thought she would have died of sheer meanness long ago," the earl mused, ignoring Charlotte's sarcastic remark. "I remember once that she rapped my knuckles with her cane simply because I utilized her garden as a shortcut. I couldn't have been more than eight years old then, and she frightened me so thoroughly that I avoided that corner of the village for the remainder of the summer." The memory sent another heart-stopping grin flashing across his handsome face. Charlotte tensed at the sight of it while Mrs. Phillips smiled indulgently at the man as he sheepishly admitted, "In retrospect, I'm fairly certain I trampled a flower bed or two, so perhaps the punishment was warranted."

"I'm positive Mrs. Merriweather has long ago forgiven you, my lord," Mrs. Phillips offered cheerfully as she bustled toward the parlor's door. "Now, you two enjoy the remainder of your visit."

Once the housekeeper was gone, Charlotte focused on the earl. "I prefer to finish this matter as quickly as possible, Lord Ashcroft. If you plainly state what you wish from me, I will do everything possible to accommodate your wishes. Within reason, of course."

Lord Ashcroft's smile dimmed a little, and Charlotte wondered if he was irritated by her direct nature or at the reminder of his reluctant visit to the countryside. The arrogant popinjay was probably sulking that his fun in London had been cut short to handle the estate's affairs.

"The Church diocese will apparently replace your father with a new vicar, but because the cottage in which he will reside sits on Ashcroft land, my family has long retained the right of approval for applicants." The earl paused. "This responsibility goes beyond my area of expertise. Obviously, I know nothing about vicars."

"Obviously," Charlotte agreed with a tiny smirk. "At last, we agree on a point."

"Touché," Lord Ashcroft murmured before continuing in a brisk voice. "Here is my proposal, Miss Windsor, and I do hope you consider it very carefully, for it solves problems for the both of us. In exchange for the occupancy of the cottage, I request your assistance in choosing a suitable replacement for the position of vicar. Help me with this, and I will readily forgive whatever monies you owe Ashcroft."

CHAPTER FIVE

Lucien

"I DO NOT owe anything, my lord."

Miss Windsor's musical voice contained obvious notes of frustration, and Lucien shared it. He was quickly losing patience with her stubborn assertions.

"Shall I call in my barrister, Miss Windsor, and take the matter to the law?"

She stared at him, then visibly wilted at the threat, sinking back against the settee as an air of defeat settled over her pretty features. "I do not have the funds to defend myself, as you are fully aware." Her gaze lifted to his, the dark-blue orbs glistening with tears. "It seems I have little choice but to do as you demand."

Lucien's chest grew painfully tight at the sight of her distress. Perhaps he should soften his approach a bit more. After all, the girl was an orphan. And apparently responsible for her younger sister as well. He could afford to show a bit of charity, couldn't he?

"Your duties would be simple ones. Review the applicants' qualifications with me and attend the interviews I must conduct. This will allow you to offer opinions regarding their character. I'm sure there are certain elements one looks for in an exceptional vicar." Lucien watched Miss Windsor pick up her teacup and take a delicate sip. The gloves she wore, while spotlessly white, had been patched around one forefinger. He found himself curious regarding the condition of her hands if she truly engaged in the sort of chores she mentioned. He couldn't imagine any ladies of his acquaintance lowering themselves to manual labor, regardless of the reasons behind it.

"How long would you require me to do this?"

"For as long as it takes to select a new vicar. I hesitate in setting a timeline, but naturally, I would hope this can be accomplished in a short timeframe. I am anxious to return to the city."

"I have many other duties, Lord Ashcroft, requiring my attention. You cannot possibly expect that I have the capability of being available for an unspecified time frame." She regarded him from over the teacup's thin, gilded edge, her eyes wide with incredulity.

"Believe me, Miss Windsor. I am as eager as you to have this business behind me. I am not suited for country life and certainly I have no desire to stay at Ashcroft longer than necessary." He arched an eyebrow in what he knew was an imperialistic gesture. His friends accused him often enough of acting like a king when it came to things he wanted. "We will begin tomorrow afternoon. The first applicant, a Mister Earnest Russell, will arrive at two o'clock."

Miss Windsor set her cup down with a tiny shake of her head. The cup rattled on its saucer with the force she put behind the action. "I have other obligations tomorrow. I am sorry to disappoint you, Lord Ashcroft."

"Cancel them."

Her plump lips pressed tight as if she struggled to avoid stating her thoughts out loud. "My sister and I must eat. Mrs. Merriweather pays me a generous sum to weed her garden. I cannot afford to cancel. Besides, as I will soon be forced to find new lodgings, I must save every coin I can. So, again, I am sorry, but I cannot come tomorrow. Indeed, being at your beck and call is an unrealistic demand on your part."

Lucien was not accustomed to being denied. It was an unfamiliar feeling, to be sure. One he did not like at all. But aside from that, for some strange, bewildering reason, he also did not like the idea of Miss Windsor toiling away in Mrs. Merriweather's garden for a few shillings.

"I shall send someone in your stead, Miss Windsor."

"That is out of the question." Her head tilted as she stared at him. "I still must have the coin the task provides. And Mrs. Merriweather is very particular when it comes to her garden. She appreciates my dedication to attention and the fact I pull weeds rather than flowers."

"Blast it all, but you are a stubborn young lady. Very well, if it will move things forward, I shall pay you for the time you spend helping me. And rest assured, it will be considerably more than the paltry amount the widow pays."

Miss Windsor's burst of incredulous laughter rang out in the spacious parlor, surprising him. When she tried stifling a giggle behind her gloved hand, Lucien scowled in confusion over the source of her amusement.

"What is so funny, pray tell?" he grumbled, unable to ignore how enchanting her smile was. Her eyes sparkled so prettily, and he wondered why his face suddenly felt so warm—and damned if his hands were not damp with sweat.

"You, Lord Ashcroft," she grinned with utter delight. "First, you demand that I repay an imaginary debt and then you offer to pay me for my time. Can you not see the irony of your proposal? How at odds one is with the other? My father would call that a quandary of massive proportions and I would agree with his assessment."

"I shall pay you ten guineas for one month."

Charlotte's mouth dropped open in shock. "Are you mad, my lord? That sum is more than an upstairs maid makes in an entire year."

"Is it?" Lucien frowned, then shrugged. "The amount seems

exceedingly low to me. Should I raise it?"

"No," she said in a firm voice. "You should lower it. Regardless of the position, it is far more than what my services are worth."

"I would pay a mistress ten times that paltry amount, so in my mind, I am receiving a bargain."

Miss Windsor shot to her feet. "Lord Ashcroft! What an outrageously inappropriate thing to say!"

Lucien smiled, unabashed and intrigued that his bluntness seemed to cause such a stir with this young lady. It was... entertaining. He wondered if this might be an avenue to explore during his time in the country. Shocking the vicar's daughter and relishing her reactions could provide the perfect solution to avoiding the awful boredom of this provincial wasteland to which he'd been banished.

"I'm well known for being outrageous and inappropriate, Miss Windsor. And I'm afraid this is just the beginning of your delicate sensibilities being shocked. Now. Please sit down so that we may work out the details of what I expect from our arrangement."

⊱⊱⊰⊰

BY THE TIME Miss Charlotte Windsor left Ashcroft Manor that afternoon, Lucien was sure of one thing.

The vicar's daughter was infuriating. And so charming that it was surprisingly easy to overlook that fact.

Sitting in the manor's enormous dining room, eating his solitary dinner, Lucien contemplated the many nuances of his interaction with the young woman. She was undoubtedly beautiful. Painfully smart. Indignantly righteous. And annoyingly innocent. Had she the wealth, family name, and connections to have funded a London season or had a sponsor, she would have been snatched up and married off before the end of her first year.

When he had gripped her arm and tugged her close, the bolt of sensation coursing through his body caught him unawares. He did not expect his own reaction to touching her. Did not expect the almost giddy elation that swept through him. And he could not stop thinking about Miss Windsor's reaction to him.

Having an intimate knowledge of women, he immediately recognized that she was attracted to him. And while she would not understand the foundation of that magnetism, Lucien certainly did. She had not snatched away from his grasp. She had not rebuked him or recoiled in distaste. No, just the opposite. She had leaned toward him with a breathy, little gasp of surprise, her blue eyes wide, her soft, lithe body melting into his before she stiffened. He was positive she'd felt the same jolt of electricity, only she wouldn't comprehend that it was sexual in nature.

"She's a dangerous one," Lucien murmured, swirling a glass of claret. He took a sip, pushing his plate aside so the servants could clear the dinner service away. After a few moments of their quiet bustling, he was left alone. Contemplating this unexpected snag in his plan and how best to handle it.

He would have to be careful not to stumble headfirst into an unavoidable trap while undertaking this task of vicar hiring. Because Miss Windsor, for all her intoxicating innocence, was an unmistakable threat to a man's bachelorhood heaven.

His worries upon waking each morning were simple and selfish. What wagers had been placed at his clubs, what manner of female companionship he would find that evening, and if the supply of brandy was sufficient enough to see him through the night's amusement. That's what his life consisted of and that was all he could hope for, with the added bonus of the endless riches his family's position and titles afforded him. Nothing could be allowed to disrupt the future he believed he wanted.

But even while reminding himself to be on guard around her, Lucien could not help but anticipate when he would see Miss Windsor next. After securing her agreement to help him, he commanded that she arrive the following day in his study to evaluate their first applicant. Her eyes flashed with quiet rebellion before she pursed those plump lips and nodded consent while muttering beneath her breath how arrogant and overbearing he was.

Lucien shifted uncomfortably in his chair. Refilling his glass from the decanter left behind on the table, images of just how he would reprimand the surprisingly impudent Miss Windsor flooded his mind. Had she been his mistress, he would have wasted no time in drawing her across his lap and striking that pert bottom of hers until she cried out her apology and begged him to stop. Then he would have swept his hand up under skirts, his fingers questing until they reached high between her legs. Then, he'd know for sure just how truly chastened she was.

She would be wet for him, of course. He'd not encountered a woman in all of his conquests who did not appreciate a bit of sensual spanking before intercourse. It seemed to heighten the experience all the more. Lucien greatly enjoyed the feel of a woman's soft flesh beneath the palm of his hand. He liked seeing the pale flesh turn pink after a few strikes. He adored the whimpers and moans that let him know the woman found it pleasurable, as well as the tiny yelp when he struck a little harder just so he could soothe away that unexpected zing of pain. All of those things were incredibly intoxicating, and making a woman reach orgasm with just his hands and fingers was a task he took very seriously.

Miss Windsor, with her sheltered life and lack of carnal knowledge, was a temptation indeed. He could very clearly see himself introducing her to the lovemaking—his brand of lovemaking. The kind where the bite of pain made the pleasure all the sweeter. She would be so easy to teach. To mold. To train. No doubt, after a few sessions where he would impress upon her the value of being properly submissive, she would find a way to contain her impudence and allow him to use her as he wished.

A groan escaped him at the thought of silencing her with his cock stuffing that sassy mouth. Damned if he wasn't aroused by the idea of wrapping his fists in the thickness of her blonde hair and thrusting until he exploded, and she was forced to swallow him down.

Gulping down the remainder of the claret, Lucien cursed and bolted up from his chair. He grabbed the bottle by its neck and exited the dining room with a violent push of its heavily carved double doors. He required a bedchamber's privacy to meet his body's incessant demands. Once that was done, once he purged those images and lecherous thoughts with the stroke of his own hand, he could erase from his mind the many depraved ways he wished to fuck the lovely Miss Charlotte Windsor.

He hoped so, at least.

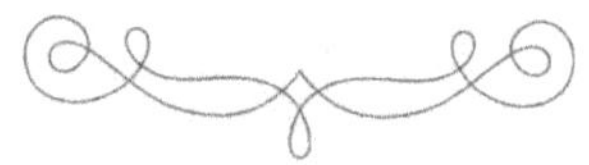

CHAPTER SIX

Charlotte

"WHY CAN'T I come with you?" Faith asked for the hundredth time as Charlotte pulled on her gloves with a frown. The stitching from the last patch was starting to come undone again. With a sigh, she added the problem to the list of many things that needed to be taken care of. Things that this ridiculous task of assisting Lord Ashcroft would take her away from fulfilling.

"I told you, darling. This is not a social visit. It is a duty that must be done, and I cannot afford you there as a distraction. You see, the quicker this is over, the better. I've no wish to drag this out."

"Is he that much of an ogre?" Faith's blue eyes widened. "Is he forcing you to go along with this… this… scheme?"

Charlotte shook her head. "He's not forcing me. No, it's more of a situation where I have no choice. I believe it's best that I humor his wishes rather than argue."

"But you like arguing. And you are so very good at it. I rarely win when you and I disagree," Faith exclaimed, flopping onto Charlotte's bed and rolling to her stomach so she could observe her older sister.

"Thank you, dear. You're becoming an expert at it yourself. Take this situation for instance. You've almost convinced me that

I should allow you to tag along. Almost." Charlotte's smile was indulgent as she patted Faith's dark-blonde head. "But alas, you cannot. I don't think it would be prudent for you to be anywhere near Lord Ashcroft."

Faith propped her chin in the palm of her hand. "Why not? Is he mad? Like old Mrs. Potts at the bakery? She threw a pastry at me the other day. Threw it right at my head and shouted that I was a cheeky girl. Thankfully, I was able to catch it. And Mr. Potts said that since it touched my hair, he could not, in good faith, sell it to an unsuspecting customer. It was strawberry with the most delicious icing."

"Faith," Charlotte tsked. "Mrs. Potts is not mad. She's just cantankerous and sometimes has a bit of trouble remembering where she is. But she's not mad." Of course, it wasn't the first time Mrs. Potts had thrown some sort of baked good at Faith. Charlotte suspected the elderly woman treated her interactions with Faith as a game of sorts. "And Lord Ashcroft is not mad, but he has exhibited a severe case of moral turpitude."

"Really?" Faith perked up, scrambling until she was in a sitting position. "Aren't you at all frightened to be around him, Charlotte?"

"Of course not!" Charlotte tugged her bonnet on and grabbed a parasol Mrs. Merriweather had given her as a birthday gift the previous year. It was a dear, flouncy little thing, and she so rarely had an opportunity to actually use it.

"You said he was quite handsome," Faith said, tilting her head. "And it goes without saying that he is rich. Maybe you can marry the earl. Then we would not have to leave Hollyhock Cottage."

Charlotte laughed out loud. "Do you think Lord Ashcroft would enjoy living in such close quarters?"

Faith huffed. "I suppose not. But you could still marry him. I'll stay here at Hollyhock while you live in the manor with the earl."

"You've worked out all the details, have you?" Charlotte

affectionately ruffled Faith's hair. She needed no reminders of either Lord Ashcroft's handsomeness nor of her unmarried, spinster state.

"Well, not all of it. You'd still have to convince the earl to propose marriage," Faith mused. "And I suppose his turpitude might be a problem. It certainly sounds like something not easily cured." The girl looked Charlotte over. "You look very pretty in that dress."

"Thank you, darling. Now, don't forget to check in on Mrs. Merriweather's garden. I want to be sure that whomever Lord Ashcroft sends over there does the job correctly."

Faith jumped off the bed, wrapping her arms tight around Charlotte's waist. Tilting her head back, she gave her sister an adoring smile. "Don't worry, Charlotte. I'll inspect it myself. Um, while you are there, will you ask if Cook has any leftover teacakes?"

Charlotte hugged her back, giving her a little squeeze so Faith wouldn't see how nervous she was about seeing Lord Ashcroft again. She had tossed and turned all night thinking of the blasted man's husky voice and sculptured jawline. "Of course I will."

"Good. And Charlotte? Do you think you can convince His Lordship to let us stay? I don't want to leave Ashcroft Village. Who would take the time to place flowers on Mother and Father's graves if we were not here to do it?"

"I don't want to leave here either, darling." Charlotte embraced her sister tighter. The reminder that their parents' graves would go unattended made her heart clench with overwhelming sadness. Hoping the worry in her voice wasn't too evident, she kissed Faith on the forehead and patted her smooth cheek. "I'm afraid I have no control over what happens once a new vicar has been chosen."

"YOU'RE CERTAINLY PUNCTUAL, I'll grant you that. It's a quality I greatly admire in a woman."

Charlotte clenched her teeth at Ashcroft's sardonic chuckle as Mr. Phillips escorted her into the earl's study. It was a room paneled in rich, dark-stained oak and gleaming brass accents. A low fire crackling in a hearth crafted from fieldstone cast the space in a warm, welcoming glow. Lord Ashcroft rose from his seat behind an enormous wood desk and strode forward to take her hand.

He kissed her knuckles, his lips barely brushing the material of her wrist-length gloves. But Charlotte felt the warmth of his breath as it drifted over her skin and barely suppressed a shudder at the sensation. Her belly felt as though it erupted with butterflies as he released her with a smile. Motioning toward a chair closer to the fireplace, he waited until she was seated before returning to his side of the desk.

"Mister Russell should be arriving shortly. Would you like some tea in the meantime?" Lord Ashcroft asked as he searched the papers on his desk. Pulling a sheaf from a stack, he handed it to her along with a pencil. "Glance over that so you will be familiar with his qualifications. And take notes if you so desire."

"Tea would be lovely, thank you," Charlotte murmured, her gaze scanning the paper. "It says here that Mr. Russell is thirty years of age."

His Lordship stepped over to push an ornate brass button set into the wall behind his desk, then took his seat, his gaze expectant as he regarded Charlotte. A glass of something rested next to his hand. A liquor of some sort, no doubt. Its color was softly amber, and as she watched, he took a small sip. "Too young or too old?"

"Perhaps just right."

"Explain." Lord Ashcroft's brow furrowed as he awaited her response.

"Ideally, you would not want the man to be too young. A great deal of what makes for an outstanding vicar is the experiences he brings with him. A young man will be lacking in those experiences. It may be difficult for some parishioners to feel connected. On the other hand, a man who is well into his years might not have the energy required to meet the demands of his flock." Charlotte continued perusing the page. "The gentleman is also unwed."

"An advantage, I'm sure." Lord Ashcroft smiled at her intake of breath.

"A disadvantage, actually. A man with a wife, indeed, even a few children, will naturally be viewed as more mature. Such a man will be far more apt to put down roots and serve the village for a long time to come. By contrast, with no obligations holding him back, a younger man may seek more lucrative positions elsewhere after a few years. I cannot say this is the case with Mr. Russell, but it is something that must be considered. My father, for example, came to Ashcroft with myself and my younger sister in tow after losing my mother to a brief illness. He welcomed the opportunity to serve in this village and raise his daughters in the fresh air and with the simple lifestyle that comes naturally with country living. A younger man might feel... trapped... for a better word."

Lord Ashcroft's head tilted as he took another sip from the glass. "I never thought of it that way. That is an excellent point, Miss Windsor. How very clever you are."

Charlotte nodded as she continued reading, her cheeks burning pink with the man's unexpected praise. "His credentials are quite impressive."

"Enough that I can justify hiring him on the spot?"

Charlotte sat up straighter, handing the paper back over and folding her hands primly in her lap. "I would not go that far, Lord Ashcroft. You should at least interview the man before making a hasty decision."

Lord Ashcroft sighed heavily. "I was hoping to avoid all the fuss. I will rely on your judgment in this, Miss Windsor. If you indicate Mr. Russell is suitable for the position, then we shall forgo the rest of the applicants, and our task will be completed. I'm sure you want that as much as I do."

A quick knock on the open door interrupted Charlotte's response. One of the undermaids hovered in the opening. "You rang, my lord?"

"Ah, yes, Trudie. I'll stick with my scotch, but will you bring a pot of tea for Miss Windsor? Include a cup for Mr. Russell as well. I'm sure when he gets here, he will appreciate a bit of refreshment."

"The gentleman just arrived, my lord."

"Excellent. Have him shown in at once." Lord Ashcroft smiled at the pretty, young maid while glancing in Charlotte's direction. "And add some teacakes as well, if Cook has some prepared. Miss Windsor enjoyed the ones we had yesterday. So much so that she took quite a few home with her."

"Those were for my sister, Faith," Charlotte blurted out, strangely embarrassed that he might think the treats were all for her. Not to say she had not eaten her share, because she had. But that was beside the point. It was rude of the man to make note of her appetite for sweets.

"Of course," Lord Ashcroft replied before his eyes flickered back to the maid. "Thank you, Trudie. That will be all." He shuffled his papers and flashed Charlotte a smirk of a smile. "Now we shall see if you are worthy of your salary, Miss Windsor."

Charlotte's gloved hands clenched into tiny fists. The man practically forced her into this position and now had the gall to gloat about it. *He is beyond insufferable!* "It is a salary you insisted upon, my lord. I would much rather be up to my elbows in weeds while tending to Mrs. Merriweather's garden. An afternoon spent on my knees is far preferable to this torturous exercise."

Ashcroft was in the process of taking another drink of scotch, but he immediately began choking as though the liquid had gone down his windpipe. With his breathing momentarily arrested, Charlotte almost considered rushing to his side and pounding his back to help alleviate his discomfort before she decided otherwise. The man deserved a bit of discomfort. Imagine drinking spirits while interviewing a man of the cloth! His irreverence for the seriousness of this task was a character defect as far as Charlotte was concerned. Lord Ashcroft was a prime example of the perils one could expect from a life overindulged and corrupted by sin and excess.

When Ashcroft finally recovered, he glared at her as if she were to blame for his coughing fit. She glared back, trying not to notice how his green eyes darkened to the hue of rich emeralds. His jaw clenched tight, a muscle ticking along its firm line. For some reason, Charlotte got the impression that His Lordship was holding back from unleashing something profound... or more likely profane, considering his lack of moral character. Even his hands were currently balled into fists, the glass in his hand in danger of becoming crushed.

"Do not tempt me with thoughts of how fetching you would look while down on your knees, Miss Windsor," he finally gritted out in a low, dangerous-sounding voice. "Such outrageous statements are akin to waving a red flag at a bull."

Charlotte swallowed hard, a hand rising to the modest neckline of her sunshine yellow-hued walking gown. She felt as if she should prepare herself to ward off a direct attack. She wasn't sure what the earl meant by that, but from the huskiness of his growl, she imagined it was quite lecherous. Before she could respond, however, the butler was ushering Mr. Russell into the room. She released a shaky breath of relief when Ashcroft's attention shifted away from her and landed on his guest, but not before the earl murmured words reached her ears.

"We shall continue this discussion, Miss Windsor, when the vicar has departed."

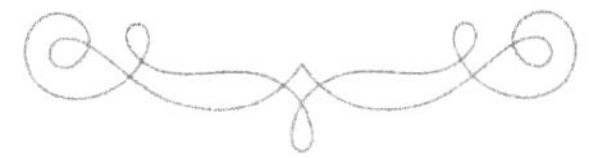

CHAPTER SEVEN

Lucien

LUCIEN HAD NEVER truly experienced envy before this moment. In general, he believed it was an emotion reserved for fools. For poets. For silly girls and schoolboys. For men suffering insecurity and searching for ways to excuse their own shortcomings.

But watching the vicar awkwardly flirt with Miss Windsor lit a fire inside his belly. It was so intense that he hovered on the verge of throwing up. The reason behind this unexpected response to the spectacle playing out before him was bewildering. But every smile exchanged between the couple and every nod of Miss Windsor's head as she silently conveyed her approval of Russell's answers to her questions fanned the flames inside Lucien higher. He eventually fell silent as the interview proceeded without his involvement. The longer he sat there, forgotten and ignored, the more resentful he became.

For the most part, Miss Windsor did not seem interested in the man's obvious attraction, but Lucien knew women to be experts in feigned disinterest. How often had he witnessed the same ploy used to force a man's hand?

"Is that agreeable to you, Lord Ashcroft?" Miss Windsor asked a second time, her gaze quizzical when Lucien's attention finally snapped to her.

"Pardon my inattentiveness, Miss Windsor. Is what agreeable?" Lucien grumbled.

Miss Windsor's head tilted. "Mr. Russell would appreciate the opportunity to view his living arrangements so that he may prepare for the possibility of moving to Ashcroft. In the spirit of moving things forward, I have suggested he pay a visit to Hollyhock Cottage sometime next week. That is, if you are in agreement."

Lucien leveled an icy glare on the hapless vicar as the man squirmed in his seat and tugged his collar. "Will you be alone with Mr. Russell?" The question came out in a faint sneer. He wanted to bite his own tongue off for that, but he couldn't seem to help himself.

The silence that fell over Lucien's study was crushing. Miss Windsor's mouth first dropped open in shock, then clamped shut into a thin line as she realized what he was insinuating.

"I cannot fathom how any of that is your business, Lord Ashcroft, but the answer is no. My sister, Faith, will be in attendance."

Lucien scoffed. "She's, what, ten years old? Hardly a suitable chaperone."

The vicar leaned forward, his brow furled into a disapproving frown. He was a handsome enough chap and possessed a pleasant manner. With a thick head of brown hair and brown eyes as earnest as his given name implied, he gave the impression of being younger than thirty years of age. "Lord Ashcroft, whatever impression I may have given during this interview, I can assure you it is incorrect. I've nothing but the utmost respect for Miss Windsor. I had the pleasure of meeting her father before he passed away, and he spoke very fondly of his children. One could tell that he cared and loved them deeply, and it greatly impressed me. Because of that respect for Vicar Windsor and for myself, I would never dishonor the man by acting inappropriately with his daughter."

"Mr. Russell," Charlotte interjected, her blue eyes burning

like sapphire flames as she continued staring at Lucien. "If you are staying at the local inn for a day or two, I would be delighted to invite you to dinner at Hollyhock Cottage this coming Saturday. Say, around four? You may look around the cottage at that time."

The vicar stood from his chair, turning his back on Lucien to take Charlotte's hand. She had removed her gloves while using a tiny pencil to jot down notes during the interview, and Lucien noticed how smooth and unblemished her fingers were. Whatever menial tasks she'd been forced to do, she'd done a fine job protecting her skin. Her fingers were pale and delicate within the other man's grip. A wave of jealousy shook him at that moment, and he had to take a deep breath to quell the urge to leap forward and yank her away from the vicar.

"It would be my honor, Miss Windsor. I look forward to making the acquaintance of your dear sister as well." The vicar gave her a sheepish smile before directing his attention back to Lucien. "Good afternoon, sir. I sincerely hope the unpleasant turn of this conversation today has no bearing on my taking the position if you offer it. I shall trust your judgment on the matter and pray that I have not offended Your Lordship."

He gave a short bow in Lucien's direction and smiled once more at Charlotte as he prepared to exit. "I hope I am not being too forward in my request, but it would be my honor to have you address me by name, Miss Windsor. I feel that we have already become friends."

Charlotte smiled at the man, apparently charmed by Mr. Russell's shy overtures. "Of course… Earnest. And you must call me by mine as well. I look forward to having you visit Hollyhock Cottage. I'm sure you will find it more than suitable for your residence if you are selected as Ashcroft's new vicar. My sister and I have been exceedingly happy there."

Earnest grinned with unabashed delight. "Until our next meeting, then."

The moment the door closed behind him, Charlotte was on her feet. Bracing her hands on Lucien's desk, blue eyes flashing like sparks from a wildfire, she hissed, "How dare you behave in such a coarse, brutish fashion, Lord Ashcroft. How dare you imply that something illicit was being planned between the vicar and myself. I extended the man a courtesy—one that you failed to exhibit. The Lord only knows why you chose to sit and stew like a spoiled child during Mr. Russell's interview, but I refuse to allow your rude behavior to be viewed as an extension of me."

Lucien rose to his feet, towering over her until she hastily stepped back. Advancing upon her, he was gratified that Charlotte retreated until her shoulders finally connected with the bookcases set into the wall. Good. Now she was trapped and glaring at him with an anger so tangible that she bristled with it like an adorable, spitting kitten.

And once again, there was that mysterious feeling of light-headedness when Lucien gripped her elbow. God, she smelled sweet. It was a heady scent reminiscent of fresh strawberries and sun-drenched linen. It made his head swim until he wondered if he was becoming ill with some unknown malaise.

"You've not invited me to Hollyhock Cottage, Charlotte," he murmured in a low snarl, deliberately placing emphasis on the use of her name. It irked him that she'd not given him leave to use it, but an impoverished vicar had her apparent approval and had been invited to dinner.

"And why would I?" she breathlessly shot back. "You may visit it anytime you please. After all, it's your property."

"Yes. It is my property. Everything within it belongs to me."

Her gaze flew to his, a strange light in the dark-blue depths that made him slightly ashamed of his thoughtlessly rash statement.

"What a horrid thing to say," she whispered. "Not everything on God's green earth belongs to you, Lord Ashcroft. No matter how much you wish it to be so."

"Call me by my given name, Charlotte," he urged, moving closer despite the warning in his brain telling him this was not wise.

"You know that would not be proper, my lord."

"Do it anyway. Why should the vicar have the pleasure of hearing his name on your lips? I demand the same." Lucien braced his free hand on the shelf above the crown of her head and waited until her face tilted upward. She possessed the most intriguing spattering of freckles across her pert nose, and he was tempted to catalog each one with a fleeting kiss. "There are so few delights to be found in the countryside. This might be one of them. I shall say please, if you are moved by hearing me beg."

"You have the uncivilized manners of a goat, Lord Ashcroft," she retorted, but her lips curved slightly despite herself. Her breathing stilled until her chest rose in shallow pants.

"One of my few flaws, if you must know the truth."

"You are terribly arrogant, too," Charlotte sniffed. "But… is it true you would really beg?" She sounded mystified by the idea, but Lucien pressed the matter. He'd beg for a smile at this juncture if it meant getting what he really desired. A compliant, sweet Charlotte in his lap with her arms looped around his neck as he kissed her into oblivion.

"I would. And I will. Please, Charlotte. Call me by my name." His voice deepened into a husky rasp that couldn't be helped. Charlotte Windsor was soft and warm. Her mouth was the perfect shape for kissing, and the flash of her eyes blended both rebellion and innocence into a tempest he could not resist. His head dipped closer to hers, delighted by the flutter of her dark lashes sweeping down. Their breaths mingled as his mouth lowered until it hovered above hers.

Lucien's gut tightened in anticipation of tasting her. Of sweeping her up into his arms and devouring every whimper and sigh. He'd thought of nothing else since the day before.

"Your Lordship…"

"My name, Charlotte," Lucien demanded in a husky murmur. "Say it."

Conflict flashed across her face. She was in danger of snapping the pencil he had given her in two. Her knuckles were white on the wooden instrument.

"I shouldn't… Lucien," Charlotte finally whispered in soft surrender, her tongue darting out to nervously swipe her lips. They parted as if ready for his kiss, and Lucien was helpless against their lure. Everything about her was intoxicating. Damned if he could explain the attraction he felt toward her. It was impossible. She was so unlike any other woman in his orbit. And other than her beauty, she certainly had little in common with his usual choice of mistresses.

"May I kiss you, Charlotte?"

Brushing his mouth over hers, Lucien inhaled her soft gasp of surprise at the question. Without conscious intent, his hold on her elbow tightened, his body bowing toward hers until he was nearly touching her slender form from hip to breast.

Christ, she's absolutely exquisite.

Indecision froze her, but then her head bobbed with the tiniest of nods.

Lucien did not wait for her to change her mind, his mouth moving over hers with more insistence until a helpless moan vibrated in the hollow of her throat. Smiling, he nibbled her plump bottom lip, laving kisses over it in a dizzying, slow, and sensual assault. "Open your mouth for me, Charlotte. I'd like to kiss you properly, and it will please me if you can think of nothing else but this during your dinner with Mr. Russell."

His murmured command broke the spell that had fallen over them. Letting out a choked cry, Charlotte pushed Lucien away.

For a moment, they stared at one another. Charlotte's cheeks flushed pink, her lush mouth trembling with unspoken emotion. As Lucien watched, she touched two fingers to her lips as if in a daze.

Lust and regret bloomed inside Lucien. He had a sinking feeling that he'd just given this girl her first real kiss.

"Wh-why did you do that?" Charlotte asked, her tone as shaky as her hands.

Lucien released her elbow, but rather than letting her slip

away entirely from his grasp, he cupped her chin in the palm of his hand. "Because I wanted to know what your lips tasted like."

"You had no right to do that."

"You gave your consent, remember? You should be glad I stopped with just a simple kiss. I won't be sorry for it, even if you changed your mind in the middle of things."

Charlotte shifted her feet, but she did not try to tear away from him. "This cannot happen again. It isn't right, and I'm not the type of woman who goes about allowing relative strangers to kiss her."

Lucien smiled. "If we knew each other better, would you allow it?"

"No!" she burst out in frustration. "You twist my words in the most disconcerting fashion, Lord Ashcroft."

"I forbid you to call me that. I have already given you permission to call me by my name. And I will be using yours, Charlotte. We have many days ahead as we work together to approve a new vicar. Being on a first-name basis will ease this tension between us fairly quickly. After all, we do have a common goal, do we not?"

"There is no need for any of this," she insisted in a panic. "I believe that Mr. Russell is likely the perfect candidate for the position. If you approve him, we can be done with this nonsense and never need to see each other again."

"That would be utterly tragic. Besides, I can hardly approve of the first candidate, Charlotte," he murmured. "You said so yourself. And there are eight others that must be seen."

"Why can't you?" Charlotte demanded. "It was your fervent wish before! You would have approved Mr. Russell without meeting him had I not insisted you conduct the interview. It makes no sense that you have now changed your mind."

"That was before I met the man and recognized his interest in you." Lucien shrugged, moving his thumb until he could caress the curve of her jawline. Her skin was soft as a peach. The urge to slide his hand further until it cupped the nape of her neck and tangled in her hair was strong, but he resisted. Such boldness might have the undesired effect of throwing her into an absolute tizzy of emotion. "Perhaps Mr. Russell believes that the perfect vicar's daughter would also make the perfect vicar's wife."

Charlotte quivered in his grasp, obviously alarmed by both his grip and the nature of his statement. "That is a ridiculous assumption about a man you just met. There is no way of determining whether or not Mr. Russell desires a wife."

"Oh?" Lucien's brow lifted high. "How do you explain the way he was shamelessly flirting with you? He was entranced by you the moment he saw you."

"Th-that's ridiculous," she sputtered indignantly.

"We've established that you believe this situation is ridiculous, my dear." Lucien released her, but only because he heard the clickety-clack of Mrs. Phillips's heels coming down the hall. Moving a safe distance away, he picked up the papers containing the information for the remaining candidates and began perusing them as his housekeeper's head appearing in the doorway.

"Pardon the interruption, Your Lordship. Mr. Mackie has returned from Mrs. Merriweather's. He is requesting a moment of your time if you can spare it."

Lucien felt Charlotte's gaze upon him but ignored it. "Very well, send him in."

Once the housekeeper was gone, Charlotte moved closer to Lucien's desk. "You sent your master gardener to Mrs. Merriweather's?"

"I couldn't trust the task to anyone other than Mr. Mackie." Lucien sat down behind his desk. Charlotte stared at him, her expression confused. Her eyes softened a bit until he said, "I've set a schedule where he tends to Mrs. Merriweather's garden once a week. You are no longer responsible for it, Miss Windsor."

"You set a schedule…" she repeated incredulously.

"No need to thank me." Lucien waved his hand dismissively. "Now, would you like to take these home with you so you may be prepared for the next interview?" He held out the stack of papers to her, but Charlotte crossed her arms, a stormy expression darkening her features.

"How dare you," she said softly, steely determination weaving through her words. "The tasks I carry out for Mrs. Merriweather accomplish many things. I help her, and she helps my sister and me. She looks forward to our time with her as she is quite lonely. Many times, I go there to sit and talk with her. Will Mr. Mackie do that? Is he willing to weed the garden and clean the chicken coop, too? Will he help her clean her kitchen and put away the pots and pans after she cooks her dinner?"

"If need be. My staff will do whatever I require of them. And you may still visit the widow, Charlotte. No one is stopping you from that noble endeavor." Lucien frowned. She was angry, but he honestly had no idea why. He thought his gesture to be quite magnanimous. "Now, I'll need you here the day after tomorrow at ten. The next potential vicar will be arriving then."

Charlotte snatched the papers from his hand, tossed them high into the air, and stalked toward the open door, where she nearly collided with the estate's gardener. Before exiting his study, she whirled and faced Lucien, who now stood surrounded by sheets of paper fluttering around him to land on the desk and the floor.

"You are an insufferable man, Lord Ashcroft. I hope someday you realize it, but there seems to be little hope for that."

CHAPTER EIGHT

Charlotte

TWO MORNINGS LATER, she was at Ashcroft Manor at precisely ten o'clock.

However, Mr. Phillips escorted her to the library this time, explaining that Lord Ashcroft would soon join her there.

Charlotte sat on one of the settees facing the east gardens, her reticule clutched in one fist and her bonnet still on her head. She'd refused to remove it as she was sure her visit would likely be short.

The past two nights had been long, restless ones for Charlotte. She'd tossed. She'd turned. She debated on not showing up for the interview but rationalized that Lord Ashcroft, as intimidating as he was, would not scare her away from facing him and ending this farce.

For that reason, she trudged down the gravel lane which led to the manor house. Faith offered to go along with her, but Charlotte refused, telling her sister to ready the cottage for Mr. Russell's visit that afternoon. Faith's enthusiasm upon learning they would have a guest for dinner had been quite encouraging, and Charlotte was sure she was doing the right thing in inviting the vicar. Of course, there was an added sense of obligation upon learning the man had been acquainted with their father.

But now, sitting in the spacious library on the same cranberry-hued settee she'd perched just days before, nerves were setting in and getting the best of her. Lord Ashcroft's behavior during her last visit had been quite surprising. She might have thought him jealous if Charlotte had not known any better. But that was a ridiculous assumption. The man would actually need to possess some sort of feeling for her. And it was quite evident that he did not. The strange incident could only be attributed to his naturally antagonistic nature. He enjoyed needling and prodding her to obtain a reaction, and he succeeded in that rather spectacularly.

Hearing a slight commotion in the hall outside the library, Charlotte clutched her reticule even more tightly. She wondered how angry the earl would be when she told him she would not return to help him with the interviews. Would he immediately toss her from Hollyhock Cottage and the estate grounds? Would he grant her a day or two to vacate? Or would he try persuading her to remain?

The money he had offered to assist him with this endeavor was the greatest incentive to stay, and Charlotte agonized over that for many hours. She could use those funds to live on while searching for employment. And they definitely would be useful in providing for the continuation of Faith's education.

But Charlotte could not justify any other reason to subject herself to the capricious mood swings of Lord Ashcroft. The twist of his mouth when he baited and teased her was unbearably appealing. The warmth of his lips upon hers even more so.

It was that fact that disturbed her the most. Realizing how much she'd enjoyed those kisses. The sharp thrill in the pit of her stomach, when he commanded that she open her mouth to him, was surprising and confusing. How could she like being ordered about like that? What lay within her soul that made it acceptable to follow his direction? What might have happened if she'd obeyed?

"Ah, you are here on time, Charlotte." Lord Ashcroft strode into the room as though he was a commanding general in the Royal Army. "You are as regular as clockwork."

"Lord Ashcroft," Charlotte acknowledged, coming to her feet as he approached. "We must discuss what occurred during my last visit and my decision as a result of your actions."

The earl frowned at the use of his title. "We're on a first-name basis, Charlotte. We established this already."

Charlotte nearly stomped her foot at the man's stubbornness. "Your Lordship, I never gave you permission to use my name."

He smiled at that but ignored her statement. "Why did the butler not take your bonnet this morning?"

"Because I have no intention of staying," Charlotte said with clenched teeth. The man was intolerable, even if he did smell like pine needles and spice.

"Of course, you are staying. Where else would you go?"

"What I mean to say is that I will not be helping you with this. It is too distressing."

Lord Ashcroft tsked. "What a shame. And I thought we were getting along quite well." He came closer, and Charlotte steeled herself as his delicious fragrance washed over her. "Is it something I did or said? Perhaps it was the kiss we shared? Were you as disturbed by it as I was? Tell me what you felt when I kissed you, Charlotte. I truly wish to know because for my part, I experienced a great deal of pleasure. I wish the moment had gone on much longer than you allowed, and I've thought of little else since you were last here."

Charlotte gaped at him. He was actually bold enough to boast aloud of the liberties he'd taken.

"That kiss should not have occurred, Lord Ashcroft," she exclaimed, her hands fiddling nervously with her reticule.

"But why not? And I again insist that you call me Lucien."

Charlotte heaved out a sigh of frustration. If using the man's name opened his ears, then she supposed she must play along with his silly game. "Lucien… that kiss was inappropriate."

He grinned wide, his handsome face lighting up with victory. "But it felt good, did it not? When I held you in my arms and traced your lips with my own, did you not also find it pleasurable?" His voice turned huskier, his eyes darkening as he reached out and took the crumpled reticule from her fingers. "I have thought about our kiss incessantly. I suspect that has been the case for you as well."

"Th-that is beside the point," Charlotte said weakly. "You cannot just go about kissing women whenever the mood strikes you."

"I've never felt inclined to do so until now, sweet little Charlotte." His head tilted as he regarded her. "Are you aware your lips taste like strawberries and cream? It is a sinful thing, really. I wonder how you accomplish it."

"Strawberries…" Charlotte stared up at him when he tipped her chin up using his forefinger. "Are you mad?"

"Perhaps," Lucien acknowledged almost cheerfully. "I've never felt such an instant attraction to a lady before. Indeed, my interactions in the past with members of the opposite sex have been quite superficial."

"I am the daughter of a vicar, my lord. And you are a lord of the realm." The reminder was a stark one, and Charlotte hoped he would see it as clearly as she did. After all, she wasn't foolish enough to believe anything would come of an earl declaring her lips tasted of strawberries. There was a world of long-held boundaries between them. Whatever he wished to accomplish with his declaration would soon die a quick death. "You must realize that I cannot help you after that unfortunate incident. You will have to find a new vicar on your own and without my assistance. In light of this, I beg that you grant me enough time to finalize new lodgings before evicting us from the cottage."

"I've no plans to evict you, Charlotte. I am not a monster despite my well-earned reputation as a rakehell," Lucien murmured, rubbing his thumb across her bottom lip as if contemplating kissing her once more. "However, I am curious. What will you do when you leave Ashcroft? Where will you go?"

Charlotte mentally shook herself from the spell he cast over her. Her knees were weak with something undefined, something that made Lucien's eyes smolder with understanding. Why did she feel she could melt into him, and he would not only allow it but encourage it?

"I will go to London. Mrs. Merriweather has a friend who graciously offered us a place to stay until we can find suitable accommodations. I have already sent a couple of letters to households advertising the position of governess. As for Faith, there is a small school for girls that I have applied for her to attend."

"I hope I can change your mind. I've no wish for you to leave just yet."

Charlotte shook her head. "What you wish is of no consequence."

"Is the money I've offered not enough? I shall double it."

Charlotte nearly choked with disbelief at the staggering amount he was willing to spend. "It is not the money, Lord Ashcroft. It is a matter of respectability and decency. Can't you understand that?"

"Oh, I do. I just find those attributes to be frequently out of my reach. Regardless, I am humbly asking you to stay. And if you do, I will absolutely double the funds." His countenance was sincere. "I'll remind you again that I cannot do this without your assistance, Charlotte. I am at your mercy here."

Her willpower was slowly depleted by his charming smile. Every objection she had listed in her head while walking to the manor house just a half hour ago was easily demolished. She cleared her throat, smoothing a hand down her dress while trying to appear brisk and business-like. "If I were to stay... *if*, you understand... then you must swear you will refrain from attempting to kiss me again."

Lucien's jaw clenched at that, leading Charlotte to suspect no female had ever before set an ultimatum of this nature with him. But if she went against her better judgment and continued with this arrangement, then she would secure his promise that he would behave himself.

"That is an impossibility, my dear. You are so infinitely kissable. It would be a shame to deny ourselves the joy that comes from indulging our desires."

"You are a reprobate, my lord," Charlotte asserted, but still, she did not pull away from the arm he snaked about her waist to keep her close. "Unfortunately for you, I am adamant about this. Swear to me, or I shall leave this house and never come back."

"If I must..." Lucien murmured, but before he actually said the words, Mr. Phillips cleared his throat from the open doorway to the library.

"Begging your pardon for the intrusion, Your Lordship. Your appointment has arrived and waits now in the drawing room."

Charlotte jerked out of Lucien's hold, backpedaling until a few paces existed between herself and the earl. Her cheeks flamed scarlet at the thought of what Mr. Phillips might have seen and heard. The smiling steward carried a sheaf of papers that looked like the ones Charlotte had tossed into the air two days before. Striding forward, he handed them to Lucien, who appeared unconcerned that they were caught practically embracing one another.

"Thank you, Phillips. If you will have Underwood show him to the library. And please let the kitchen know we would like a tray of tea prepared." Once the man had gone, Lucien nodded at Charlotte. "Remove your bonnet, my dear."

Charlotte cursed herself, but she did as he requested. Sliding the bonnet off, she noted how his expressive eyes flared with appreciation.

Faith insisted upon doing her hair this morning, and Charlotte allowed it if only to quell the questions her sister asked. She wanted to know every single detail of Charlotte's interactions with the earl. But while Charlotte did not relate the details of the kiss they shared, she did share with her sister that she did not feel comfortable working with the man. Faith clicked her tongue as if she understood and proceeded to weave Charlotte's golden waves into a fetching coil of looped braids with a few tendrils left to curl around her face.

"You look very fetching this morning, Charlotte. That hairstyle is lovely on you," Lucien said, the admiration in his tone unmistakable.

Charlotte blushed but before she could respond, the next applicant for the vicar position was shown in.

CHARLOTTE PICKED HER bonnet up from the settee, tying the ribbons beneath her chin as Lucien silently watched from his chair.

Mr. Raymond Carver had just been shown out after a rather uneventful interview. It was obvious that this particular gentleman was not suited for the position. Not only was he much older in age, but he also carried an air of superiority about him that was distinctly off-putting. Charlotte formed an immediate dislike of the man, and Lucien picked up on that. Giving her a nod, he'd taken over with the questioning as Charlotte jotted down a few notations for future reference.

"That was a hard one, wasn't it," Lucien said in a mild tone. "Not quite sure what it was about him, but Mr. Carver certainly did not make a very good impression on either one of us, did he?"

Charlotte shook her head. "He was a bit pompous, in my opinion. Hardly the sort you would like for your vicar."

"You are an astute judge of character, my dear."

Slanting him a glance, Charlotte let a smile curve her lips. "I believe I am."

Lucien sighed. "I walked right into that, didn't I?"

"You did," she agreed. "Now, if you have nothing else for me this morning, I must return home."

Green eyes narrowed slightly before a congenial smile graced Lucien's handsome features. "Ah, yes. You have company tonight. I'd forgotten the invitation you extended to Mr. Russell to come for dinner."

"You are correct, Your Lordship. I've many things to do this afternoon, so if you will excuse me…"

"May I have the honor of walking you home?" Lucien asked suddenly. "I should like to see Hollyhock Cottage myself. After all, I should be aware of its condition and any repairs that must be made before a new tenant moves in."

Charlotte bit her bottom lip. Of course, it was Lucien's right as the landowner to inspect the tiny cottage, but she couldn't help but wonder if this was a trick of some sort. "If you like."

"Excellent," he drawled while Charlotte suspected she'd played right into his hands. "When you are ready, lead the way, Charlotte."

A few minutes later, they walked down the driveway, their feet crunching on the gravel. The morning clouds had not cleared and now a cool breeze from the north was blowing, indicating a rain shower might occur in the near future.

"Do you think it will rain?" Charlotte asked when the silence between them became pronounced. Lucien did not appear inclined to break it, and Charlotte was not one to be silent for very long. Her father had always accused her of being a bit of a magpie. It was a characteristic she and her sister shared.

"I hope not. I did not bring anything to shelter either one of us," Lucien chuckled. "It would be a shame if your dress was ruined."

Charlotte blushed. She knew her gown was hardly the height of fashion. She'd managed to save enough money here and there for a few ready-made dresses from the local dressmaker, but they were simple articles of clothing and crafted of far sturdier material than the muslins and silks that were currently popular. "You are being far too kind, sir. If anything, a bit of rain might help this particular dress. I cleaned out Mrs. Merriweather's chicken coop wearing this last week, if you must know the truth."

Lucien wore a look of horror on his face at Charlotte's blunt statement, but he quickly recovered. "Still, the hunter green is quite fetching on you. The color does wonders for your skin and makes your eyes sparkle like blue topaz."

"You certainly know how to give a compliment."

"I am most sincere in giving it, Charlotte." A strange gleam lit his green eyes. "I would not say it if I did not mean it."

"Then I thank you for it," she stammered, embarrassed that the earl, with his expensive garments and shiny black boots, would bother even to notice what she wore.

"Do you think you will have difficulty finding a position as a governess?" Lucien asked suddenly. When Charlotte's foot slid on a muddy patch of road, he quickly reached out to grip her elbow in his strong hand, steadying her until their pace resumed. She tried not to think about the warmth of his hand. It burned her skin even through the sleeve of the Spencer jacket she wore.

"I am not overly confident, but I feel I have a good chance at employment. I have many attributes which are desirable. I am young, quite knowledgeable in several different subjects, and willing to travel if need be, although I do prefer staying close to London. If Faith is accepted to the girl's school we have our sights on, I would not like to be far from her. We would miss each other terribly if I were forced to live in another town. You see, we've never been separated before."

Lucien was silent, and Charlotte bit her bottom lip, wondering what he was thinking.

"Do you have any serious prospects for employment?" he finally asked.

"I've only just recently applied for a few of the openings."

A tiny frown creased his brow as a rumble of thunder echoed in the distance. "Perhaps I could be of assistance in this area."

"Do you know many families with younger children in search of a governess?" Charlotte cocked her head.

"A few," he replied in a cryptic fashion. "Although I am of the opinion that you are too young and far too pretty for such employment." His emerald gaze passed over her form. "You would be a terrible temptation to any man, I think. Even if he were the most faithful of husbands."

Charlotte bristled. "Is that what you think when you come across an attractive maid or serving girl? That her talent and worth is only as valuable as her outward appearance?"

"No, and that was not my intention while pointing out the obvious. You *are* young, Charlotte. Attractive. Feisty. But most of all, you are intelligent and capable of engaging in lively conversation. I only mean those particular qualities will be irresistible to some men. You may find yourself propositioned often as a governess. I merely mean to warn you of dangers you might not have already considered."

"I'm becoming proficient in evading such propositions, Lord Ashcroft. I have you to thank for that," she said primly.

He surprised her by throwing back his dark head and laughing out loud, amused by her tart response. "Perhaps I've not given you enough credit, Charlotte. After all, if you can withstand and deflect my overtures, then perhaps it's possible you will hold your own with the best of them." Tucking her hand in the crook of his arm, he grinned at her. "But if you are amenable to suggestions from a reprobate, I do have a few acquaintances who may be looking for a governess such as yourself, and the husbands possess just enough character and honor that I would consider them trustworthy. Will you object if I make the necessary inquiries on your behalf?"

The wind blew straight out of Charlotte's sails. Once again, she was leaping to conclusions without hearing all sides of the story. The earl was apparently sincere in his attempts to help her, and she displayed gratitude by deliberately antagonizing him with her sharp tongue.

"My apologies, Lord Ashcroft, for being so curt when you are lending assistance with my situation. It is appreciated, and I welcome anything you can do for me and my sister."

"Good." He smiled with satisfaction, his teeth blindingly white despite the encroaching cloudiness of the sky above them. "Once I've seen you safely home, I shall send out the necessary letters upon my return to the manor. I'm positive we can find a suitable household that will not only be safe but also keep you near your sister."

"That would be lovely," Charlotte agreed eagerly. "Thank you."

"Remember you are to call me Lucien," he chided as a fat raindrop unexpectedly plopped on the crown of Charlotte's bonnet. "Of course, I will continue to honor my word when it comes to paying you to aid me in finding a new vicar. Agreed?"

"Yes, Lucien." Charlotte frowned. "It is difficult to call you as anything other than Lord Ashcroft. Remembering to use your given name may take time."

"Understandable. Now, how far is it to Hollyhock Cottage? I do hope it is close by. From the looks of that raincloud, I fear you and I are in immediate danger of receiving a thorough soaking."

Charlotte tilted her head back so she could peer up at the cloud he referred to. "Oh, dear. I believe you are right. But Hollyhock Cottage is at least fifteen minutes away."

"And you've walked this distance these last few days?" Lucien grumbled in surprise. Swearing softly under his breath, he glanced down the road in the direction from which they had walked. "It's another twenty minutes back to the estate. We don't have a chance of outrunning it in either direction."

"There is an old woodcutter's cottage just up the road. Right around this bend, as a matter of fact. It has been abandoned for some time." Charlotte worried her bottom lip between her teeth. "Perhaps we could seek refuge there until the weather clears?"

"At this point we have little choice. Unless we would like a good soaking."

A few more raindrops fell as Lucien spoke. They were surprisingly cold despite the balmy spring weather the area currently enjoyed. Charlotte knew from experience that a rain shower before late afternoon would most likely be chilly. She shivered in dread of running through freezing rain before reaching shelter.

"Come on," Lucien said, grabbing her hand tight within his enormous and comfortingly warm one. "We can make it if we run."

CHAPTER NINE
Lucien

CONSCIOUS THAT CHARLOTTE could not run nearly as fast as he could, Lucien purposefully shortened his strides. He kept a tight grip on her hand as he jogged down the road, surprised that she kept up as well as she did. The rain began in earnest before they could reach their destination. Within a minute or two, they were both drenched.

Charlotte was unlike any other woman he knew. And his admiration grew with each encounter. This girl was no shrinking violet. She worked hard to take care of herself and her sister and was obviously unafraid to meet a challenge head-on. She was barely breathing hard when they finally reached the tiny cottage some distance off the main road. Standing aside on the rickety porch, she watched as he shouldered open the door and pushed his way inside.

"It's dusty and unused, but it seems relatively safe," he called over his shoulder as he stood in the center of the single room and looked around. A fireplace with a stone hearth occupied one corner, and a single rope-style bed with no ticking or mattress sat pushed against the far wall. It was the simplest of dwellings and had not been occupied for quite some time.

"The last woodcutter died almost eight years ago. He lived here while working for the e-estate," Charlotte said, moving to the center of the room. "No one has lived here since. The new woodcutter for your family l-lives in the village with his wife and s-son."

Lucien picked up a chair that was missing one leg and quickly broke it into multiple pieces. After laying the wood in the fireplace grate, he found a box of forgotten matches on the matching stone mantel and struck the sulfur stick against the fieldstone. Within minutes, the old wood caught fire and blazed to life.

Charlotte quickly moved closer to the fireplace, laying down her reticule on the hearth and reaching her hands toward the flames. "Thank g-goodness the-there were matches."

Her teeth chattered while she spoke and Lucien quickly realized she was soaked to the skin, her dress and decorative jacket providing no protection from the deluge they'd dashed through.

"Christ, you're drenched." He quickly stripped off his suit coat and shook it out by the fire, hoping the blaze would quickly dry the material. Laying it across the hearth, he next shrugged out of his waistcoat, which thankfully was as dry as a bone.

"Wh-what are you do-doing?" Charlotte asked, sidling even closer to the fireplace. Turning her backside to the flames, she reached behind her and warmed her hands.

God have mercy.

The position she'd assumed thrust her breasts into sharp prominence, her back arching slightly as she tried warming the back of her body. With her hands behind her back, she had unknowingly arranged herself in a submissive pose... one Lucien was quite familiar with. Beneath the bedraggled bonnet, her hair had fallen loose from the braids and now curled in damp waves around her shoulders. She was a temptress sent to enchant him.

"My waistcoat is dry. I want you to wear it for a bit," he explained gruffly. "Take off that jacket and your bonnet. Neither is doing you any good at the moment."

"I'm perfectly fine," she said between chattering teeth. "It-it's not the f-first time I've been caught in a r-rainstorm." But despite her protestations, she shrugged off the garment and handed it over to Lucien so he could lay it next to his suitcoat. He did not miss how her eyes skimmed his body without the additional formal garb a gentleman usually wore. When she realized his gaze was on her, she quickly looked away, her cheeks turning pink in the warm glow of the fire. Silently, she removed her bonnet, hanging it by the ribbons from an exposed nail sticking out from the wood of the mantel.

Moving to drape the waistcoat over her narrow shoulders, Lucien brushed her hair off her shoulders. It would take very little to bare her body to him. The gown, although not as fine as the material of the ladies in the *ton*, was cut in the same fashion. The tiny cap sleeves clung, just barely, to her smooth shoulders, and the silky mounds of her breasts rose above the wet material of a lacy fichu. He could make out the thin stays beneath the material, his mouth watering when he thought of how perfect her breasts must be. They strained against the slight restraint of the undergarment, and his fingers itched to set her flesh free. Would her nipples taste as sweet as her mouth? Did he even have to ask that? There was no doubt that Miss Charlotte Windsor was the most delectable thing he'd seen or tasted in quite a long time.

"Thank you," she murmured, closing the sleeveless garment so it no longer gaped open. "Are you cold, too?"

"Not in the least." That was the truth, for his body felt like it was on fire the longer he looked at this bewitching creature.

"Do you think it will rain for very long?"

"I sincerely hope not. For my own sake, at least," he muttered.

Charlotte spun around to now face the fire, leaving Lucien staring at her backside. The light of the flames backlit her entire body in the thin, wet gown. When she bent over and slipped damp slippers off her feet, he could not help the groan that rumbled from his chest.

"Are you sure you are not chilled?" She cast a suspicious glance his way while setting the footwear on the raised hearth so they could benefit from the fire's heat.

"I'm fine," he choked out. Damn if her tiny, stockinged feet were not just as appealing as the rest of her. Raising his hand to his forehead, he checked his own temperature, wondering if perhaps he was falling ill. He was decidedly lightheaded.

"You are flushed, my lord," Charlotte accused. "At least let me give you back t-this." She went to remove the waistcoat and was halted by his hand gripping her wrist.

"Leave it on, for God's sake," he rasped. "If there's an ounce of self-preservation in your body, leave it on."

She stared at him, a dawning light of understanding in her expressive eyes. "I'm sorry."

He shook his head, exasperated by the unnecessary apology. "Don't be. You cannot help how my body reacts to seeing you like this." His grip shifted until he could twine his fingers with hers. He held her hand for a long moment, marveling at how much smaller it was than his. Her fingers were slender. Delicate. And yet, they were as strong as fibers of woven silk. She shivered in his grasp but kept her eyes downcast, which disturbed him for some unknown reason. He wanted to stare into her eyes as he tried to determine the reason for this strange attraction between them. Hell, he wanted to drown in those mysterious blue pools and never come up for air.

"I wish I had some other way to warm you," he murmured, moving closer.

Charlotte's eyelashes fluttered shut, and a little sigh slipped from between her parted lips. "You are very warm." The words came out in a whisper. "S-standing so close to you is h-helping a great deal."

Lucien noted that her teeth were not chattering nearly as fiercely as earlier. Without thinking, he slid his hands to her upper arms and began rubbing them in a soothing fashion. The friction of his palms on her bare skin sent shock waves throughout his entire body. He moved closer, still. "You must be cold as an icicle in this dress."

Charlotte nodded wordlessly, her eyes remaining closed as she swayed with the motion of his hands. For a period of time, he simply sought to warm her, and her eyes never opened. Only when he paused to check on the dryness of his coat did she peek up at him.

"You'll be a bit warmer with this on," he murmured, shaking out the coat and layering it over her shoulders. The material did not allow for the moisture to penetrate very deeply and the fire dried it enough that it could be worn now. Charlotte huddled into it with a sigh of gratitude.

"You are right. That is much better." A giggle escaped her. "If your boots were not so large, I would demand the use of those as well. I don't think I can feel my toes at the moment."

Lucien glanced down at her feet, watching as her stockinged toes curled against the cold surface of the rough, wood floor. His gaze swept the cabin, looking for something he could set her upon.

"Wait here a moment, my dear."

There was a rickety table against the far wall. It was small and must have been used by the woodcutter for his meals. Dragging it toward the fire, Lucien ensured it was close enough to the raised hearth. Then, without explanation, he circled Charlotte's tiny waist with his hands and lifted her until she sat on its surface.

"What on earth are you doing?" she asked in surprise, her arms automatically wrapping around his neck for support.

Lucien paused, his body naturally pressing between her thighs when she parted them to balance herself. Their faces were now just inches apart, their mouths so close they shared the same breath. Their position was scandalous, and if anyone happened upon them at that moment, they would find themselves married before the end of the day.

And regardless of his rakehell reputation and love of bachelorhood, Lucien could not think of a single reason to hate that idea.

"Lucien," Charlotte whispered, her eyes glowing softly in the firelight. "What are you doing?"

A crooked smile lifted his lips. "I think I'm going to kiss you. But only if you agree to it, Charlotte. You see, I am adhering to the rules you set before."

"Aren't rakehells known for breaking the rules?"

"My life has revolved around that very concept," Lucien breathed, his mouth hovering over hers until her breath came in little gasps. He watched the pupils of her eyes dilate and knew she was experiencing the same arousal he felt. "Have you ever felt desire before, Charlotte? Have you ever wanted someone so badly that you thought you might expire if you did not possess that person completely?"

Her eyes widened with his words, but she shook her head. "No. No, I have not. I imagine that you have, though. I imagine that you have experienced that with many women in the past."

Lucien ducked his head, suddenly shamed by the extent of his lascivious exploits. Charlotte's innocence was leaving an indelible mark on his soul. He found himself reluctant to ruin her for his own selfish amusements but damned if he could restrain himself around her. She was quickly becoming an obsession. A treasure he wished to possess and keep safe from a cruel, harsh world. Of course, she would never agree to become his mistress, but if he could help her so that navigating life was a little less complicated, if she would allow it, he would.

With a sigh of his own, he leaned away from her, but Charlotte frowned, her arms tightening around his neck and keeping him from retreating very far.

"Are you not going to kiss me, Lucien?" she asked, her eyes wide and guileless. Her tiny pink tongue swiped her bottom lip, and Lucien groaned inwardly.

"Are you sure you want that?"

She thought about it for a moment, then slowly nodded her head. "I think I do. I think this may be the last time I have an opportunity like this with a man such as yourself. I shall remember this moment with fondness when I am old and gray. Being kissed by a handsome earl, both of us drenched by a sudden spring rainstorm. I shall remember this ancient, dusty cottage and the warmth of the fire and the smell of the wood burning." Her elegant fingers curled themselves into his thick, dark hair at the nape of his neck, and Lucien sighed like a big cat being stroked by his master. "And I shall remember how strangely my body reacted to being kissed. How my heart pounded with such ferocity that I thought it might leap from my chest. I will remember that the man kissing me had shoulders so broad they blocked out the light from the fireplace and how his skin burned mine wherever he touched me." Charlotte met his gaze, her chin lifting as they stared at one another. "I shall remember all of this because it will never happen again, and if I have one memory of my own to treasure until the day I die, I want this one. I deserve it, I think."

"You deserve so much more, sweet little Charlotte, but if you think I will not kiss you again, you are quite mistaken." Lucien's tone was hoarse; his body reacting almost violently to her impassioned words. "I will kiss you often if you agree to it. I won't be able to help myself, and I will ensure you won't be able to help yourself either."

Charlotte shook her head, a sad smile curving her lips. "I'm afraid that will not be possible. You are an earl and a confirmed bachelor. I am a vicar's daughter who must make her own way in this world. There is no scenario where our lives entwine beyond this moment. *This moment.* Here. Now. So take your kiss, Lucien. Take it while giving me something to remember forever."

Lucien considered arguing, but when Charlotte's fingers tightened, tugging him closer, he gave in with a single purpose in mind.

He would give her something to remember for the rest of her life. Something to remember *him* forever.

CHAPTER TEN
Charlotte

THE MOMENT HIS lips touched hers, Charlotte was lost. And it was foolish of her to wish it, but the thought that the earl might be affected by their kiss in the same manner warmed her from the inside out.

Lucien's mouth moved over hers with growing urgency, molding and shaping their lips into something that could not be separated. Sparks ignited inside Charlotte, setting her insides aflame and leaving a hunger inside her that could not be denied or ignored. Her blood, cool and sluggish at first, quickly heated into a raging inferno of want and need. A craving unlike anything she had ever known licked at her until she was desperate for his mouth. For his touch.

The shock of it was all so sweet. So unexpected. She could not get enough of the way his mouth plundered hers. She ached for his hands to grip her tighter. When his palm came up and encircled her throat in a vaguely threatening yet gentle gesture, she practically disintegrated with longing. He squeezed a little harder and his kisses abruptly became far more forceful than before. He was stealing the air from her lungs, and she was glad to give it to him. A low sound of agonized desire from his chest echoed her own, and Charlotte gasped in delight when he thrust his tongue deep into her mouth.

"Fuck, I should not be doing this. I should not be doing any of this," he groaned between kisses.

Charlotte gripped him closer, frightened that he might decide to stop the delicious torment. She did not want him to stop. She wanted more of this incredible, sparkling world he was introducing her to. She wanted to climb higher and higher into the clouds with Lucien as her guide. Seeking to encourage him, she returned his kisses with awkward, enthusiastic fervor until he moved between her legs and pressed the firm heat of his body to the junction of her thighs.

The explosion of pleasure was almost too much to bear. She whimpered in response, pushing against him and silently demanding more. Every nerve in her body felt alive, the sensations an erotic mix of want, fear, and yearning. His hands on her throat were steel-wrapped silk, and she melted every time his fingers flexed.

"Can I touch you, Charlotte? Can I touch you here?" Lucien's low, husky murmur was a silken entreaty of wickedness and lust. He nibbled at her lips, demanding an answer.

"Y-yes." She did not resist when his free hand snaked beneath the edge of her gown. Her head fell back in immediate surrender, her legs falling open as if she possessed no control over them. His fingers trailing higher and higher on her bare skin made her shake in anticipation. Something wonderous was about to happen. Something from which she would never, ever recover.

"Christ, you are so goddamn sweet. Everywhere I kiss you is like tasting sugar for the first time." His mouth pressed open kisses to her neck and chest, moving lower until he blazed a trail of fire across her breasts where they mounded above the half-stays she wore beneath her gown. She had not even noticed he had pulled away the flimsy fichu to push the gown's low neckline lower, exposing more of her flesh. Charlotte jolted when his teeth grazed one nipple through the fabric of her stays, and a moan escaped her throat when he nipped the tender bud.

"Shhhh," he murmured against her throat, his fingers closing around the slender column until Charlotte found it difficult to breathe without his permission. "Just relax against me and let me show you a side of heaven you never dreamed existed." As he spoke, the hand beneath her skirts climbed steadily until suddenly, he was breaching the private space between her legs with an insistence that stole her breath. "I want to touch you here. I want to see you naked and writhing beneath me as I fuck you." He laughed softly in her ear. "Do you even know what that word means, my sweet, sheltered siren?" His fingers pushed aside the flimsy barrier of her garments until he finally touched her where the ache was almost unbearable.

Charlotte nearly fell into a swoon, so great were the overwhelming emotions coursing through her body. She was floating high above the earth, and Lucien's husky, dirty words of seduction sent her higher and higher.

"If you let me, I would kiss you here where my fingers are now. I would lick you until you throbbed for me. Until you begged me to let you come. I would feast and feast until you shook in my arms and exploded on my tongue. And after you reached your climax, I would plunge my cock deep inside you until you came again around me. I would do this over and over until we were both weak with our release. Then, sweet, sweet Charlotte, I would begin anew."

His fingers explored the blonde nest of curls no one had ever touched before. Charlotte did not understand half of what he said, the terminology he used foreign and unknown, but her body instinctively comprehended every word. She burned for him, moisture gathering along his fingertips until he hummed in satisfaction. He began circling a tiny bundle of flesh she'd never paid much attention to before this moment and every nerve ending in her body was electrified by his boldness.

"Oh, God," she whimpered, throwing her head back in surrender. Whatever he was doing to her, it was too sinful to bear. Too delicious to deny. She wanted more of him. More of this magic.

"Not God." Lucien chuckled low, sweeping one finger into the entrance of her body and gathering up the moisture there. He swirled it around her flesh in a manner that seemed designed to drive her insane. "Just a reprobate earl cursed with an insatiable desire to touch and kiss you and watch you come undone for the first time."

Then he tightened his hand around her throat and moved his hand between her legs with an intensity from which there was no hope of escape. Her body wound tighter and tighter, climbing to a pinnacle that seemed impossible. Her breath grew short, her lungs heaving for air. For redemption. For salvation. For Lucien. And just when she thought she might faint from the overwhelming pressure, from the incredible pleasure, her body exploded into a million, air-spun pieces of glittering shards of color and sensation.

"Yes," Lucien hissed against her mouth, kissing her so deep she would have gasped out loud if he'd allowed it. "Come for me, Charlotte. Come on my fingers so I can taste your sweetness later when I'm alone in my bedchambers. I'll use your silky wetness and this memory to stroke my cock until I explode in the palm of my own hand, crying out your name."

Charlotte did not understand his impassioned words, but she had a vague comprehension. With the firm pressure of his fingers still against her throbbing center, Lucien pressed his muscular body between her thighs. She could feel him there… a hard bulge of flesh that made her feel tiny and fragile in comparison to his overpowering strength. But he did no more than push against her, a tremor of restraint shaking his body when she welcomed him with a whimper. Something about the way he held himself against her, the way his fingers now gently caressed her, was so soothing and yet disturbing at the same time. She squirmed, still restless, her legs opening and flexing almost against her will.

"Christ, that was… that was everything I've dreamed of since the moment I met you," Lucien confessed softly, withdrawing his hands from beneath her dress. His hand dropped from her throat and curled about her waist, providing support as she slowly drifted back to earth. Charlotte shivered with the loss of his body heat, wishing he would envelop her once more in the cocoon of warmth he'd woven.

A frown creased his brows, and with a muttered curse, he stepped back to the hearth and stirred the fire with a piece of wood lying to the side. "Let me get this fire going again."

She watched as he worked. Once the fire resumed its cheerful snapping and crackle, Lucien turned to her.

Charlotte's breath caught in her throat at his handsomeness. Lucien was built like a Greek god, blessed with sinewy muscles and rippling bulges. Damp, dark hair curled over his shirt collar, and Charlotte blushed, remembering how she'd entwined her fingers in those silky curls just moments before. His green eyes glowed like rare emeralds as he let her gaze her fill, then with a quirk of a smile, he sank until he was seated on the hearth with the fire behind him.

Still perched on the table, Charlotte's legs now dangled off its edge, her feet hovering in the space between his thighs as Lucien scooted closer. When he took one of her feet in the warmth of his large hands, she nearly shot off the table in surprise.

"What on earth are you doing, Lucien?" Funny how easily his name came to her lips now. It was as if he'd pressed it there with his fierce kisses and there was no undoing its hold now.

He grinned up at her while rubbing her toes through the thin cotton stocking. "Warming your feet, of course. They are as cold as icicles."

"That-that-s not necessary," Charlotte stuttered, but she could not help the groan of pleasure when his thumbs firmly stroked the arch of her sole. "Dear lord, that feels heavenly."

"I take it no one has ever massaged your feet." Lucien placed her foot on the hard slab of his thigh and picked up the other to give it the same treatment.

"Of course not," she said with a breathy sigh. "This is an entirely new, novel experience."

His chuckle filled the small cottage. "I rarely offer this type of service. Tell me if I do something you do not like, as I am no expert in this particular field."

Charlotte's gaze settled on him. "I'm sure that's not true. A man like yourself, who has been with dozens of women, must have had the opportunity to practice regularly."

His hands moved from her feet to her ankle, then to her calf. When he squeezed the muscle there, Charlotte moaned with delight.

"My interactions with women have rarely included intimate moments like this." His large, warm hands rubbed and massaged, moving higher and higher until he had passed her knee and was now squeezing her inner thigh. His other hand moved to the opposite side and when he slowly but surely leaned forward, the air in her lungs became trapped with anticipation.

What on earth was he about to do?

She sucked in a breath when Lucien pressed soft, fluttering kisses to the bare skin. His mouth was hot as a branding iron, his lips exploring every exposed inch. All she could hear was his breathing, her heartbeat pounding in her veins, and the soft patter of rain hitting the cottage's roof and dripping off the eaves.

"As I expected, you taste sweet here. And if I move up just a little more, I will find the nectar of the gods." He licked the skin on the inside of her thigh, using his palms to both spread her legs wider and push her gown higher. "Will you let me pleasure you, little siren?" His gaze flickered up to meet her shocked stare. "Will you let me show you just how talented my tongue is?"

"There?" she asked in wavering disbelief. "You-you wish to place your mouth *there?*"

"You will greatly enjoy it," he promised, his eyes shimmering with sharp desire. "As will I."

Charlotte teetered between falling over the edge of wickedness with this man or staying behind in the safety of innocent ignorance. If she let him do what he wished, she was afraid she would never recover from the experience while he would move on with barely a backward glance for the girl he had ruined. Reality came rushing in with that thought. How many women had been splayed before him in such a manner? How many had lost their hearts and minds to the charm of his handsome grin and sinful kisses? She was just one of many. And losing herself, her virginity, and her dignity was not worth it.

A known libertine and rake was attempting to corrupt her, and the price he demanded for a glimpse of heaven was too high.

With the palms of her hands, Charlotte shoved at Lucien's shoulders with enough force that he quickly sat up. His palms gripped her knees to steady himself. Otherwise, he might have tumbled backwards straight into the fire.

"What the devil?" he muttered beneath his breath as he regained his balance.

"You must stop, my lord. I cannot allow you to continue with this wickedness," Charlotte said in a shaky voice. Dragging her feet off his thighs, she hopped down off the table and then stood trapped between his knees. Lucien did not budge, his broad shoulders blocking her escape.

"Wickedness?" he echoed, eyes glinting like green embers. "A bit of pleasure is what I've given you, Charlotte. It's not wicked in the sense you believe it."

"It *is* wicked. We are neither man and wife nor are we engaged to be. There is nothing between us other than the relationship of employer and employee. I will not be your toy, my lord. Something you play with to ease the boredom of your time at Ashcroft."

His hands lifted to her waist, hard fingers digging in through the thin material of her dress to keep her still. "I'm not toying with you."

"Yes, you are," Charlotte replied in as icy a tone as she could manage when her insides sloshed around like warm jelly. "This means nothing to a man like you, but it means a great deal to me. We must not go any further with this madness."

The rain had stopped, and the smell of wet earth and green

leaves permeated the air seeping into the little abode. It mixed nicely with the crackling woodsy scent of the fire, but the weather was a reminder that the little interlude was over. Charlotte waited, barely breathing, for Lucien to release her. She wasn't sure what she would do if he refused… if he decided to take what he wanted from her. Her position was incredibly vulnerable. If his intentions turned nefarious, she would not have the strength to stop him. Her hands curled into fists, preparing for a struggle if need be.

Lucien's frustration was obvious in the clench of his teeth when he stood, allowing Charlotte the opportunity to sidle a couple of steps away. He regarded her for a long moment, raked his hands through his damp hair, then reached for her a second time.

"Madness is an apt description for what I'm feeling right now," he *tsked* while tucking his suit coat tighter beneath her chin. After ensuring she was ensconced within the overly large garment, he smiled ruefully. "And I'm afraid there is no cure for it."

CHAPTER ELEVEN
Charlotte

WHEN THE RAIN finally stopped, Lucien banked the fire so it would smolder harmlessly into a pile of ash and soot. As they exited the small cottage, Charlotte refused to look back at the building. She was on the verge of tears as it was. A very special memory had taken place within those humble walls. It hurt knowing she was the only one who would glance at the cottage and remember what had happened there. Lucien, she was sure, would ride past it and never give the interlude they shared this rainy, spring morning a second thought.

"Are you all right?" Lucien asked, his gaze sharp as he threw her Spencer jacket over the crook of his arm. "Your face is very pale."

Charlotte buried her nose into the depths of his coat, fighting an overwhelming urge to deeply inhale the spicy aroma of his cologne. "I'm fine," she managed with a small sniffle. "Just cold."

Lucien let out an unintelligible grunt before saying more clearly, "Let's get you home. You will need a warm bath and a glass of brandy to warm you."

"Brandy?" Charlotte repeated with a wrinkle of her nose.

"Yes. It's just the thing to warm you from the inside out."

"We do not keep spirits in Hollyhock Cottage," she informed him in a prim manner. "I shall have a cup of tea, however. I'm sure that will do just as well."

Lucien stared at her. "No brandy? No... no wine or anything of that nature? You must at least have some sherry on hand. All ladies drink sherry."

"Then I must not be a lady because I do not drink it or spirits of any sort."

"That's incredibly sad. Sherry is completely harmless. I mean, it's almost medicinal, if you want to know the truth."

"Well, it's a blessing that I'm not sick. Because I still would not drink it, my lord."

"Damnit," Lucien swore under his breath. "We're back to that again, are we?"

"Yes, we're back to that. You are Lord Ashcroft, and I am simply Miss Windsor," Charlotte said, not waiting to see if he followed her onto the main road. "What happened must be forgotten by the both of us. It's for the best."

Lucien caught her by the elbow, tugging her until she had no choice but to face him. "Forget it? I'll carry that memory until the end of my days, little siren. If you think I can forget how you sighed my name when you came apart in my hands, then you are as delusional as you are beautiful."

Charlotte pulled away from his grip and walked faster, huddled into the warmth of his coat and wishing her shoes were dry. "I prefer that we never mention th-that incident ever again. We shall pretend it never happened. And we will each go on with our lives all the same despite it."

"*Pretend it never...*" Lucien echoed her words before jogging to catch her a second time. "You may be able to erase this from your mind, Charlotte, but I will not. I cannot. I'm going mad just thinking about kissing you again."

Charlotte leveled him with serious glare. "Then I suggest that you finish your business here quickly, my lord, and return to London in order to save your sanity. Because what just happened will not occur a second time. I promise you that."

Lucien fell into step beside her on the winding road, and they were both quiet while navigating around mud puddles.

"I will send a carriage for you tomorrow. It is unacceptable that you have been walking this distance these past few days," Lucien said, and Charlotte took his offer as a conciliatory measure to ease the tension between them now.

"Completely unnecessary. I enjoy walking," she replied, then ruined her independent declaration with a sneeze.

"It will be a wonder if you don't catch your death of cold after this morning's disaster," Lucien scoffed, placing a hand in the low of Charlotte's back when she stumbled on a loose rock.

"I sincerely doubt that is a possibility."

A tiny lane that led away from the main road loomed ahead as they rounded a curve. This was the road to Hollyhock Cottage and Charlotte gave Lucien a grim smile as she came to stop at its head.

"Thank you for your escort, Lord Ashcroft. Hollyhock Cottage is just beyond that strand of woods so now is as good a time as any to take our leave of one another."

"I shall see you safely inside, Charlotte."

"There is no need," she said matter-of-factly. When she went to shrug out of his suit coat and the waist coat as well, he suddenly gripped her arm, halting her movements.

"Keep it on," Lucien gritted from between clenched teeth. "That wet gown is still very much transparent and your flimsy jacket is hardly enough to provide coverage."

Charlotte blushed, suddenly excruciatingly aware of her body's exposure in the damp clothes. "Only my sister is at home, Lord Ashcroft. No one will see me in this state."

His smile caught her off guard. "Excellent. I would like to meet your sister. My gardener told me she was very involved with making sure he performed his job to her specifications at Mrs. Merriweather's. She seems like a conscientious young lady."

"She's a tyrant, if you want the truth of the matter," Charlotte replied absently as they continued walking up the short lane.

"Then we should get along quite well," Lucien chuckled.

"I do hope you won't stay very long." Charlotte knew she was being rude, but the morning's turn had her not quite feeling herself. She sneezed again then said, "We have much to do today with Mr. Russell coming for dinner."

Lucien's gaze darkened. "I've not forgotten that, Charlotte. You have my word I will not overstay my welcome."

"Good," Charlotte said, clearing her throat in the uncomfortable silence that fell between them. The cottage coming into view saved her from continuing the awkward conversation.

"Very charming," Lucien said in a low voice. "I can see its appeal."

"Faith and I love it very much." Her voice cracked a little bit, but she quickly recovered with a tiny laugh. "I do not love the gate, however. I've repaired it three times already over the past two months. It's a temperamental thing."

"I shall send someone to take care of it immediately," Lucien promised, reaching for the gate's latch and swinging it open so that Charlotte could walk through. "It is the estate's responsibility, after all."

Charlotte did not reply, choosing instead to continue striding toward the cottage. Upon reaching the front door, she slipped off her wet shoes before turning the handle.

"Faith? I'm home, dear."

Her sister came running from the direction of their small kitchen, the apron she wore covered in flour. "Thank goodness! I thought I might have to cook dinner all by myself for Mr. Earnest." She drew up short at the sight of the man standing in the tiny parlor, her blue eyes wide with shock. "You are early, sir. We haven't even started to roast the chicken. And why are you all wet?"

Charlotte smiled, pulling her sister closer. "This is Lord Ashcroft, Faith. He offered to escort me home and unfortunately, we were caught in that earlier rainstorm."

"How do you do, Faith?" Lucien took the young girl's hand, gallantly pressing a kiss to the back of it. "Your sister has spoken of you often over the last few days. Indeed, I feel as though I already know you."

Faith dipped a curtsey and then frowned at Charlotte. "You said Lord Ashcroft was not a person I should be around. That his morality was missing. Does this mean you've changed your mind? I hope so. His Lordship is quite genial and not at all the ogre you said he was."

Lucien's brows shot upward as he gave Charlotte a questioning look.

"That was before I… uh… knew the man very well, dear." Coughing over her discomfort, Charlotte squeezed Faith's shoulder. "Remember your manners, Faith."

"Will you be here for dinner, too?" Faith eagerly asked the earl who watched the interplay between the two sisters very intently.

"Of course not," Charlotte interjected. "Lord Ashcroft has other important matters to attend. I'm sure dinner here would be a much more humble affair than he is accustomed to."

"On the contrary," Lucien said slowly while flashing that ridiculously charming smile at Faith. "I would love nothing more than to have dinner with two such lovely ladies. And roast chicken happens to be a particular favorite of mine."

Charlotte's lips pursed. "I do not believe that is a good idea. I mean, Mr. Russell is not just coming this afternoon for the pleasure of our company, Faith. Remember, I told you he would like to examine the cottage since he may be the new vicar."

"I won't get in the way of his exploration." Lucien laughed, waving off Charlotte's weak objections. "Besides, it will give me further opportunity to become better acquainted with Mr. Russell. After all, he is in the lead for the position, although we still have several applicants to interview."

Faith cocked her head, studying Lucien. "I've never met an earl before. You are the first, my lord."

"I am honored." He smiled at the younger Windsor girl before his gaze cut to Charlotte. "I particularly enjoy being first in all things. It is a quirk of mine."

Charlotte nearly choked on an indrawn breath at the brazen insinuation of his declaration. Before she could protest any further, Faith clapped her hands in delight.

"This shall be the best dinner ever! Your Lordship, I have so many questions about life in town. That is, if I may ask them of you and it is not too impertinent. I find the idea of endless parties and balls and soirees quite fascinating. Is it true that ices of every flavor imaginable are available in town? I should so like to try pineapple ice. All I've had is the lemon kind."

"I'm happy to answer any questions, my dear, regarding flavored ices and parties when I return tonight." Lucien bowed at the waist and flashed Faith a wink. "Now, your sister should change her clothes and get into a warm bath. She was soaked through to the skin, and we wouldn't want her catching a cold now, would we?"

Faith blinked, suddenly realizing that Charlotte was barefoot, wearing the earl's suit coat, and her hair hanging in messy, damp curls down her back.

"Oh, poor Charlotte! How awful for you!" Faith twirled to leave the room, calling over her shoulder. "Let me pop the teacakes into the oven and I'll run you a bath at once!" Pausing in the parlor's doorway, she dipped another curtsey to Lucien. "We will see you tonight, then, my lord. So pleased to meet you."

"It is my honor, Faith. I look forward to dinner."

When they were alone, Charlotte slipped her arms from the coat and the waistcoat and held them out to the earl. It was difficult to take her eyes off him as he stood in the midst of Hollyhock's tiny parlor. He was so… overwhelmingly male. He took up every available inch of space. Ignoring such blatant masculinity, especially one in nothing but a damp, crisp white shirt and fawn-colored breeches, was nearly impossible.

"I want you out of those clothes and into a hot bath, Charlotte," he said, his husky voice sending an unwanted and unexpected shiver down her spine.

"That is so inappropriate, Lord Ashcroft," she breathed in response, watching as he shrugged back into his garments. Within seconds, he was impeccably attired, to the point one would have never guessed he'd been dashing through a rainstorm, breaking up furniture, and building fires in an abandoned woodcutter's cottage.

And seducing innocent women, her inner voice added.

His smile was more a smirk than anything else. "I've not even begun to show you how inappropriate I can truly be, little siren."

Charlotte's eyes briefly closed. "Y-you should not call me that." She wrapped her arms around her midsection, remembering that her gown was still transparent.

"Why not? It's what you are. A siren, luring me into unknown and uncharted territory." He moved closer, using the tip of his forefinger to tilt her chin up. "I'm being truthful when I tell you that I've never felt such a pull toward a woman before. I'm not sure what to do about it."

Charlotte stood silently, trembling when he used his thumb to rub along her bottom lip. Good lord, the things this man made her feel were too dangerous. And the fact that his hands had been up her skirts showing her what his idea of heaven looked like… without her objection… was downright frightening.

Leaning forward, Lucien pressed a soft kiss to her mouth and then quickly backed away.

"Get warmed up, Charlotte. I'll be back around four to help welcome Mr. Russell to Hollyhock Cottage."

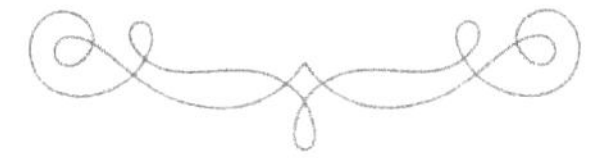

CHAPTER TWELVE
Lucien

L UCIEN FOUND HIMSELF counting the hours until the carriage was brought around to Ashcroft Manor's front steps.

After cleaning himself up and donning fresh clothes, he now had time to spare before he was to be at Hollyhock Cottage. He wondered if Charlotte was as anxious as he was and he cursed himself for being so eager to see the young lady who was turning his world upside down.

The things he'd done to her in that woodcutter's cottage went beyond the pale. It was completely irresponsible and callous of him to take advantage of the situation to press his attentions upon an innocent, sheltered woman like Charlotte. And if anyone found out about that little interlude and everything that had occurred, he'd end up hitched before he could blink twice.

But she is complicit in her downfall, too. She wanted me to touch her. Begged me to kiss her. What mortal man could even hope to resist such temptation? She knows my reputation and still, she wanted what happened between us. Just remembering how sweet she was on my fingertips, on my tongue, might possibly be enough to have me swearing off bachelorhood forever.

"Don't be a fool, man," Lucien muttered under his breath at the outrageous idea that was persistently rattling around in his head the last few days. Since making Charlotte's acquaintance, he had found himself contemplating the ramifications of a serious commitment to a woman and what it might feel like to be so restrained.

Going against the principal cornerstones of the pact with his two friends was not something he was eager to do. Remaining single, free and unattached was the goal and allowing a gorgeous face and two pretty blue eyes to sway him was tantamount to the worst betrayal.

"I won't fall into that trap. I simply won't," he vowed silently. "Wylder and Simon are depending on me to stay the course. There is no chance in hell that I will fail them and their faith in me and our pact."

Swinging himself up into the back of the carriage, he could not help the thrill that electrified him at the thought of seeing Charlotte, however. She was like an exotic drug and God help him, he could not wait for his next dose.

"To Hollyhock Cottage, Jenner," he instructed the coachman as a footman closed the door behind him. A click of Jenner's tongue had the coach lurching forward and Lucien settled back, hoping the moments would pass quickly. He was eager to see his little siren.

PULLING COMPLETELY THROUGH Hollyhock Cottage's small, curved driveway was impossible. The way was blocked by a small two-wheeled carriage drawn by an old horse that looked grateful for the chance to stand still. The vehicle was a bit worn but the trappings were polished and clean. Lucien's jaw clenched. It appeared that Mr. Russell had come a bit earlier than four o' clock.

Why that disturbed Lucien was not difficult to understand. He did not like the idea of the vicar enjoying Charlotte's pleasurable company with no one around to monitor them. It was ludicrous to count her younger sister as a suitable chaperone.

He vaulted from the carriage before Jenner could dismount from the driver's seat and open the door for his descent. Standing before the gate, which was currently tilted slightly askew, he debated on continuing up the cobblestone steps to the cottage's front door or walking around the building itself to see if perhaps Charlotte was giving the vicar a tour of the grounds.

Hearing voices from somewhere around the corner of the cottage, Lucien decided to wait where he was and observe the interaction between Charlotte and the other man.

"As you can see, Earnest, the garden, although small, is quite sufficient for one's needs. It suited the three of us very well, so as a gentleman alone, it would provide very well for you," Charlotte's sweet voice drifted on the slight afternoon breeze. She sounded just a little bit hoarse, however, and tired. Lucien's chest tightened with concern.

"We had a bumper crop of radishes last year."

Lucien recognized Faith's voice… bright and enthusiastic.

"As well as tomatoes. And shallots," Charlotte added helpfully. "Mrs. Merriweather was kind enough to give us seeds for the tomatoes. They grow almost without any tending at all."

"I'm not one for gardening," Mr. Russell confessed with an embarrassed chuckle. "At my last position, the women of the congregation kindly provided me with all manner of foodstuffs. In fact, I rarely had to prepare my own meals. Someone was always willing and ready to share theirs with me. I am hopeful that the same goes for here. Until I marry, that is. Then, of course, my dear wife would handle those duties."

"Of course," Charlotte said, a note of doubt in her tone that wasn't difficult to discern. "I'm sure there are those in the village who will happily help the new vicar with such things until he is settled. My father was a firm believer in repaying the generosity of others with a helping hand whenever it was needed. If someone required assistance in rethatching their roof or building a stone wall, he always wanted to help. There is no doubt the congregation will be willing to do the same in your situation,

Earnest."

"I'm not sure how valuable it would be to have me mending fences or laying stone walls. I don't know of any vicars required to do such physical labor in their positions as spiritual advisors to their flock."

As he spoke, Mr. Russell emerged from the side of the building with Charlotte and Faith in tow behind him. Catching sight of Lucien standing at the gate, Charlotte's face lit up with relief before her expression turned guarded.

"Good evening, Lord Ashcroft," Earnest said, somewhat surprised. "I had no idea you would be stopping by this evening. Charlotte was just giving me a tour of the grounds. It's quite charming, if a little small and neglected."

Faith scowled at the man. "Charlotte and I work very hard at keeping it up, Mr. Russell. And it's not neglected… it's just…" she floundered for a moment, searching for the right term before crossing her arms in a decidedly hostile gesture. "Gently used is a much better description."

"Faith, it's all right," Charlotte murmured, wrapping her arm around Faith's narrow shoulders. Clearing her voice, she addressed Lucien. "Hello, Lord Ashcroft. You are a bit earlier than we expected, but your timing is perfect. I was just about to show Mr. Russell the cottage. Won't you come inside?"

"I'm sure there is no need for the earl to concern himself with the inside of the cottage, my dear. I'm confident that any repairs or modifications that must be made will be handled quickly and efficiently before I take up residence," Earnest said with a nervous laugh.

Charlotte appeared stricken at the thought of anyone altering the cottage. Her mouth dropped open as if to dispute Earnest's assertion, but Lucien swooped in before she could utter a word.

"*If*," he said silkily. "If you are given the position, Mr. Russell. Charlotte and I still have seven applicants to interview before I make my decision." Lucien strolled past the gate and advanced on the trio as they paused at the door to the cottage. "We want to make sure we have the right person for the position, after all. And being that you were the very first to be interviewed, you can understand my reluctance to settle right away."

"Of course," Earnest stuttered, his face morphing into a pale red shade that was not flattering at all. "I did not mean to imply anything with my statement, my lord. I felt at home the instant I saw the property and my natural instinct was to react as though it were already mine. I hope I did not cause offense."

Lucien ignored the man's stammering excuses to reach for Charlotte's bare hand. He pressed a kiss to it, noticing the warmth of her skin. Frowning, he peered at her face and saw her face was feverishly pink. She ducked her head under the weight of his perusal and moved to stand behind Faith.

Lifting the younger sister's hand, Lucien gallantly repeated his actions, giving hers a kiss a well. "Thank you for the dinner invite, ladies."

"You-you're staying for dinner, too?" Earnest nearly squeaked.

"Yes, roast chicken is one of my favorites," Lucien replied in a casually indifferent tone, his gaze traveling over Charlotte's flushed cheeks.

"Shall we all go inside?" she asked before suddenly sneezing. A pained moan escaped her before she smiled brightly at the two men. "It will not take very long at all for Earnest to see the cottage. Then we can sit down for dinner. It's all ready."

"I did mostly the whole thing myself," Faith crowed, leading the way into the house. "Charlotte slept for most of the after-noon. But one cannot blame her, seeing how she isn't feeling well at all. Even after a warm bath, she still isn't quite herself, are you, Charlotte?"

"I'm perfectly fine. Just needed to catch up on a bit of sleep. Unfortunately, I tossed and turned all night and I'm paying the cost for it today." Charlotte's voice was even hoarser than before. Lucien caught her gaze as concern filled him. He certainly was no physician, but it was easy to see that she was sick. His jaw clenched tight. As he had predicted, she'd caught a cold from the soaking received in that rain shower.

"You did not need to follow through with the evening, Charlotte. It is understandable if you canceled dinner. In fact, Mr. Russell and I should take our leave so that you may get some rest," Lucien said.

"Are you ill?" Earnest asked in obvious surprise.

"She and Lord Ashcroft were caught in a rain shower this morning. Poor Charlotte was positively soaked by the time he brought her home," Faith offered, taking the two men's hats and overcoats from them.

"Indeed," Earnest said, his gaze now bouncing between Lucien and Charlotte, his cheeks hollowing in as he contemplated this bit of information.

"Faith," Charlotte chided gently, "You may place the gentlemen's things on the coat tree. And perhaps we should begin with dinner and leave the tour for after?"

"Yes, let's do that," Faith cheerfully agreed. "I'm terribly hungry and I promised I would take a plate of chicken over to Mrs. Merriweather's."

"You know I don't like the idea of you going there this close to dusk. It's not safe," Charlotte said, leading the way to the small dining room. Lucien wondered if he was the only one who noticed that she was a little unsteady on her feet.

"I shall run fast as a cat there and back," Faith swore before smiling at Lucien. "Lord Ashcroft, it is only proper that you sit at the head of the table. After all, you do own Hollyhock Cottage."

"I would leave that place of honor for your sister," Lucien replied with a small bow in Charlotte's direction. "She has done a wonderful job of making this a warm and welcoming home. Along with your help, no doubt, Faith."

Faith beamed from ear to ear with the compliment as Lucien pulled out the indicated chair, nodding for Charlotte to sit. Earnest awkwardly took a seat to her left while Faith scampered off to the kitchen, exclaiming that she would soon appear with their dinner. Lucien sank into the chair on Charlotte's right side.

While Earnest fussed over his napkin and the correct placement of it in his lap, Lucien took Charlotte's hand in his beneath the table. He squeezed it gently.

"You are sick, Charlotte," he said in a low voice that only she could hear. "You should be in bed rather than entertaining guests."

"Always trying to entice a woman to bed." Charlotte smiled weakly, her hand remaining in his for a heartbeat before she pulled free of his grasp. "I assure you I am quite all right, Lord Ashcroft."

"I don't believe you and I don't like being lied to."

She said nothing to that, choosing instead to address Earnest. "What do you think of the house thus far? It is small, but one must admit it is cozy. Faith and I have been quite happy here. And of course, my father loved this little cottage as well." Lifting her glass of water, Charlotte took a long drink of it, eyes closing in appreciation of the cool liquid.

Lucien was fighting an overwhelming urge to scoop Charlotte up into his arms and carry her to bed. And while such plans usually involved nefarious purposes, his intentions now were to simply see to her comfort. Under the fevered flush of her skin, she was as white as the tablecloth.

"It's quite adequate. A bit provincial compared to my last residence, but it's not without charm," Earnest said, gazing about the room as if evaluating its contents. "Will the furniture be included in the post, Lord Ashcroft?"

Lucien faltered. He honestly had no idea. He quickly looked at Charlotte for an answer, but she had her eyes closed. "Charlotte?"

"Hmm?" She blinked at him and licked her upper lip. It was beaded with sweat.

"The furniture," Lucien prodded gently. "Does it stay with the cottage?"

She frowned in confusion then gave a slight shake of her head as if to clear it. "The furniture? Does it stay? Yes, with the exception of a few pieces which have been in our family for generations."

Lucien shot a glance at Earnest. "There's your answer."

"In my old position—" the vicar began before Lucien cut him off.

"Yes, we know. Your old position was far superior to this one." Lucien nearly snarled at the man, irritated that he could not seem to see their hostess was so ill she could barely sit upright. "Might I suggest you return to your old position, Mr. Russell? I'm sure you will be far more satisfied there than you could ever be here at Ashcroft. You've found fault in the smallest things, and I would not have an unhappy, dissatisfied vicar on my hands."

"Sir, nothing could be further from the truth," Earnest floundered, holding a hand to his heart. "I'm sure I would be quite happy here. In fact, I sincerely hope I am offered the position. I also most fervently hope that Charlotte and her sister are inclined to remain in the area if I am to be the new vicar. I would welcome their help in meeting the congregation and easing my settlement into the community." The man smiled at Charlotte. "I should hope I could count on you to lend me aid in that area, Charlotte."

Charlotte smiled blankly at the vicar and Lucien realized she was not truly aware of what he was suggesting. The man was subtly and inexpertly asking permission to court her under the guise of begging for help.

"My understanding is that Charlotte and Faith will be relocating to London once I have chosen a new vicar," Lucien said, his tone icy.

Disappointment flashed across Earnest's face. "Perhaps I can convince her to stay if I am afforded the opportunity to serve you, my lord."

Faith bustled back into the dining room before Lucien could respond to that. She carried a large tray and balanced upon it was a platter of roasted chicken slices, a bowl of creamed potatoes, and a second bowl of green peas crowned with a large pat of butter. Setting the platter down, Faith quickly removed each dish so that it now occupied the center of the dining room table. When Charlotte went to help, Faith waved her off but when she saw how pale her sister was, her demeanor changed to one of utmost concern.

"I can do it, Charlotte. You sit back and play the lovely hostess."

Charlotte smiled at her little sister, her features softening with affection. "You've done a beautiful job, dear. I fear I wasn't much help at all today."

Faith impulsively hugged Charlotte's neck before taking her own seat beside Lucien. "You take care of everything here. This was nothing compared to that."

Everyone served themselves from the food offerings, although Lucien insisted on filling Charlotte's plate for her. But she did not eat. Moving the food around her plate with the tines of her fork, she simply nibbled on a bit of chicken and drank water.

"I must insist that you come back and tour the cottage another day, Mr. Russell. It is not convenient tonight, for obvious reasons," Lucien said in a low voice to the vicar. Faith sat unusually quiet while he spoke. Her delicate features relayed the concern for Charlotte. Several times during the meal, she attempted to engage her sister in conversation but was unsuccessful.

"I fear you are right, Lord Ashcroft," Earnest said, finally seeming to understand the situation. "I am disappointed, of course, but as you said, it would be best to postpone."

Charlotte shook her head, a frown creasing her brow as she patted her face with her napkin. The flush of her cheeks left no doubt now that she was feverish. "That's ridiculous. There's no reason we cannot continue on with the plans, Earnest. If everyone is done with their meal, we may finish the tour. I'm sure you do not want to stay another day in the countryside just for this."

She stood from the table, then immediately swayed with the motion of getting up. Before she toppled over, Lucien leaped from his chair and caught her in his arms.

CHAPTER THIRTEEN
Lucien

"OH, DEAR," EARNEST said, eyes wide with alarm.

"Charlotte!" Faith cried, rushing to Charlotte's side. "Oh, dear Charlotte! Whatever has happened to her?"

"She's fainted." Lucien gathered Charlotte's slight figure closer, cradling her against his chest. She was burning up with fever, her skin so hot it nearly scalded him through his clothes, and yet, violent tremors shook her body. "Faith, run upstairs and quickly pack a valise for your sister. A dress or two, but mostly nightgowns and a robe. Russell, you will ride to the village and fetch the doctor. Faith will accompany you as she knows the location of the man's residence. Bring him straightaway to the manor. Do not delay. Faith? Is there a blanket I can wrap her in?"

Faith ran to a cabinet in the corner, pulling a well-worn quilt from the bottom drawer.

"Shouldn't I bring him here?" Earnest asked dumbfounded as Lucien carried an unconscious Charlotte from the dining room to the parlor. "I mean to say, wouldn't it be safer to have the good doctor examine her here? Or better yet, shouldn't we take her to him?"

"The items needed to bring her fever down will be at Ashcroft Manor. And I won't waste time carting her all over God's green earth when she will only end up at the manor anyway,"

Lucien explained, his voice tight with irritation at being questioned. He took the quilt from Faith, taking the time to swipe at the girl's tears with the pad of his thumb before wrapping Charlotte in the soft material. "She'll be all right if we work quickly, my dear. I promise." Giving Earnest a cursory nod, he further explained, "Faith cannot possibly care for Charlotte alone, and I have a whole houseful of servants who can see to her needs. Now, do as I say and do not tarry."

"Charlotte has never been sick before, my lord," Faith whispered in a forlorn voice. "At least not that I can remember."

"I will take good care of her, Faith. I swear my oath to you on that," Lucien said, inwardly wincing at his own words. His oath had never really been worth much in the past. A rakehell did not have much need for such honorable things, but right now, he meant it with every fiber of his being.

Faith nodded solemnly then flew at him, her thin, childish arms wrapping tight around Lucien's waist. Her strength was surprising, but he felt her quivering with fear. She was being terribly brave in light of what was a terrifying situation. He allowed the embrace, feeling something melt inside him.

"Thank you, my lord. I shall trust you and when Charlotte is better, I will tell her how chivalrous you were at her moment of need." She let him go then, running up the small flight of stairs to where their bedrooms were.

Earnest had already gathered their overcoats and hats and now stood waiting at the door for Lucien.

"I'll follow you out to your carriage. Once you have her settled, Faith and I will do as you say." His lips curved in a rueful smile. "The old nag I rented from the livery won't be much for speed, but I'll do what I can without resorting to beating the creature."

Charlotte chose at that moment to moan softly, her head lolling back on Lucien's forearm. Her eyes cracked open slightly and she stared up at him as if he were a pleasant apparition.

"What a lovely dream," she mumbled, raising a hand to

touch Lucien's face.

"Shhhh, Charlotte. Rest easy now." Lucien carried her out of the cottage, striding toward his carriage. "Jenner, let down the steps. Miss Windsor has fallen ill, and we must take her immediately to the manor." Vaulting in the vehicle, he braced himself on the seat and settled her firmly against his body. Earnest reached in, laying Lucien's coat and hat on the opposite seat.

"I'll see you shortly, my lord." The vicar's concern was quite palpable as he regarded Lucien and Charlotte curled up in his arms. "I will say prayers that the illness is short lived."

Lucien nodded then turned his attention back to the woman he held. "Quickly, Jenner," he called out to his coachman. "Take us home."

OTHER THAN A few instances where Charlotte woke in fitful discomfort, she slept until the next afternoon when the fever finally broke for good. During those intervals, Mrs. Phillips, Faith, and two of the upstairs maids kept her body surrounded by icepacks and cool cloths based upon the advice of Doctor Taylor.

Lucien had spent that time endlessly pacing, sometimes within his study, sometimes in the confines of his own bedchamber, but usually in the corridors outside the guestroom where he'd placed Charlotte. It destroyed him each time he overheard Charlotte's whimpers of pain, and he fought against the overwhelming desire to shove his way into the room so that he could be at her side. Even Doctor Taylor's insistence that she would be fine, although her fever was certainly a serious matter, was not enough to persuade Lucien of her ability to recover. The illness had come on so forcefully, it did not seem possible that within a day or two she would be back to normal.

"Just the average spring cold and fever, Lord Ashcroft." Doctor Taylor closed his physician's bag, his age spotted hands trembling slightly as he clicked shut the brass clasp. "When Miss Windsor is able to sit up, she may begin eating once more. Soup, bone broth. That sort of thing. Tea with no cream. And perhaps a bit of toast, if she cares to have some. I will check on her again tomorrow. I'm sure that with enough rest, she will recover quickly. Young, healthy folks like her usually do."

"May she have a strawberry tart, Doctor?" Faith asked, slipping her hand into Charlotte's and holding it tightly as she slept. The younger sister's little face was tired, showing signs of fatigue on her youthful visage. She'd spent the night working as hard as anyone else when it came to lowering Charlotte's fever. When Charlotte had woken briefly an hour before, Faith had burst out crying and hugged her tight.

"No, child." Doctor Taylor smiled indulgently. "Not just yet. Maybe in a couple of days she can abide it."

Faith nodded. "She will be better by then?"

"I don't see why not." Doctor Taylor turned to Lucien. "If I may speak with Your Lordship in the corridor?"

Lucien followed the elderly man out into the hallway as Mrs. Phillips bustled past them carrying out the damp cloths used to cool Charlotte's body and the used bed linens.

"I'll get the kitchen started on preparing some bone broth right away, my lord," she said, descending the stairs with her arms piled high with cloths. One of the two maids trailed behind her, similarly burdened.

"My thanks, Mrs. Phillips," Lucien acknowledged before turning his attention to the doctor. "What do you wish to tell me, sir?"

"Simply that I would advise watching for signs of illness in the younger sister. I've been told you and Miss Windsor were caught in a rainstorm, but it is a bit unusual for an illness to take hold this quickly. It may be a situation where the two girls were contaminated some days before and it has only now manifested itself."

Lucien considered that, and although he strongly believed the doctor was incorrect in his assessment, he nodded in agreement.

"Of course, Doctor Taylor. I understand your concern and will certainly keep a close watch over both girls. I intend on having them both stay here until Miss Windsor has fully recovered from this ordeal."

"Yes, well, that is quite admirable of you, my lord," Doctor Taylor harrumphed, as he began descending the stairs. He held tight to the ornately carved banister with one hand while Lucien bracketed him on the side. "It does my heart good to see someone taking care of those two girls. They have done untold kindnesses for the people of this village and have felt the loss of their father these past few months quite keenly. It was from him that they were blessed with an abundance of compassionate and gentle character."

"I shall take care of them to the best of my abilities."

Doctor Taylor paused on the stair step, giving Lucien a shrewd once over and nodding his head as though he was satisfied with the results of his perusal. "I don't know if you realize how perilous Miss Windsor's situation truly was. Although I have every confidence in her full recovery, if you had not taken the initiative of bringing her to your home and immediately beginning the process of cooling her body down, she may very well have succumbed to the high fever. It is certainly not hyperbole to say you were instrumental in saving her life. Well done, Your Lordship."

Lucien bowed his head in acknowledgment, continuing the doctor's escort to Ashcroft Manor's double doors. After being assured the doctor would return the following day to check on his patient, Lucien bounded back up the stairs and entered the guest room after giving the door a quick, respectful knock.

Charlotte sat propped up against the pillows, her face pale as the clean sheets she lay on. Faith had taken it upon herself to pull her sister's unruly blonde waves into a thick braided plait of hair that lay over her shoulder.

"Mrs. Phillips will bring some tea for you, but in meantime, would you like a glass of water?" Lucien asked, coming closer to the bed. Charlotte had been changed into a fresh nightgown and robe, and Faith rose from the bed, tugging the bedclothes up higher, fussing over her like a little mother hen.

"Faith poured me some already. Thank you," Charlotte said, her voice weak and trembly. Clearing her throat, she tilted her head. "What exactly happened? I don't recall much of dinner other than the part when Faith carried in the food."

Lucien moved closer, drinking in the sight of her. Even in a weakened state and obviously still suffering from the illness, Charlotte was a vision of loveliness. He couldn't take his eyes off her. Knowing that she might have actually died made his heart clench tight inside his chest. He'd only known her for little more than a week but for some reason, that did not matter. She was as familiar and as dear to him as if he'd known her all of his life. It was such an odd thing... and it left him feeling unsettled and more than a little confused by the ferocity of his emotions.

"You ate a little bit, tried to stand up, and fainted almost immediately. If I had not caught you, you would have had a rather nasty fall."

"*You* caught me." Charlotte studied him. "And then you carried me here?"

"Yes." Lucien clasped his hands behind his back. "You required immediate attention, and it was faster to bring you here for that. Doctor Taylor agrees with my actions. You were... *are*... very sick."

"I was scared to death when it happened, Charlotte, but it was honestly the most romantic thing I've ever seen," Faith exclaimed before yawning wide behind her hand. "You stood up, wobbled a bit, then *swoop!* Lord Ashcroft caught you right in his arms before you could even land on the floor. It was most impressive. Even Mister Russell was astonished."

Lucien's face felt hot as Faith spoke. The praise and obvious admiration made his insides warm and yet uncomfortable at the same time.

"You should get some rest, Faith," Charlotte said softly. "I know you are exhausted, and as you can see, I'm quite all right for the moment."

"You are right. I am terribly tired." She kissed Charlotte on the cheek and went to the door connecting the guest room with the one beside it. "Isn't this clever, Charlotte? Our rooms connect… this way I can come running in case you have need of me during the night."

"I know you've taken very good care of me, my darling. Now, go get some rest."

"Good night, or rather good afternoon. It is still daylight outside, after all. Lord Ashcroft, will someone wake me for supper?" Faith asked, pausing with her hand on the door handle. "Cook promised me a special treat."

Lucien grinned at her. "I'll make sure you are awakened in time for supper. Now, do as your sister says and try to get a little sleep in the meantime."

Once he was alone with Charlotte, Lucien sank into the empty chair beside the bed. "I don't have to tell you how worried we all have been since yesterday. Faith, especially, has been beside herself with concern. I am grateful to see that you are on the mend."

Charlotte's eyelashes fluttered down, sweeping the tops of her high, pale cheekbones. "You've been incredibly kind, Lord Ashcroft. I don't know how I can repay you, but I shall do my best."

"There is no repayment necessary," he replied in a gruff tone. He reached out, capturing her hand and lacing his fingers through hers. "It is because of me that you became sick in the first place."

Her gorgeous blue eyes locked on his, confusion flitting through the clear depths. "How are you responsible, my lord? Did you cause the rain shower? Did you not utilize every method available at the time to warm me? It is not your fault. If anything, the blame can be laid at my own feet. I should have carried a parasol with me that morning."

"That would have been of little consequence," Lucien huffed.

"The rain would have drenched through such flimsy protection. No, I should have requested a carriage to carry you back and forth each morning and afternoon. And had I known you were walking such distances to reach Ashcroft Manor, I would have insisted upon it."

"I find walking enjoyable. It is hardly unusual for me to cover that distance on a regular basis." Charlotte plucked at the embroidered vine pattern on the coverlet. "And under the circumstances, I would not have accepted your offer for fear it would only add to the debt you say I owe."

"Damnation, Charlotte!" His words came out in a hiss. "I'm trying to accept some responsibility for my actions. For my thoughtlessness. I may be a rake of the first order, but I'm hardly a monster who would delight in adding to your troubles."

Charlotte was silent, her brow creased into a frown as she contemplated his fervent statement. "I do not understand you at all, my lord. I do not understand this pull between the two of us, nor why you would feel compelled to help me in any manner. It is appreciated, but of course, I must return to my own home. I cannot stay here and expect either you or your household to care for me."

Lucien squeezed her hand tight. His eyes bored into hers, willing her obedience. "You will stay as long as I deem it necessary for your health, Charlotte. And you will be a model patient and allow me to take care of you." His tone softened in a cajoling tone he'd used before on women in his orbit. "Let me do this for you, little siren."

"I cannot abandon my home, Lucien," she whispered. "Nor my obligations to others."

"Let me worry about that. I'll take care of everything. All you must do is get better."

Worry etched lines across her forehead as she regarded him. "Why would you do that? You said you wished to be done with this place. That you wanted nothing more than to return to town where your carefree life can go on, uninhibited by responsibility.

Why does it matter to you if I am well? Or if Hollyhock Cottage is taken care of? Why would you concern yourself with Mrs. Merriweather's chicken coop, or the blacksmith's two daughters who come to me for tutoring? Why would any of it matter to you?"

Lucien lifted her soft, white hand to his lips. He kissed it gently before laying it back in her lap and standing up from the chair. "I don't know why, Charlotte. That's the damnable truth of this situation I find myself in. But seeing to your welfare is a burning need inside me. One that must be appeased. And maybe, once you are safe and content wherever you land in life, I can move on as well."

CHAPTER FOURTEEN
Charlotte

CHARLOTTE FLUFFED HER pillows, cursing herself for being so weak as to fall under Lord Lucien Westley's spell.

The Earl of Ashcroft was an excellent negotiator. Skilled in enticing women to do his bidding with a flash of dazzling green eyes and a hint of a charming smile. In one week's time, he had successfully managed toppling her into his bed with scarcely a word of protest from her lips.

"A guest bed but a bed belonging to him, nonetheless," she muttered, reluctantly acknowledging the difference.

"What was that, dear?" Mrs. Phillips asked from the other side of the room. The housekeeper had put away items used for Charlotte's earlier bath and was now drawing open the heavy curtains. Sunlight flooded the room, leaving it bright and cheery in contrast to the dim and somber sickroom it was just four days before.

"It is of no consequence." Charlotte sighed dramatically. "I'm just tired of being abed. Bored to tears by a lack of activity. And I know you and Faith both mean well, but please do not suggest I read another book." She gave the stack on the bedside table a withering glare. "None have kept my interest and that is quite depressing." The only time she found the books even remotely interesting was when Lucien visited in the evenings and read to her for a while. His husky voice and the soothing cadence as he read aloud was the most exciting part of her days as a patient.

"I know, dear. But it wasn't that long ago that you were at death's door. Doctor Taylor says you need a little more time to recover. If you resume your usual activities too soon, you very well could suffer a relapse. And wouldn't that be just awful?"

"It was a simple spring cold," Charlotte grumbled, crossing her arms over the front of her clean nightgown and matching robe. "The likelihood of falling that ill again within a few days is astronomical. Nearly impossible. Practically inconceivable."

Mrs. Phillips smiled, stepping to the bedside table and fluffing the flowers in the vase there. "Perhaps, but the doctor does know best in situations of this nature. And I declare. Isn't this just the prettiest bouquet of flowers you've ever seen? His Lordship selected and picked each bloom himself this morning. Such a thoughtful gesture."

"They are lovely," Charlotte grudgingly admitted. She'd feigned sleep that morning when Lucien quietly entered the room with a crystal vase filled with roses, lilies, and snapdragons. There were even a few stalks of hollyhocks in the arrangement. He'd stood over her for a long moment, silently watching as she breathed deeply and pretended to be lost in slumber. When he passed a gentle hand over the crown of her head, she had struggled to contain a moan of contentment.

The earl was barreling through all her defenses. Incinerating all the barriers she'd put in place over the years as a way of protecting herself. It was difficult to ignore the surprising kindness he had shown her and her sister. And it was particularly difficult to pretend his touch… his kisses… had not set her soul on fire.

The last few days provided plenty of time to reflect on the time they had shared in the woodcutter's cottage. And although she blushed now, remembering her own boldness in asking Lucien to kiss her, she'd made a grave error when she had allowed him to continue. The intimacy they shared had changed her irrevocably… and definitely for the worse. Because now, she knew the dizzying pleasure to be found in his touch. Now she wanted more. And to want more of Lucien Westley's attention in any form was inherently dangerous for any woman, especially one as innocent and naive as herself.

Sounds of a commotion outside Charlotte's bedroom shook her from her reverie. There were raised voices accompanied by a strange thumping noise that seemed to be rhythmically ascending the stairs at the end of the corridor. Mrs. Phillips frowned, giving Charlotte a quizzical glance.

"Whatever could that be?" the housekeeper muttered.

"I do hope it's not Faith getting into mischief," Charlotte fretted, wishing she possessed the strength required to leap from the bed and see for herself what the fuss was about.

"She has gone with Cook to the village market this morning and won't return for a while." Mrs. Phillips strode to the bedroom door, opened it, immediately pressed a hand to her chest in shock, and murmured, "Oh, dear."

"I'm telling you; I will see her with my own two eyes, young man. And if you think a set of stairs will stop a stubborn, old woman like myself, you'd best think again!"

Charlotte's jaw dropped in recognition of that voice. "Mrs. Phillips, that cannot be who I think it is…"

Before Mrs. Phillips could verify the visitor's identity, Mrs. Merriweather's cane thumped again followed by a muffled howl of pain.

"Are you intending to help me up these stairs or throw me down them to my death, Lord Ashcroft?" Mrs. Merriweather demanded in a loud voice. "Take my arm, sir. No, my other arm. Are you daft? Or simply incompetent?"

"If you would stop striking me with that blasted cane, I could better aid you in climbing these stairs, madam," Lucien grunted in annoyance. "There, just a few more steps and you shall see for yourself that I've not allowed the patient to expire."

"It wouldn't surprise me, young man, if she wasn't singing at the pearly gates already. If you've this much trouble helping an old woman up a flight of stairs, I cannot imagine how you've managed to keep that dear girl alive," Mrs. Merriweather huffed, her voice thin from a lack of breath and exertion. "I have heard from good sources that she was near death when you carried her here."

"Mrs. Merriweather, how kind of you to come for a visit!" Mrs. Phillips exclaimed, bustling into the corridor to lend assistance. "Charlotte will be so pleased to see you. She's just in here…"

Mrs. Merriweather eventually appeared in the doorway, clutching Lucien's arm with one hand and her ornate walking cane in the other. Her lined faced lit up when she saw Charlotte propped up in the bed and she righted her large bonnet which had somehow been knocked askew.

Charlotte's eyes filled with tears. "Oh, Mrs. Merriweather… I can hardly believe you are here. You know you should not be walking around with your back hurting like it does." The fact she'd left her home simply to visit her was incredibly touching. Charlotte could not remember the last time the lady had ventured out into the village or even for church services. She was content to putter around her tiny home, tending to her chickens and gardens. Beside Charlotte and Faith checking in on her and helping with various tasks, a few generous souls in the village also pitched in when needed.

The elderly lady pushed her glasses up on her nose and peered at Charlotte while shuffling closer. Lucien's expression was one of resigned torture as he walked with her, lending the support of his muscled arm. Charlotte flashed him a grateful smile, trying to convey with the simple gesture just how much his patience toward their cantankerous visitor meant to her.

"Hmmm," the lady snorted, sinking into the chair beside Charlotte's bed. Once she settled, Lucien quickly sidled away. He eyed the old woman's cane as if contemplating throwing it into the fireplace. "I fear you will never change, my dear. Here you are worrying about others when you are the one laid up in a sick bed. And of course I came to Ashcroft Manor. I had to see for myself that you were all right."

"I'm much better now," Charlotte assured her, wiping the tears with the back of her hand. She sniffled and laughed. "How on earth did you get here anyway? Surely, you didn't walk all that way!"

"Walk! Ha! I'm no ninny. I convinced that poor excuse of a gardener, Mister Mackie, to bring me in one of the estate carriages. I figured he's done such a fine job of ruining my garden, the least he could do was bring me here as a gesture of atonement," Mrs. Merriweather said, thumping her cane on the hardwood floor for emphasis. "The fool cut nearly all of my prize rosebushes back to mere stumps."

Charlotte bit back a grin. "For years I've tried convincing you that must be done. At least a trim, anyway."

"Yes, well, it seems I had little choice. The man was most insistent," the elderly lady grumbled, casting a suspicious glance around the room. "Well, are they taking good care of you, my dear?"

"Yes, Lord Ashcroft has been the epitome of an accommodating host when it comes to the sickroom," Charlotte said, her gaze flickering to meet Lucien's baleful glare. "Although I do feel I'm well enough to go home, it has been decided that I must stay a bit longer to fully recuperate. It's quite silly, I think. And unnecessary."

"Men do like to control the reins, so to speak. Especially those of Lord Ashcroft's caliber." Mrs. Merriweather dressed the gentleman in question with a critical stare before admitting in grudging admiration, "Although I must admit you very well might owe your life to the man and his heavy-handed ways. It's been said in town by that visiting vicar that you would have died, were it not for Lord Ashcroft here."

Charlotte shook her head, her lips pursed. "That is a gross exaggeration, Mrs. Merriweather."

"It's the truth of the matter," Lucien growled, stepping forward. "Miss Windsor was delirious with fever and has no inkling of just how sick she truly was. It is a miracle that she has recovered so quickly and is able to converse with us today. It was a very tenuous situation. If I have any say over the matter, she will remain under my care and that of Doctor Taylor for much longer than just a few days, although I do recognize the fact she is eager to return home."

"It's a good thing that you have no say-so over my life, Lord Ashcroft," Charlotte returned with a snide smirk. "If it were not for the good doctor's advice to remain here for just a bit longer, I would be gone already."

"Miss Windsor…" Lucien's tone contained a warning no one could possibly mistake or ignore. "I would expect and hope for a bit more gratitude for my obvious concern for your health."

Mrs. Merriweather's eyes narrowed, speculation evident in her expression as she glanced from him to Charlotte and back again.

Mrs. Phillips loudly cleared her throat, giving the three of them a bright smile. "Would you care for refreshments, Mrs. Merriweather? I'm sure after your journey here, a bit of lemonade or a spot of tea might just be the thing."

Mrs. Merriweather waved her hand in dismissal, her gaze still on Lucien. "Thank you, Mrs. Phillips, but I cannot stay long. I merely wanted to assure myself of Charlotte's well-being. And now that I see she is quite on the mend, I shall be returning home."

"Oh, can't you stay a bit longer?" Charlotte exclaimed, putting aside the tension that had seeped into the room. "Faith will be so disappointed she missed your visit."

Mrs. Merriweather laughed, rising from her chair and leaning over Charlotte to give her a kiss on the cheek. "That child has come to check on me several times, so don't you worry about that. Now, if Lord Ashcroft will lend his arm once more, I shall take my leave so you may get some rest. You do look a bit peaked, my dear." Her snowy white head tilted as she gazed down at Charlotte. "I am loath to admit it, but perhaps Lord Ashcroft is right. A few more days here will do you good, I'm sure of it."

Lucien mumbled something under his breath and Mrs. Merriweather, whose hearing was still sharp as an embroidery needle, shot him a questioning look. But Lucien smoothed his features into a mask of polite attentiveness and strode closer to help the lady turn about.

"I'll go make sure the carriage is at the ready," Mrs. Phillips offered. She practically ran from the room in a swish of skirts, eager to be absent and out of range of the widow's razor-sharp tongue.

"Goodbye, then, Mrs. Merriweather," Charlotte said, her tone morose as she watched Lucien escort the lady to the door. "The next time I see you shall be at your own cottage, I swear it."

"When I return, I will have a word with you, Miss Windsor," Lucien said smoothly, his eyes flashing like green fire as he stared at her. "I can see there are some things we must iron out during your convalescence."

Charlotte nearly wilted into the pillows, biting her lip in consternation. There was no way of escaping whatever lecture Lucien intended on administering. She was as captive as a fox caught in a trap and, pompous rakehell that he was, he would take advantage of that fact.

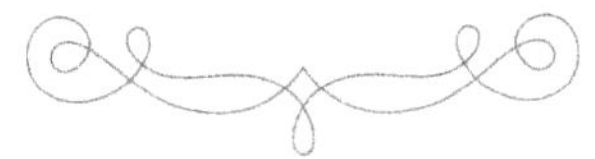

CHAPTER FIFTEEN
Lucien

LUCIEN KEPT HIS temper in check for the length of time required to see Mrs. Merriweather off safely. The old woman rode off in one of his carriages as though she were a visiting queen, his own damn master gardener acting as an escort. Once he stood on the front terrace steps alone, his attention immediately returned to the problem awaiting him in the north wing guest room.

Saucy little chit. I've been far too lenient with her. If she cannot understand the seriousness of her health, then I shall be forced to make it unequivocally clear.

He practically vaulted up the wide marble stairs leading to the second floor of the manor. Apparently, word of his displeasure had already flown through the household. There were no signs of Mr. Phillips nor of Underwood, Ashcroft's stoic, elderly butler. All the upstairs maids had vanished as well. The corridor leading to the guest wing was as quiet as a church vestibule.

Opening the door to the room Charlotte occupied, he found her seated in a chair beside the large bank of windows. Her eyes were closed as she basked in the sunshine and Lucien immediately likened the picture she presented to that of a small kitten enjoying a patch of sunlight. A soft blue robe encompassed her slender body, and she snuggled down into its folds as his low exhale of exasperation echoed in the stillness of the room.

"What in damnation are you doing out of bed?" he barked, shutting the door behind him.

Charlotte cracked open one eye, glaring at him as he stalked closer, his boots thumping angrily on the gleaming wood floor. "I am enjoying the sunshine, my lord. And if I possessed the strength, I would have flung these windows open to let in a bit of fresh air as well."

"You should not be taxing your strength in this manner." The words came out in a growl. "Stand up so I may assist you in returning to your bed."

She opened her eyes, studied him for a long moment, then serenely closed them once more. "No."

"Pardon?" Lucien's eyebrows rose high. Surely, he misunderstood her. It was inconceivable that someone might tell him no.

"I said, no." A tiny smile lifted the corners of her lush, bee stung mouth.

Lucien's hands clenched into helpless fists, struggling for patience. God, this woman was driving him to the brink of insanity. What did he care if she were sick or recovered her health? With or without him, she would continue living her life as she saw fit and there was not a damn thing he could do about that.

But you do care, a small voice inside him insisted. *If you did not, you would not be in this current situation. If you didn't care, you wouldn't be so worried that she might swoon and hurt herself in a fall. Just days ago she was deathly ill, and now she needs you to help her understand that her wellbeing is important to you.*

He required a different tactic, one that was miles away from his normal autocratic, arrogant self.

He decided to plead with her.

"Charlotte, please return to the bed. You are still weak and—"

Her eyes flew open, the blue depths sparkling bright with anger. "I'm not weak, my lord. I simply have not recovered all my strength. I refuse to be treated like an invalid, and I'm hardly a child. So, no matter how prettily you beg it of me, I will not return to bed. I shall go when I'm good and ready and not a moment before."

"Beg you…" Despite his best intentions to remain calm, Lucien's frustration spiked even higher. "Charlotte Windsor, if you do not return to that bed voluntarily, you shall find yourself across my knee instead. A few swats of my hand on that tempting backside of yours will no doubt do wonders in reducing your insolence."

"What an outrageous thing to say!" Charlotte gasped at the threat, her eyes narrowing on him. "You would not dare. Especially since you've labeled me a fragile, sick creature."

"If you insist on behaving like a child, I have no qualms in treating you as such," Lucien retorted in a silky tone. "Now, will you do as I say? Or shall I follow through on my word?"

"Fine." Charlotte conceded abruptly. "You are nothing more than a bullying tyrant, Lord Ashcroft." She jumped up from the chair, her movements quick and angry, her eyes flashing fire at him. Then just as suddenly, she wavered, her face turning a pale ivory. Grabbing hold of the tufted arm of the chair, she swayed on her feet much like she'd done the evening she fell ill. "Oh, dear," she murmured in a thin, weak voice. He knew it pained her to look to him for aid, but she did just that… her helplessness calling out to the knight in shining armor that somehow lurked deep within him.

"Goddamnit," Lucien swore, swooping her up into his arms. "You just proved my point and made the need for further conversation on this subject useless. You are in no condition to be without round the clock care and supervision just yet. So, you will do as I say, Charlotte Windsor, and remain abed under my care until I deem otherwise."

But for some reason, rather than carrying Charlotte directly to the bed which was only a few feet away and the most logical place to put her, Lucien instead sank into the chair she'd just vacated. Cradling her against his chest, he held her tight until her breathing leveled out and the small, involuntary noises of distress escaping her throat faded away. Even then, he did not put her aside but continued holding her as if she were the dearest treasure in the world, his face nuzzling into her freshly washed hair. He breathed deep, committing to memory every nuance and emotion invoked by embracing her so intimately. Realistically, he knew that if anyone strolled into her room and saw them this way, there would be no avoiding the consequences of his actions.

Maybe that's what I want. Maybe that's the only way I can keep her from leaving me.

"Lucien…" Charlotte whispered. "You should not be holding me like this. It's… it's improper."

"Be quiet," he admonished with a heavy sigh. "I swear to God, Charlotte, you have me so twisted about in my own head, I'm not sure what's proper and what's not. I only know that I've been dying to hold you and the only thing stopping me before was the fact you've been ill. Just a few more minutes like this, and I promise I'll let you go."

Charlotte relaxed against him, inexplicably snuggling closer and resting her head against his chest. She did not say anything more, her breathing becoming easier the longer Lucien held her.

They sat like that for a while, the sun warming their bodies until Lucien drowsily realized Charlotte had fallen asleep. Gently, he shifted her body so that she lay across his forearm, and he could see her face as she slumbered.

His heart softened, melting into a puddle of ice-water at the sight of her beauty and the trusting manner in which she slept in his embrace. He could feel himself changing and he wondered if he dared pursue what his heart demanded. Along with that question came the niggling doubt if what he felt for this girl was genuine or simply a basic reaction to the unaccustomed loss of female companionship.

Perhaps this unusual situation might prove useful when it came to appeasing his father's demands to seek a wife. After all, he was attracted to Charlotte, and she seemed to share that with him. An arrangement where she posed as a potential fiancée would satisfy the old earl while also keeping her within arm's reach. It would give him a bit of time to untangle his feelings. Would Charlotte agree to such a scenario? Maybe a dismal future as a governess could sway her into believing that sham relationship was worth it.

His arms tightened around her. The idea that she would be his, even in an imaginary situation, had his heart pounding hard. He would have more time with her.

Once a new vicar was chosen, she would be gone.

Charlotte stirred, her eyes opening to clash with his. For a long moment they simply stared at one another. Then slowly, Lucien lowered his head until his mouth hovered above hers.

He waited. Waited for her to make the next move. Waited for her to make the choice that would seal her fate. If she struggled to free herself, if she turned her head away, he would let her go and abandon this crazy, half-formed plan.

But Charlotte did not pull away. She watched him with those pretty blue eyes, so wide and innocent while her tongue darted out to swipe her lips as if in anticipation. Lucien barely contained a groan as everything inside him roared to life. She lifted her head so that her mouth could meet his on an exhaled breath. She kissed him softly, shyly, hesitantly, but insistently, until Lucien began kissing her back with all the raging hunger bedeviling him since he laid eyes on this girl.

Charlotte's hands gripped the front of his coat. She held tight, fingers clenching the material as if it were the only thing that kept her floating away from reality. Lucien deepened the kiss, his tongue stroking hers and retreating until everything else melted into the background. His large hand cradled her jaw, his fingers tangling in the braid her hair was woven into. He kissed her over and over, shifting her body until she was curled in the circle of his arms with no way of escaping.

Drawing back just enough to break contact with her mouth, he began pressing scorching hot kisses along the slender column of her neck. He pulled his hand free of her hair and moved until his palm covered her breast. When she moaned in submission, he shaped her flesh until it fit his hand then lightly pinched the nipple that was puckered and tight beneath the thin cloth of her night rail and robe.

Her sharp intake of breath was all he needed for an answer. Greedily, he plucked and pinched the tender peak until it strained to meet his fingers. If he could have laid her across the bed, he would have given the other breast the same treatment but their positions in the chair only gave him access to part of her body. Beneath her curvy rear-end, his cock was hard as stone and demanding that he take what he wanted.

"Oh, Lucien," she whimpered, throwing her head back until more of her throat was exposed to his mouth. "What are you doing to me? What spell have you woven around me? You make me forget who I am. Make me forget why I must not allow such indecencies."

"Nothing about this is indecent, little siren. This is right. You, here in my arms, is right. My mouth on yours," he kissed her fiercely as if emphasizing the point, "is right. If I could kiss you every second for the next thousand years, every heartbeat of that time would be right."

"I cannot think rationally when you hold me. And every time you kiss me, my brain refuses to work properly," Charlotte confessed sadly. "I feel as if I am going mad."

"Then we are going mad together. Because you've invaded my every thought and everything I thought once important no longer means a thing." Lucien stopped kissing her although his fingers continued with the sensual torture of her breast. "I want to ask something of you."

She gave him a quizzical look then slowly nodded her head that he should continue. A gasp escaped her when he tweaked her flesh a bit harder, but she arched into his hand and Lucien knew the flames inside her burned as bright as the ones raging inside him.

"I want to court you," he said slowly, tracing the outline of her lips with tiny kisses when she began to voice a protest. "Do not fret. It would not be real, little siren, and it would be to our mutual benefit. Already, I am helping you with the money I promised when it comes to hiring a vicar. This would be something different. If you agree, I will tell my father I am pursing a relationship with a suitable woman while you remain in Ashcroft Village for the indefinite future."

"You-you wish to lie to your father by pretending to seek an engagement with me?" Charlotte breathed in disbelief, covering his hand with hers and stopping all movement. "I cannot be party to such deception, Lucien. It wouldn't be right."

"A small deception that benefits us both and harms no one. You won't be able to live at Hollyhock Cottage, of course, but we will set up alternative arrangements. And remember, the monies I am paying you are substantial. You could save it for your future and the expenditures you will have with Faith attending the school you desire."

Charlotte groaned, pushing his chest and sitting upright. "You do not seem to see the inherent wrongness of what you are asking of me, Lucien. Real or not, it would be the same as requiring me to become your mistress."

"It is not the same," Lucien bit out, frustrated that she could not... or would not... see the benefits of his proposition. "You would not be required to engage in any form of intimacy with me, and I would publicly acknowledge you as a romantic interest. I'll even go so far as to introduce you to my parents. Just so there is an air of respectability to our courtship."

Charlotte's eyebrow arched high. "No intimacy? So, you will refrain from kissing me like this?" She squeezed his hand where it still lay on her breast and pulled it away from her body. "You will stop touching me?"

"As the woman I am courting, I would expect there will be moments of physical interaction. Instances where our mutual affection will be on display," Lucien argued. "What I have suggested is not unreasonable."

Charlotte rolled off his lap, struggling to stand while Lucien stared at her. "Your only care is what *you* want, my lord. Whatever eases your particular problem and makes the way clear for you is of utmost importance. To you. Only you. You have given no thought as to what this would do to me. How such an act would affect my life. Your wish is to place me in a little treasure box nearby… one that you can fling open whenever the situation calls for it. I would *still* be your toy. I cannot do this, Lucien. No matter how much you protest that it is to my benefit." Wrapping her arms around her waist, her mouth trembled as though she might burst into tears at any moment. "I have no right to demand it of you as I am a guest in your home, but I'd like you to leave my room now."

"Damnit, Charlotte, if you would only listen to reason…" Lucien scowled, a twinge of guilt eating at his stomach for the callous way he had put forth his proposal.

"Please leave." She turned her back to him and shuffled a few steps toward the bed. "I don't want to talk to you right now. I don't want to talk at all."

Lucien rose from the chair, reaching out to cup her elbow. She flinched at his touch and that only made the shame boil higher inside his gut. He was making a damned fine mess of things without any effort at all.

"At least let me help you back into bed before I go. I don't want you nearly fainting again," he muttered, leading her toward the bed. She was stiff as he walked with her, a far cry from the soft, pliant creature he'd held in his arms just moments before.

Once she was settled with the pillows propped behind her, Lucien gripped Charlotte's chin between thumb and forefinger, forcing her to meet his gaze.

"I know my proposal offends you. I understand why. But I ask that you at least consider it for its practicality and the benefits of keeping Faith in a place she has known her whole life." It was dastardly of him to use Charlotte's love for her sister as a means of gaining what he wanted, but Lucien truly believed it was in their best interest as well as his own. "Think it over, siren."

Rather than answer him, she closed her eyes, silently dismissing him and his arguments. Lucien cursed softly, released his grip on her, and left the room without another word, closing the door softly behind him.

CHAPTER SIXTEEN
Charlotte

CHARLOTTE WOKE UP to Mrs. Phillips bringing in a lunch tray of artichoke soup and a bowl of fresh strawberries. She only managed a few bites before turning over onto her side. Ignoring the housekeeper's *tsk* of sympathy, Charlotte buried her head in the pillow while she listened to the matronly woman bustle about the room.

"I'm sure your appetite will return soon, dear. Maybe by this evening you will feel a bit better. I suspect that the visit from Mrs. Merriweather was far too taxing for you."

"Thank you, Mrs. Phillips," she sniffled. "I'd like to be alone now, if that's all right."

"Of course, dear," the housekeeper said quietly. "You need your rest if you are to get better."

For a long time after the woman departed, Charlotte pondered the events of that morning, remembering everything the earl said during their heated discussion. She questioned whether she was too hasty in dismissing Lucien's proposal and if she'd done the right thing in rejecting it. There was really only one reason to even entertain such a ridiculous arrangement and that was for the sake of her sister. Agreeing to Lucien's suggestion meant keeping Faith in Ashcroft Village just a bit longer. Wouldn't it be better for her sister to continue being brought up in a familiar environment rather than the unknowns of a girl's school where she wouldn't know a single soul?

When she heard Faith rustling around in the connecting room Charlotte propped herself up in the bed, dashing any evidence of tears from her cheeks.

"Charlotte?" Faith poked her head through the connecting door's opening. "Are you awake?"

Charlotte smiled, waving a hand to indicate Faith should enter the room. "Did you have a good time going to market with Cook?"

"The best time. I didn't want to leave." Faith leaped onto Charlotte's bed. "They had the dearest little lambs there today. Black and gray ones. They were so funny… you should have seen them jumping on bales of straw and upturned buckets. Why, a few times they jumped on the older sheep and used their bodies to leap into the air."

"I bet that was a sight to see." Charlotte laughed softly. "If I know you, you probably had a dozen of them picked out to bring home as new pets."

Faith grinned. "Only half a dozen. Our garden is certainly not large enough for a dozen!"

Charlotte tweaked Faith's nose. "Cheeky miss."

Faith grew more somber. "I went to Hollyhock Cottage today. Cook asked the coachman to take me there on the way back from the market. She helped gather more clothes for the two of us. Everything was so rushed when you got sick that I did not get everything we needed."

"You did a fine job that night, Faith. You took care of me and knew just what to do."

Faith's head tilted as she studied Charlotte. "Mr. Russell has been looking after Hollyhock. While he certainly has no idea how to mend a gate, he has made sure things are secured and in their proper place." A small grimace darkened her angelic face. "He's acting like he lives there already."

"It is a high likelihood he will be the new vicar, Faith," Charlotte's tone was gentle. "I believe Lord Ashcroft will no longer require my help in interviewing any further applicants for the position. I think his mind is set on hiring this one."

"Ugh," Faith said with an exaggerated frown. "I did not like how he stared at you over dinner. Like he considered you part of the furnishings being left behind for the new tenant."

Charlotte stilled. "Do you mean Mister Russell or Lord Ashcroft?

"I mean the vicar, of course. He went on and on about what he used to have while disparaging our few belongings. It was hardly a flattering look for the man… to be so critical."

"I'm sure he meant well. I think he's just a bit awkward and doesn't realize he is saying things the wrong way."

"He told me today he intends on visiting you soon. I think he likes you," Faith said with a dramatic rolling of her eyes before she squealed and grabbed Charlotte's hands. "Oh! I'm such a silly goose! I've forgotten to tell you the most exciting news!"

"Let me guess. You bought me a lamb today."

"Don't be silly," Faith admonished. "I haven't the money for a lamb. If you want one, you should ask Lord Ashcroft for the funds. He would do anything for you."

"Faith," Charlotte chided her sister. "That is not true. He barely knows me. And I would never ask him for funds for any purpose." Her heart pounded with the insincerity of that remark. Wasn't she thinking of becoming the earl's hired fiancée?

"He knows you well enough, I think!" Faith trilled, flopping onto her stomach in the middle of the bed. She propped her chin in her hand. "Anyway, you shall never guess who has come to Ashcroft Manor, Charlotte. All the house is abuzz with the news since Cook and I came home from market."

"Hmmm," Charlotte pretended to ponder for a moment. "Ah! I know! The Prince Regent himself!"

Faith giggled, rolling onto her side and gazing at Charlotte with mischievous eyes. "Better! And far more handsome than Ole Prinny could ever hope to be."

"I give up…" Charlotte raised her hands in surrender.

"The Mayfair Rakehells themselves, Charlotte! The other two, that is. Both of them are here! They only just arrived sometime after lunch. Have you not heard the news from a maid or something?"

"Where did you hear that moniker, Faith?" Charlotte asked with a disapproving frown. "That is not something a young miss like yourself should even be aware of, much less repeat."

Faith pouted. "But they *are* the Mayfair Rakehells. Cook said so. She was all flustered at the thought of them being here for dinner, so she rushed off to the kitchen to compose a menu. And I saw them as I was coming up to see you. They did not see me, though. I stayed close to the wall as I came up the stairs and I watched as they went with Lord Ashcroft into his study. Then they shut the door, and I couldn't see them anymore." Faith cast Charlotte a sly smile. "They are very handsome. I wager some women probably swoon at the sight of them. All three standing together was a sight to behold… they could all be brothers, that's how much they look alike. Lord Ashcroft told them there was not much to do here in the country, but he was sure he could find something to hold their attention."

"You should not have been eavesdropping, nor spying, Faith," Charlotte said, her heart beating fast. Why would Lucien's friends leave London? It was the height of the Season. Parties, soirées, balls… it was a whirlwind of activity right now and taking one's self out to the country was not the norm. "Remember, we are guests in this house. I will not tolerate rudeness to our host."

"I'm sorry, Charlotte, but the fact there are three of London's most eligible bachelors currently under Ashcroft Manor's roof cannot be ignored. We've gone without anything exciting happening in the town for so long and now here comes a trio of handsome, wealthy men who are no doubt in search of wives."

"Wives?" Charlotte shook her head in wonderment at the calculating gleam dancing in her young sister's bright blue eyes. "Where on earth do you come up with the outlandish things you say? That is a subject you are far too young to discuss."

"But Cook said—" Faith began indignantly, sitting up to better argue the point.

"Never mind what she said. I don't want you repeating whatever you may have overheard from her or anyone else." Charlotte's tone was firm. "Now, you should go and get yourself washed up and change your dress while you're at it. You have mud on the hem there and you smell like one of the lambs you were holding. Go on, now."

"Oh, all right," Faith said, hanging her head as she slid off Charlotte's bed. "I'm going. But don't say I didn't warn you the first time you see the Mayfair Rakehells standing together as a group. I may only be ten years old, but I swear even my heart skipped several beats."

CHAPTER SEVENTEEN

Lucien

"THE OBVIOUS SOLUTION is to evict the girl and install the first vicar you interviewed," Wylder said, drawing deep of his cigar before blowing the smoke up into the air until it drifted away in a hazy plume.

"It would seem the most expedient way of getting what you want most, Ashcroft," Simon agreed. Pouring himself another whisky, he grinned at Lucien over the edge of the glass. "You *do* wish to return to London, don't you?"

"Of course I do." Lucien scowled. "But it's not so simple a matter as you think. She has a younger sister to care for."

"So?" Wylder seemed puzzled by Lucien's concern.

"So, I cannot just throw them out into the streets. Regardless of my reputation, I'm not that heartless." Lucien tossed back the remnants of whisky in his own glass.

"I hear you are paying the girl a pretty penny for her expertise," Wylder drawled with customary cynicism.

Mere seconds later, Lucien had his friend pinned against the wall, his fists gripping great handfuls of the man's coat to the point the fabric was torn.

"What the damnation… what is wrong with you, Lucien?" Wylder said, truly astonished by Lucien's actions.

"Don't fucking talk about her like that, do you understand

me?" Lucien snarled, giving Wylder a shake to emphasize his fury. "She's not a whore, and I won't stand for anyone insinuating that she is. *No one.* Not even my closest friends. So, mind your tongue and your manners when it comes to her, or so help me God, I'll rip your head from your shoulders for use as decoration on Ashcroft's entrance gates." Casting a glance over his shoulder at a strangely calm Simon, Lucien growled, "That goes for you as well, Simon."

Simon tipped his glass to Lucien. A tiny smile of dawning comprehension tilted the corners of his mouth. "Point taken. Wylder, apologize before our dear friend goes apoplectic with indignation."

Wylder's eyes narrowed on Lucien, his chin setting higher with natural stubbornness. "As soon as I receive one for him ripping my coat. I just received it from the tailor and now I shall have to take it right back."

Lucien scowled, but he slowly released Wylder, watching as the man swore soundly over the tear in the coat's shoulder seam. "Pardon for ruining your coat, Wylder."

"It's hardly ruined but it is rather inconvenient to return it for repair," Wylder grumbled. "And my apologies for my statement regarding the girl. It was said in jest. I had no idea you felt so strongly in regard to her situation."

Raking a hand through his thick, dark hair in frustration, Lucien retreated. His visceral reaction to the perceived insult to Charlotte's character was shocking. Normally, he would have made his own snide comment and let the matter pass, but not when it came to Charlotte. His little siren deserved better than his friends thinking the worst of her.

The fact Simon and Wylder had come for an unannounced visit had Lucien feeling unaccountably conflicted. One the one hand, he was happy to see his two best friends. They had voluntarily traded the gaiety of London for the slow, plodding passage of time in the country. And while he should have been ecstatic to have a pleasant diversion from the responsibilities his father had thrust upon him, he could only muster a lackluster excitement for their visit.

But it was an undisputed fact that their presence complicated matters. In fact, he was frustrated that his attention could not remain focused solely on Miss Charlotte Windsor. She was all he thought of now, day and night, and any other distraction was not welcomed right now.

"This is unlike you, Lucien. You've never been one to let a woman distract you. Please tell us this is simply a diversion created to avoid the boredom of country life." Wylder snubbed out the cigar and shrugged the coat off his athletic form. He frowned at seeing the size of the tear in the fabric before throwing the garment into a chair with a snort of disgust.

Lucien sank into a leather-wrapped club seat, thrusting his fingers again through his hair. "I will admit I am not quite myself. I don't know what it is about this girl, but she has me tied up in fucking knots."

He missed the alarmed glance Wylder and Simon shared between them.

"Then there's only one thing to be done," Simon said in a careful tone. "You must fulfil your duties here quickly and return to the social whirl of town. Once you are back engaging in your favorite activities, any lingering feelings you might have for Miss Windsor will be erased soon enough."

"My favorite activities?" Lucien snarled. "And which of those noble pursuits should I miss the most? The whoring? The gambling? The endless rounds of meaningless parties and horse races and boxing matches?"

"My vote would be for the whoring," Wylder offered amicably.

Lucien glared at the man. "There's more to life than fucking every woman who lands in your bed."

"My guess is you've not been fucking at all and that is the source of your ill temper." Simon chuckled then sobered when Lucien turned a baleful stare on him. "My guess is you've not had a woman since your last night in London at The Scarlett Petticoat."

Lucien neither denied nor acknowledged the truth of Simon's statement but his silence was answer enough.

"Good God, man," Wylder breathed in equal parts horror and admiration. "Do you mean to say you've not tossed a woman's skirts for nearly three weeks now?" Flinging his dark head back, he let loose a sharp laugh. "This is so astounding, I find myself bereft of words. Truly, this is a monumental event."

Lucien's jaw clenched tight. He loved these two men as though they were blood brothers, but he would not sully what passed between himself and Charlotte by relating their previous interlude simply for their amusement. And certainly he would not use it as assurance that he was still the same skirt-chasing rake he'd always been.

But the memory of debauchery and wickedness committed at The Scarlett Petticoat with Simon and Wylder right alongside him that last night in London, made Lucien's skin heat in the most uncomfortable manner.

Because all he could think about in that moment was using Charlotte Windsor as a willing participant in reenacting those moments. He imagined how stunning she would look bound in ropes and on her knees, her mouth open to receive his cock. He imagined spreading her milky white thighs with his hard hands and devouring her sweet little quim until she quivered beneath him and helplessly called out his name. He imagined thrusting into her body, savoring the tightness of her channel and the soft little whimpers of lust he knew would escape her throat as he claimed her. He imagined fucking her until she was incapable of breathing without him. It was a terrible twist of irony that he was beginning to wonder if he could survive without her.

"Lucien," Wylder said, snagging his attention. "Is your fascination with her because of who she is as an actual person? Or is it because you've been deprived of female companionship for longer than a reasonable man should go without?"

Lucien sagged in his chair, rubbing his forehead in defeat. "I don't know."

But that wasn't the truth at all. He did know. He was obsessed with the thought of Charlotte being his. He wanted her. Her, and no other.

But there was only one way to claim a girl of Charlotte's caliber. And despite the internal angst twisting his gut, he wasn't prepared to take such drastic lengths.

"Then come back to London with us, Lucien. Install this Mister Russell as Ashcroft's new vicar, thank Miss Windsor for her father's service," Simon murmured thoughtfully, "And get the hell out of here while you can."

⋙⋘

THERE WERE TWO extra place settings at dinner that evening.

Lucien looked askance at Mrs. Phillips as he, Wylder, and Simon sat down at the enormous formal dining table.

"There seems to be two unnecessary seats prepared, Mrs. Phillips." He frowned. "It is only the three of us dining tonight. There's been an error, obviously."

"No, Your Lordship," Mrs. Phillips said, her lips pressing tight together. "There is no mistake."

Before Lucien could argue the point with the uncomfortable housekeeper, the dining room doors swung open. Faith bounded into the room, twin pigtails bouncing on her shoulders, her blue eyes sparkling with mischievousness.

"Good evening, Lord Ashcroft." She dipped a perfect curtsey to the men. "And good evening to you, Lord Camden. Lord Wyldewood."

"Good evening, Faith." A slight frown creased Lucien's brow. Why the child was attending dinner with three bachelors was a mystery. Granted, societal norms were a bit different in the country, with formal rules relaxed in certain cases, but this was highly unusual. "I did not know you were attending dinner with us."

Before Faith could reply, a soft, husky voice came from the doorway and the three men scrambled to stand from their chairs.

"I do hope it is all right that Faith and I join you tonight, Lord Ashcroft. Mrs. Phillips assured me that it was no problem to set two extra plates." Charlotte glided into the room, looking sumptuously ethereal in a soft, mint-green gown. She wore gloves and her sunshine-colored hair was pulled into a flattering bun high atop her head. Curling tendrils fluttered about her pale face while her eyes burned bright with determination.

"Char—" Lucien cleared his throat, eyes darkening as he realized his own error. Quickly correcting himself, he continued, "Miss Windsor. You are not well enough to be out of bed, I think."

"And I think I was growing quite tired of having only myself for company," Charlotte replied, coming closer to the table and choosing one of the empty place settings as her spot. It happened to be the seat beside Simon, and he made a great show of taking her hand and bending over it, his dark-blue eyes glowing with amusement.

"Good evening. You must be Miss Charlotte Windsor." His gaze flickered to a scowling Lucien before he said, "I am Simon Blackthorne, Earl of Camden."

"Pleased to make your acquaintance, Lord Camden. This is my sister, Faith." Charlotte nodded toward her younger sister to take the seat on the other side of the table next to Wylder.

Her eyes widened as Wylder left his chair, advancing on her to tug her hand from Simon's grip.

"Wylder St. Clair, Earl of Wyldewood at your service." Wylder kissed her hand, his firm mouth erasing the memory of Simon's lips where they had just touched her skin. "You are even more lovely than Ashcroft described."

Charlotte's gaze locked with Lucien's. A smile of triumph tugged at her lips, leaving him with the overwhelming desire to toss her over his lap and administer a much-needed spanking for her reckless behavior. "Thank you, my lord. And the three of you together is even more formidable than Faith led me to believe."

Both men burst out with surprised laughter, but Lucien's frown was thunderous. She and Faith had discussed his friends? What was said between the two of them? And why in God's name did Charlotte believe she was well enough to come downstairs? She should still be abed, being tended to and coddled.

Simon held her chair out for her, and the three men remained standing until she sank into the seat. Wylder retreated to his side of the table and pulled Faith's chair out for her as well.

Lucien barely hid his fury. Only he seemed to notice how wan and fragile Charlotte appeared. How her gloved hands shook the tiniest bit as she removed the articles and placed them in her lap. She was still so damned weak, and his heart clenched painfully when she coughed delicately into a linen napkin before drinking a bit of water from a crystal goblet.

What she hoped to prove by showing herself in his dining room, he could only guess. But if he had to hazard insight into her motives, he would say she wanted to prove she was well enough to leave him.

I'm not ready to let her go just yet.

The servants began bringing in the first course and everyone was silent as bowls of white soup were placed before them.

"I adore white soup," Faith declared, picking up her spoon with the intention of digging into the meal.

"One moment, dear," Charlotte murmured. "Wait for everyone to be served."

Faith laid her spoon down, her expression forlorn. To her credit, she'd been mostly silent since entering the dining room and Lucien knew she was on her best behavior, determined not to embarrass her sister.

"It's quite all right, Faith. Go ahead," Lucien said, nodding at the young girl while Charlotte flashed him a look of gratitude. "Seeing that we are most informal here at Ashcroft Manor, we will not hold to the *ton's* silly rules."

"I second that, Ashcroft," Wylder remarked, his silver gaze sliding over Charlotte from across the table. The expression he wore was perplexed, as if he were attempting to solve a riddle but catching sight of Lucien's frown, he smiled widely. "Things are very different in the country. Rules are relaxed and sometimes they are even ignored."

Lucien's hand tightened around his goblet. He knew what his friend insinuated with that cleverly disguised comment. The fact Charlotte was currently staying in his home without benefit of a proper chaperone could become a minor scandal if one chose to make it so.

Charlotte did not respond to that, simply ducked her head and lifted a spoonful of soup to her lips.

"Have you been to many plays at the theatre, Lord Camden?" Faith asked, her eyes wide as she directed her question at Simon. "I do hope to see one in the future. Have you been backstage before? Do you know any of the actors?"

Simon's laugh was indulgent and while he answered Faith, Lucien's gaze remained on Charlotte, watching intently for a reason to banish her back to bed. But she defied him by eating the entire bowl of soup. By the time the second course of roasted capon in a wild mushroom cream sauce arrived, her face was not quite as pale as before and she engaged in a spirited discussion with Simon over the merits of Mozart versus Beethoven for the opera.

So things went as the evening progressed until the final course of dessert was served. Faith let out a cry of delight when a bowl of pineapple ice was set before her.

"How thoughtful of you, Lord Ashcroft, to remember my longing for pineapple ice. It is the most amazing thing to ever happen to me. I shall never forget this moment."

"You've not even tried it, darling," Charlotte said with a grin. "You may find it horrid."

"No, I won't," Faith declared. "It shall taste like sunshine; I just know it." She pursed her lips at her older sister. "If you do not like yours, may I have it, Charlotte?"

"We'll see," Charlotte replied, dipping her spoon into the dessert and bringing a small taste to her lips. "Mmmm," she sighed dramatically. "It tastes far better than I expected."

Faith dug into the frozen concoction while Lucien's eyes helplessly fixed on Charlotte's mouth and the spoon that she gave a small, discreet lick. His cock hardened painfully as he fantasized Charlotte's mouth worshipping his body with the same delicate reverence. Blood rushed in his ears, and he struggled to control his reaction to her innocent actions.

Christ above…

"Careful, Lucien," Wylder leaned closer to whisper in his direction without Charlotte overhearing. "You are practically salivating over the lady and the way she eats dessert from a damn spoon."

"I cannot fucking help it," Lucien hissed back under his breath. "Everything about her fascinates me. It's a goddamn curse."

Wylder leaned back, an assessing gaze passing over Charlotte that had Lucien gritting his teeth with the force of his possessiveness. "If that's true, you are in more trouble than we could have ever imagined."

CHAPTER EIGHTEEN
Charlotte

MISTER EARNEST RUSSELL came to call three days later. Carrying a bouquet of flowers that Charlotte suspected came straight from her own cottage garden the man was so nervous when handing them over, he promptly dropped the bunch on the floor at her feet.

"I beg your pardon, Miss Windsor," he sputtered, picking the bouquet up and looking about the west parlor. "I thought perhaps there would be a vase readily available but I see there is not."

"No need to fret." Charlotte smiled at him while addressing Ashcroft Manor's housekeeper. "Mrs. Phillips? Is there a small vase I might use for these? Something that is not too dear of a piece?"

"I'm sure I can find something in the kitchen, miss," Mrs. Phillips replied, her expression stern as she stared at the young man.

"Do take your time, madam," Earnest said. "I've much to discuss with Miss Windsor and a bit of privacy would be greatly appreciated."

"You'll get the same sort of privacy any other gentleman caller would receive, Mister Russell. An open door to the corridor and myself acting as chaperone." Mrs. Phillips's tone was as chilly as her glare, but she said nothing more as she exited the parlor with a humph of exasperation.

"Come have a seat, Mr. Russell." Charlotte indicated he should sit on the brocade upholstered settee and from his position, it was obvious that Earnest expected her to occupy the space beside him. Instead, she slid into a Sheraton-style chair opposite him and quietly folded her hands in her lap. She ignored the flash of disappointment on Earnest's features while plastering a pleasant smile upon her own.

Faith had warned her that Earnest intended on calling soon so Charlotte was not surprised at all to see him in Ashcroft Manor's parlor. What did surprise her, however, was the fact the Earl of Ashcroft was not in attendance as well. Learning the earl and his two guests had gone for a morning ride Charlotte pondered his new lack of interest. The logical conclusion was that Lucien had finally realized the difference between their lives and the social constraints that existed between them. Was it any wonder that he quickly turned to the distractions offered by the arrival of his friends? She was no longer a source of entertainment for him and while grateful that her life could now return to normal, Charlotte found the fickleness of his affection horribly painful.

Mrs. Phillips had earlier relayed the news that the fourth applicant for the vicar position would arrive the next afternoon. Charlotte had decided she would attend the interview as she had done before. Until Lucien selected a vicar, she was obligated to continue the arduous task of helping him choose one. Especially since she still needed funds to leave Ashcroft Village. The monies he'd promised her would help immensely when it came time to relocate.

What about playing his pretend love interest? Will you consider it so that you have no need to leave?

The question haunted her, but Lucien gave no indication that he was still interested in following through with that proposal. Reluctantly, she decided the opportunity was no longer an option.

"Mr. Russell, it is so kind of you to visit and inquire of my wellbeing. I assure you I am feeling much better. In fact, I have made plans to return to Hollyhock Cottage soon." Charlotte smoothed the front of her dress, avoiding the longing gaze Earnest settled upon her. "As you can imagine, Faith and I are anxious to be back home. You have our thanks for looking after the cottage in our absence."

"It was no hardship, Miss Windsor. Indeed, it was my honor." Fumbling with his gloves, he removed them and shoved them into his pockets. "I have something to ask of you, and I hope you forgive my forwardness in posing this question while you are still recovering from your illness."

"Of course, Mr. Russell. You may ask me anything. I shall try to answer to the best of my abilities."

"Would you... what I mean to say... is would you consider a marriage proposal, Miss Windsor, if I am selected to serve as vicar here?" Earnest stumbled over the words, but even as Charlotte listened in a dazed state of shock, the man rose from the settee and landed on his knees at her feet. "I know we've been acquainted for only two weeks, but you have captured my heart with your quiet, demure ways. I feel certain that a union would benefit us both." He stared up at her with worshipping eyes, his hands capturing hers and holding them tight. "It would be my honor if you said yes."

Charlotte swallowed hard. "Mr. Russell, I cannot give you an answer on a question like this. We hardly know one another and—"

"We would come to know one another, and it is a fine match. One cannot discount the fact that it would solve your problem of having someplace to go, and my own in establishing myself as vicar with the townspeople who adore you. Of course, if I am not chosen for the position, I expect that you would break off the engagement. I would not expect you to follow through with a wedding in that case."

Charlotte's irritation grew as the reality of his statement sunk in. He was not proposing marriage for the sake of marrying *her*, but simply because it would make his task easier to have her as a wife when it came to the people of Ashcroft Village. "Mr. Russell, I think this is a hasty proposition and one I cannot entertain right now. I am not without the means to take care of myself and Faith, and I see no reason to tie the two of us into a loveless marriage simply for the sake of convenience."

"Marriages of convenience are terribly commonplace. Ours would not be unique, my dear Miss Windsor." He chose that moment to press wet, warm kisses to the backs of her hands. Charlotte almost snatched her hands away.

"Mr. Russell, you overwhelm me with practical reasons for this proposal, but I cannot say yes. I am very sorry to disappoint you with an answer you do not want." She would have risen to her feet in a tactful escape, but Earnest was kneeling on the hem of her gown, leaving her effectively trapped in her seat. Unless she caused a scene by pushing him backward, she was stuck for the time being.

Earnest frowned. "I don't understand. I have a great deal of affection for you and for your sister. Indeed, I would not even require that you send her away immediately, considering her tender age. Eventually, she could be placed in a boarding school while we continue the work here of administering to the fine people of this town."

"Please get up off the floor, Mr. Russell," Charlotte asked with quiet firmness. "I cannot say for certain you will even gain the position of vicar so putting forth a proposal at this stage is certainly premature."

Earnest's brown eyes lit with immediate hope. "Does this mean you shall accept my hand in marriage if I am offered the position?"

Before Charlotte could form an answer, Mrs. Phillips came bustling back into the room. She carried a simple glass vase with the bouquet artfully arranged but spying Earnest on his knees before Charlotte, she nearly dropped the entire thing.

"Mr. Russell!" she exclaimed, frantically looking for a spot to set the vase. "What on earth has happened? Did you trip? Should I call the butler to assist you? Or the doctor?"

Earnest flushed bright red with embarrassment. Scooting off the hem of Charlotte's gown, he stuttered, "Miss Windsor and I are in the midst of a very serious matter, Mrs. Phillips. A marriage proposal that is of the utmost importance to us both. Would you please give us just a few more moments of privacy? You see, the lady has yet to say yes."

Charlotte took advantage of the unexpected opportunity, leaping to her feet and leaving Earnest kneeling on the floor. "Oh, Mrs. Phillips. What a lovely arrangement. Here..." Charlotte quickly strode across the room to the elderly woman to take the vase from her hands. Lowering her voice, she whispered, "Please do not leave me alone with Mr. Russell. I've already turned him down, but he is quite persistent, as you can see." Continuing in a normal tone for Earnest's benefit, Charlotte said, "I think the sideboard there by the window is the perfect spot for these."

Earnest rose to his feet, brushing off his trousers with one hand and pushing his sandy brown hair back off his forehead with the other. "Mrs. Phillips, I humbly implore you to leave us..."

Mrs. Phillips shook her finger at the man. "I most certainly will not! I shall stay in this room as a proper chaperone." The housekeeper flashed Earnest a look of disappointment. "Really, Mr. Russell, your actions are most improper. It's a good thing I returned when I did otherwise Miss Windsor's reputation would surely have suffered."

Earnest appeared as though he wished to remark on that, perhaps to point out that Charlotte had spent the past few days as a guest at Ashcroft Manor without a true chaperone. But his lips pinched tightly together, and he remained silent.

"Please sit back down, Mr. Russell," Charlotte said softly, wondering if she was doing the right thing by giving the man false hope. "Let us continue with our visit and leave the other matter for future discussion."

AFTER EARNEST HAD departed, Charlotte spent the rest of the morning packing her and Faith's few items into two threadbare valises that once belonged to their parents. It was sometime after lunch when she made her way downstairs once more with a plan of sitting in the garden for a while. The house was oddly quiet, the many servants taking their own meal break except for Underwood. The elderly butler stood at the ready by the front door in case of unexpected visitors. He gave Charlotte a smile when she passed him and entered a corridor leading to the garden access.

This route required passing the library. Charlotte decided she might as well select a book to enjoy during her time outside. Once she and Faith returned home, she doubted there would be very much free time available to her. Her days would once again revolve around the simple task of surviving. That meant working with Mrs. Merriweather again. Picking back up the tutoring of the blacksmith's daughters. Concocting her elixirs and potions for the sick and infirm. It was her very own invention of a potent salve that had helped her regain her own health so quickly following her illness. Faith had been smart enough to bring it to Ashcroft that night and every morning had rubbed a bit of the aromatic stuff onto Charlotte's chest.

And of course, she would busy herself once again writing letters to procure employment as a governess somewhere. Even though Lucien had promised to help in that area, Charlotte refused to rely on that. She was used to doing things on her own and this would likely be one of those times when her own persistence would pay off.

The double doors of the library were closed as she approached them. It wasn't until she slipped inside that she realized the room was not empty. Not wishing to see Lucien, or anyone else for that matter, Charlotte hesitated, prepared to flee when the two men speaking caught her attention. She froze, listening with incredulity to their conversation.

"This is an unquantified disaster, you know."

Charlotte recognized the man's voice as that of Lord Wyldewood.

"Nothing like a little disaster to sort things out and make a man see clearly," Lord Camden replied.

"He's been caught in the parson's noose. And by the parson's daughter, no less."

"A vicar's daughter, if accuracy matters at a time like this." Simon's calm voice was a direct contrast to the irritation in Wylder's tone. "And he's not completely trapped yet. There is still hope he comes to his senses."

"I barely recognized him at dinner last night… the way he was acting. I've never seen a man so besotted. There's no doubt she's bewitched him," Wylder growled.

"Bedeviled, you mean," Simon scoffed. "We both know Lucien is not the sort of man who would fall head over heels without having some sort of spell cast over him. And she's a beautiful little sorceress, I'll give her that."

"What are we going to do about it?" Wylder demanded. "We can't just sit by while he acts the fool mooning over her."

"I'm not sure there is anything we can do… other than doing our best to convince him to come back to London with us when we leave here. However, my fear is that his father will simply apply more pressure until Lucien capitulates to his demands of settling down and producing an heir. Obviously, we are all in danger of losing our freedom but our dear friend is standing right on the precipice." Simon sounded contemplative and Charlotte held her breath, waiting to hear what else his friends were plotting on his behalf. "I do feel half the battle here is overcoming the fact he has not bedded a woman in weeks. His fixation on Miss Windsor could simply be a matter of pent-up denial and frustration."

"How can we help that? We cannot very well bring a

lightskirt here to Ashcroft to fuck Lucien back into the rational man we know."

Charlotte smothered a gasp with her hand. Wyldewood's crudeness was not a complete shock, for she sensed the man's nature tended to be a bit darker than his two friends, but still. To hear such vulgarity spoken aloud was shocking.

But Lucien has said worse... and you did not object too strenuously. She argued with herself. *That was different. Lucien said those things in the heat of the moment. Not while coldly planning a rendezvous with a woman of fallen virtue.*

"True, but it makes me wonder. If not a lightskirt, then perhaps a rival for his affections? I have it on good authority that Lord Nichols's daughter, Joanna, is at their family's country residence. The rumor is Lady Nichols has objected to the fast pace of the *ton* and hopes to shield their daughter from the perils of too many parties and balls. She has demanded that Joanna take a small break. Considering the baron's estate is only a few miles away, this could be a convenient solution to our unusual problem. We introduce a bit of female distraction and remind Lucien there is a vast array of women back in London to choose from." Simon said. "Perhaps we should ask her to come visit while we are here?"

Charlotte swallowed the bitterness as it swelled in her throat. The betrayal she felt, although certainly unwarranted since the gentlemen were hardly friends of her own, was intense. She had liked both men upon meeting them the night before and genuinely believed they held her in the highest regard. To overhear their plans of sabotage was incredibly disheartening. She wanted to burst into the library and inform the pair of them that she had no designs on Lucien. She did not want him pursuing her. Did not want his distracting kisses nor the fiery branding of his touch on her skin. She knew full well that she was no match to the ladies of the *ton*, but neither did she have any desire to be. The pair of them should hardly concern themselves with saving Lucien from her clutches when she never wanted his attention to begin with.

As quietly as Charlotte could manage, she backed out of the library without catching the gentlemen's notice and raced down the corridor until she reached the doors leading down onto a wide stone terrace with steps disappearing into the gardens.

Only when she finally stopped running, her chest pounded with exertion. She was breathless, her limbs trembling and weak after her illness. Taking refuge in a leafy alcove hidden from view of the manor's many windows, she sank onto a marble bench so she could calm herself. It was only then that she realized tears were streaming down her cheeks. Her heart felt as though it was being ripped in two.

And the reason for her sorrow only made her sob harder.

CHAPTER NINETEEN
Lucien

S HE WAS IN the garden somewhere. He merely had to search for her within the maze of towering hedges and tidy rows of flowering rosebushes and rhododendrons.

His boots crunched along the gravel paths as he stalked Charlotte. He could barely see the impressions left by her tiny, slippered feet but there was enough evidence she'd passed this way. He followed her trail deeper into the maze until finally he heard the unmistakable sounds of crying.

His jaw hardened. Why was she weeping? Beyond what he already knew of her visitor that morning, what had happened to throw her into such a state of distress?

Damned if he would not wring Earnest Russell's neck with his bare hands if he were the one responsible for her tears.

Approaching the alcove, he silently watched Charlotte swipe the moisture from her cheeks and smooth the front of her gown. She was unaware of his presence which allowed him a few precious moments to observe her. She looked like a beautiful angel framed by the deep green of the hedges behind her and the ivy vines crawling up and tumbling over the framed alcove.

"Why are you crying, little siren?" he asked softly. With cautious movements, he advanced toward her.

Charlotte's gaze flew to meet his, a gasp of surprise escaping her parted lips. "Your Lordship…"

Lucien frowned at her dogged use of his title, but his tone remained calm. "What has upset you so dreadfully, Charlotte?"

Her eyelashes fluttered downward, hiding her gaze from his scrutiny. She wiped at her cheeks and sat straighter on the bench, squaring her shoulders as if prepared to do battle with a foe. "I am not upset, my lord. I simply stopped to rest here for a moment and enjoy a bit of solitude." Her eyes narrowed as she shot him a baleful glare. "You've ruined that, you know."

With a smirk, Lucien stepped into the alcove and sat on the bench beside her. "Lying does not become you, little siren."

Her chin tilted in defiance, but she ignored his statement and countered with one of her own. "Why are you here, my lord?"

"I had news to relay and no desire to wait until this evening. Underwood informed me you had headed in the direction of the gardens earlier so naturally, I began my search here." Reaching out he placed a forefinger beneath Charlotte's chin, lifting until she had no choice but to look at him. From this angle he could see the sparkle of tears in her blue eyes, turning them the dark color of rare sapphires. Her pale cheeks were flushed pink, and her mouth was ripe and red from her teeth worrying her bottom lip. "Tell me why you are crying. Does it have anything to do with Earnest Russell's visit this morning? Did he upset you in some way? Tell me the truth, little siren. Because if he is the cause of your unhappiness, I will personally horsewhip the man."

"It has nothing to do with Mr. Russell," she admitted in a voice strained thin with anger.

"If that is true, then I am glad to hear it. I just gave him the position of vicar and would hate to fire the man before he can even begin to work."

Charlotte closed her eyes, a pained sob escaping her chest that she could not conceal. "You-you selected him as Ashcroft's new vicar?"

Lucien's heart clenched at the sorrow in her voice. He knew this was news she never wanted to hear. It meant she must vacate

Hollyhock Cottage in the very near future, although it would be at least a fortnight before Mr. Russell would take up residence. "I did."

"Then there is nothing further to discuss, my lord. Our arrangement is over."

Her sadness was wrenching Lucien's heart to pieces but she bravely met his gaze, her white teeth nibbling her bottom lip as if the action would keep her tears from flowing again.

"It doesn't have to be, Charlotte," Lucien insisted huskily. "You can stay here in Ashcroft or come to London where I will assist in establishing you in your own apartment. With the funds I have placed in an account solely for your use, you have the ability to decide."

"Funds?"

"Yes. I have paid the sum we previously agreed upon… along with a bit extra. It is yours. Do with it as you see fit." Without meaning to, his hand slid until it cradled her jaw. Charlotte's breath hitched at the movement, but she did not pull away. "I want to continue seeing you, Charlotte. Have you reconsidered my proposal of an engagement? Not only will it be beneficial in dealing with my father, it will be a profitable venture for you as well."

"Mr. Russell has asked me to marry him," Charlotte blurted out. Her eyes were chips of ice as she stared up at him. He felt the heavy weight of her censure. It felt like she blamed him for the man's uninvited proposal.

"And what was your answer?" Lucien already knew but he wished to hear it from her lips.

"I told him I could not entertain the idea unless he were selected to fill the position as vicar." Her gaze was accusatory. "Did you know this before you offered it to him? Is that why you chose him?"

"I learned of it afterward," he admitted softly. It was why he had decided to give her a choice: remain in Ashcroft or come to London.

"And if I accept his proposal, I will never see you again, will I?" Charlotte choked. "You will find every reason you can think of to stay far away from Ashcroft Manor. It won't even take the subterfuge of your friends to accomplish it."

"What do you mean?" Lucien asked, puzzled. "We are uncommonly close, that I will admit, but Camden and Wyldewood have nothing to do with my decision to hire Russell."

"Don't they? After all, it's painfully obvious that they must grant their approval of your endeavors. It is the only way of ensuring you all share the same future," Charlotte cried out, gripping his hand and trying to tug it away from her face. Lucien held firm however, determined not to release her as she continued with her indignant tirade. "Loveless, lonely bachelor existences where you hop freely from whore's bed to whore's bed, gambling den to gambling den, gentlemen's club to gentlemen's club," she sneered at him. "A lifetime of emptiness shared with them and only them. I honestly feel sorry for the three of you. You are so wrapped up in your own glory as dissolute rakehells, you will never find true happiness."

Lucien jerked her closer, his eyes narrowing at her words. "I don't know what the hell you are talking about when it comes to Camden and Wyldewood, but this is the truth of the matter. If you marry Russell, you can be damned sure I *will* stay away from Ashcroft. Do you understand why? Let me enlighten you. Because it will kill me to watch another man lay claim to you. And I cannot promise I would not harm him for the simple act of calling you his wife. I will stay far, far away and spare us both the carnage I would wreak. The hell I would bring. The scandal that would inevitably come after." His gaze searched hers, his mouth hovering above the pouty, full lips that were slowly driving him mad. "You have a choice, siren. It's *your* choice. Marry Earnest Russell and stay in your beloved cottage, in the town you adore, or come with me to London where I shall pursue you as my romantic interest with the eyes of society watching every move we make. I will pay you handsomely for your participation in this sham while maintaining an air of respectability. And when you tire of our arrangement, or when I've used it to my satisfaction, we will end it."

Charlotte's eyes flashed like blue fire at the casualness of his words. As if it would be a simple matter to end their affair. "I'll be ruined."

"No, your honor will not suffer if you are the one to break it off. When we reach that point, I will be the heartless cad and you the injured party. The *ton* is so deranged this will only enhance your appeal. You may even find yourself marrying for love with a gentleman smitten with you. It's a far better future than toiling away as a governess for a family who does not appreciate you. You must admit that my offer is far more advantageous." He ignored the fact he'd just touted the fact she might someday marry for love with a gentleman of the *ton* when mere seconds ago he'd threatened bodily harm to any man who took her as a wife.

"Your friends believe I have bewitched you," Charlotte bit out abruptly. "They mean to convince you that your interest in me is a fleeting one. That your interest is based on boredom and malaise. I think they are right. We are not meant to be together, Lucien. Not in this world or any other. So, you may take your money and go to the Devil with it. I told you once already that I will never be your whore."

There was a roaring in Lucien's ears while he listened to her. Most of what she said did not make sense, but he had a sinking feeling that the accusations regarding Wylder and Simon lay rooted in truth. His friends had not minced words in relaying their thoughts on Charlotte. They believed Lucien should return to London where his dissolute lifestyle would resume while keeping with the pact they'd made together. Now that he had hired Earnest Russell, he was free to do just that. Even his father would reluctantly concede Lucien had done his duty in the matter.

But leaving Ashcroft meant losing Charlotte forever.

"So, you are choosing Russell over me," he accused wooden-ly. "Is that it, Charlotte? Is that what you want? A lifetime with a man who doesn't understand you? One who will never set your body on fire as I can?"

"I am weary of the world burning down around me," she replied, dodging his accusations. "Now, I must do what is best for me and Faith."

"What's best is that you choose me, siren," Lucien growled. "Or is a taste of heaven necessary to convince you? A taste of heaven before you resign yourself to a life of cold, hellish mediocrity with a man you'll never love."

"Love?" She laughed, the sound sharp and so cynical it did not sound like his little siren at all. "Love is for those who do not know any better and for the lucky few who don't care. And we both know you do not love me any more than I love you."

"Charlotte," he ground out between clenched teeth. "You speak of things you have no knowledge of. But I'm going to show you. Right here on this garden bench. I'm going to prove you wrong."

Something in Lucien's eyes alerted her. She pushed against his chest with ineffective fists, her tone rising with panic. "Lucien... we cannot... it won't help either of us..."

His mouth crashed down on hers before she could utter an-other word and for a moment, she resisted by remaining stiff in his arms. But within seconds, the inevitability of the kiss melted her, turning her into a compliant wisp of femininity in his unyielding embrace. Letting out an anguished cry of surrender, her arms wound about his neck, and she clung to him, returning his fevered kiss without hesitation.

Lucien's mouth moved ruthlessly over hers, his tongue plunging deep inside to twine with her own. It was a savage kiss, one born of frustration, denial, and passion.

She tasted of sugared strawberries, the flavor sweet and lushly ripe. When he tore his mouth from hers, Charlotte gasped as he blazed a trail of kisses up and down her neck, pausing occasionally to take the lobe of her delicate ear between his teeth. He lightly bit the flesh then sucked it into the heat of his mouth. Charlotte moaned helplessly, wiggling closer to his muscled form.

"I will soon do the same to your beautiful breasts, little siren. I will lick and suck them into my mouth. I will trace the shape of your nipples with my tongue until they are burned into my memory. I'm going to devour you in every way imaginable." He kissed her deeply again and murmured, "Let me show you, Charlotte. Let me show you what pleasure is. How addictive it can be. Let me show you how insane you've made me because I vow, I've never felt this way for any woman before you."

While he spoke, Lucien unwound her arms from around his neck, gently pushing Charlotte down until she was reclining on the bench. His heart raced with gratitude that she did not fight him. Instead, she watched him with heavy-lidded eyes, her mouth parted and little pants of air escaping her throat. His hand encircled the slender column of her neck, his fingers squeezing slightly until her lashes fluttered shut.

"This is a sin, Lucien," she moaned softly, her pulse beating wildly against his fingertips. When she swallowed, he felt the movement and his cock jerked as he imagined sinking deep into her mouth and to the back of her throat.

"Then sin with me, little siren." he murmured, pushing her skirts until the tops of her thighs were exposed to his gaze. With gentle reverence, Lucien dipped his head and kissed the pale flesh there. She trembled in response, her hands weaving into the thick waves of his dark hair. His eyes locked on hers as his mouth explored her silky skin. "I want you too badly to feel shame for any of this. And I won't let you feel it either. This is simply two people finding pleasure in one another's arms. There will be no lasting damage or adverse consequences if we continue, I swear it. I'm hardly reckless enough to make love to you the way I desire, but we can find satisfaction in what I'm about to do to you. Will you let me, Charlotte? Will you say yes?"

She hesitated, obviously torn between the devil and salvation, but when he leaned over her and slowly pushed the bodice of her dress down until her half corset was exposed, she moaned softly. And when his fingers dipped down into the fabric and tweaked her nipples, her hands came up and thrust into his hair. Her body arched under his touch, a whimper of delight escaping her lips.

"Lucien…"

"I need your words, Charlotte. Tell me you want me to touch you. Say you want my mouth on your breasts, between your thighs. Say you need to come undone at the tips of my fingers." Lucien shoved her corset down until her breasts swelled over the fabric. Seeing her pale pink nipples, he groaned and immediately fastened his lips around one budded peak, muttering as he feasted, "Tell me what I want to hear, Charlotte. Now, before it becomes impossible to stop."

"Y-yes." She shuddered as he sucked and bit at her flesh. "I want you to touch me. To show me what madness means. Damn you for exploiting my weakness, but it is impossible to deny you or myself. I only ask one thing of you."

"Anything, my siren. Ask me anything and I shall give it to you," Lucien vowed, moving to her other breast and laving the tip with the flat of his tongue.

A tremor passed over her, and her words were so soft he could hardly hear her. "Please do not hurt me. My-my heart could not bear it."

CHAPTER TWENTY
Charlotte

BARELY BREATHING, CHARLOTTE waited for his reaction. Part of her hoped he would realize how crazy this was. The other prayed he would not stop kissing and touching her.

The sparks igniting her from the inside out were catching fire in other areas of her body. Her breasts ached for his kisses while the area between her thighs trembled at the thought of his fingers sweeping over her. Her head was spinning, and the very real possibility of being discovered made the pleasure unexpectedly sharper.

Lucien stilled, his gaze meeting hers. The seriousness in the green depths of his eyes relaxed Charlotte even as the rest of her body wound tighter and tighter.

"I'll never hurt you, Charlotte," he swore in a low voice. "The things I'll do to your body will cause pain… always balanced by pleasure… but I will never hurt you." He paused, then said, "Believe me, little siren, when I tell you I've never promised a woman anything before."

She still did not understand when he said things like that, however Charlotte closed her eyes, giving a little nod of acceptance.

But Lucien would not allow silence when it involved her own ruin.

"No, Charlotte. You will not close your eyes for this. You will watch and you will learn what it means to be mine… even if only for a short period of time. You will learn how to beg me for more but know this… the moment you ask that I stop, I will. I will let you go. Not willingly, and I will hate myself for it, but I will release you at once. But until that occurs, you belong to me. Now, you will tell me what you want. Tell me what you need. I need you to say it aloud."

Swallowing hard, Charlotte met his piercing stare and in the tiniest, softest voice, she replied, "Touch me, Lucien. Please. I want… I want you to kiss me… and God help me, I want you do anything you desire—anything you want with me."

Lucien let out a groan complemented by a strangled laugh. "You cannot comprehend the danger in flaunting such temptation before me. Swear that you will do exactly as I say, and I will give us both unimaginable pleasure."

Charlotte's resolve wavered but steeling herself, she clenched her fists and said in a stronger voice, "I promise."

His eyes searched hers for a long moment. Charlotte felt he was looking for the answer to something locked and hidden deep inside her. When he found it, his gaze darkened even more even as his mouth softened enough that his lips quirked upward.

"Good. Now, help me hitch your skirts up. I want them gathered around your waist and your legs on either side of this bench."

Lucien sounded so stern, his voice calm, yet also husky with lust. Did he really mean that she should do something so scandalous? So indecent? Charlotte's heart skipped then began beating with such rapid intensity that she felt faint. Her hesitation resulted in an even cooler response from Lucien.

"Why are you not obeying me, Charlotte? Do you wish to continue or stop?"

"I'm afraid… what if someone sees—"

"No one will enter this garden, Charlotte. If you worry that your sister may stumble upon us, don't be. I know as well you that Faith is spending the afternoon with Mrs. Merriweather and will not return until supper. Wylder and Simon have no interest in traipsing about through the hedges unless in pursuit of a romantic entanglement with a willing lady. They will not come looking for you. My servants? They would not dare disturb me when I left strict instructions against it. It is just you and I. No one else." Lucien gripped her chin in the palm of his hand, studying her intently as he gently commanded, "Now. Will you obey me, or must we stop before we even begin?"

Charlotte shivered. "Y-yes."

"And you are still certain this is what you want?"

"I am certain," she said firmly although her insides clenched at thoughts of what he would do now that he'd been granted her express permission.

When Lucien released her, she sank back onto the bench. Lifting her bottom, she silently aided him as he slowly pushed her skirts up, exposing her lower half to his gaze. She heard him suck in a breath then he said, "Put your arms above your head, siren. That's a good girl. Now, one leg here, and the other, just like this, here."

Within seconds, Lucien had her displayed like a sacrificial offering on a pagan ceremonial altar, her legs on either side of the marble bench. Although she still wore her stockings, she was incredibly exposed by the practical split design of the delicate underdrawers. Her cheeks burned with mortification, her eyes squeezing tight when she felt his hands trail up the inside of her thighs. His fingers gently traced an intricate pattern over her skin, drawing ever closer to the center of her body. She trembled, linking her fingers together so they would not tangle in his thick hair and force him closer.

"Christ, you are so beautiful here," Lucien murmured, his strong fingers moving to spread the fabric apart for his perusal. She wanted to squirm under the heated weight of his stare but forced herself to remain still. When he finally dragged a forefinger through her damp folds, she gasped in shock as her body melted into a puddle of need. Swirling her wetness around sensitive flesh, he pressed hard against the small bundle of nerves and laughed softly when she cried out her pleasure. "Such a responsive little siren. So wet for me. So needy and so willing to be corrupted. I cannot fuck you like I want to, but I can taste you. Will you let me do that, Charlotte? Will you allow me to lick your sweet, little quim until you come undone for me?"

Charlotte whimpered, her hips bucking upward to follow the path set by his teasing fingers. She wanted to feel that madness again. Wanted it to wash over her and drown her. Never would she have imagined herself like this. Spread out for a man's enjoyment and her own.

"Ah-ah," Lucien chided, his tone amused. "Use your words, siren. Tell me what you want me to do."

Embarrassment suffused her. Surely the heat of it was turning every inch of her exposed body to a strawberry pink hue. "Please."

His laughter echoed in the alcove. "Not good enough, Charlotte. You can do better than that, can't you?"

"*Please*, Lucien." The words were a shaky whisper. "Put... put your mouth on me. I *need* you."

Lucien moved until his shoulders filled the space between her thighs, his mouth hovering over her core. He was so close that Charlotte could now feel his warm breath as it stirred the dark-blonde curls there. She moaned again. Even to her own ears, the sound was desperate and greedy with desire.

"Such a good girl. You deserve a reward for obeying me." A second later his tongue lapped at her with languid intent.

Charlotte tensed under the onslaught, every nerve, blood cell, and heartbeat fixated on the feel of his mouth exploring her there. She shuddered, her body submitting to Lucien. "O-oh, oh, *God*."

"Still praying to be saved," Lucien muttered, flattening his tongue against her until another shocked gasp escaped her burning lungs. "It won't work, little siren. You should know by now there will be no redemption for either one of us."

He began feasting in earnest then, his mouth an instrument of wickedness that Charlotte could not resist. He drove her to a swift climax that left her lost in a world of sensation then quickly worked her body into a frenzied state again within moments of the first. This time, however, he inserted one thick finger into her pulsating channel, crooking it so that it rubbed against a sensitive spot just on the inside wall. His tongue ruthlessly lashed her flesh, his finger working in tandem until suddenly, everything went white-hot and bright. The leafy green canopy above her, spotted with patches of blue sky and puffy white clouds, seemed to shatter into shards of pleasure so sharp and so exquisite, she wondered if she was still on this earth and not floating away.

"Lucien..." she moaned his name in a breathy whisper that drifted on the slight breeze around them. *"Lucien..."*

"Yes... come for me, little siren. Give me your surrender. Give me all of it. God, you are so sweet. Dripping down my chin like liquid honey. I've never tasted anything so goddamn delicious as you, Charlotte. If you allowed it, I would pleasure you all day, every day. I would spend my hours drinking you in as though you were the rarest of brandies. I would enjoy counting how many times you come for me. Enjoy hearing my name on your lips as you beg for more."

Charlotte nearly drew her legs up at the intense pleasure, but Lucien growled, his hands moving until he gripped her thighs tight. He kept her spread open, his tongue darting out to tease and taste her folds. "Don't you dare close your legs right now. I want another climax from you."

"No, I-I can't." Her hands came down, plunging into his hair. The thick, dark strands were so soft, so luxurious sliding through her fingers that she forgot about tugging him away from her sensitive flesh. "I don't think I can..."

His head lifted long enough to study her, and Charlotte knew she would never see such beautiful, lustful madness ever again. Lucien's eyes glowed with possessiveness, his mouth wet with her release and his jaw clenched until it appeared made of the same marble she reclined upon. He licked his lips while she watched in dazed satisfaction and when a small grin curved his mouth, bringing out the dimples in his cheeks, Charlotte felt herself melting yet again.

"You don't think I know how much you can take?" he murmured, his hands holding her hips still when she tried shifting away. "You think two glimpses of heaven are enough? We'll see about that, siren, because now… now it's my turn."

CHAPTER TWENTY-ONE
Lucien

WITH A SWIFTNESS that had Charlotte gasping, Lucien curled an arm around her waist and flipped her until she lay on her stomach, facing away from him. She'd left her hair hanging free down her back, with the sides pulled back and secured by small clips. It was a hairstyle that reminded Lucien of the day he first saw her on the road leading to Ashcroft. She'd looked like an angel that day and she looked like one now as a shaft of sunlight penetrated the alcove and illuminated her body. Spread out on the bench's white marble, she was an absolute vision and Lucien's cock throbbed with insistent hunger, demanding he claimed this woman forever as his own.

Remember your promise. Remember you will not take anything from her that cannot be given back.

Wrapping his hand in the thick mass of waves, Lucien tugged her head back as he too, straddled the bench. Sliding closer to her body created the right angle to thrust inside her. He wouldn't let things go that far but damned if he could stop himself from teaching her what her body was capable of while finding his own pleasure.

Her back arched as he leaned down and whispered in her ear, "Are you ready for me, Charlotte?" He bit the lobe of her ear until she hissed in a mixture of pain and arousal.

"Lucien..."

"Shhh. No talking now... unless you wish to tell me to stop." Keeping a fist tangled in her hair, he quickly unfastened the fall of his breeches with his free hand and withdrew his shaft. Then he swept his fingers up into her heated core, reveling in her soft squeal of surprise as he gathered some of the moisture there and spread it over his length. For several seconds, he worked his hard cock using her release as lubrication. The sounds that filled the alcove were unmistakable evidence of their mutual passion. Charlotte's harsh breathing and whimpers mingled with Lucien's own low groans of lust as he imagined fucking her rather than the palm of his hand.

Sitting back, he gazed down at her body. The sight of his hand tangled in her hair was visually stunning. It looked as though he had swaths of sunshine wrapped around his fist. His jaw clenched with possessiveness and something oddly tender. Charlotte was allowing him to do as he pleased. Surrendering. Submitting. His cock swelled as he thought of sliding into her tight little channel, using it while spanking her bottom until it was pink and warm from the weight of his hand. *One day... not now but one day I'll do just that. I'll show her how pleasurable that can be for us both.* But rather than frighten her with the depths of his admitted depravity, he instead gripped her hip, pulling Charlotte until she fit snugly into the cradle of his hips. With this angle the head of his shaft and much of his length now glided against her clitoris rather than entering her body.

Charlotte froze but when he again slowly slid her forward and back along his cock, she moaned and tentatively rocked against him.

"Fuck... just like that, Charlotte," Lucien grunted, in disbelief how hot and slick her body was and how damn good it felt. The throbbing of her clit against the topside of his shaft and every slide of her body on his was driving him closer to the edge of oblivion. "You feel incredible... so hot. So soft. So willing to give into what we both need. You're going to climax again, aren't you, little siren?" He blew out an incredulous laugh. "You're going to explode on my cock, and I haven't even properly fucked you."

She mumbled in response, but they were not true words. Just a tangled jumble of sounds and moans and soft cries of frustration as Lucien deliberately kept her from tumbling over the edge.

But Lucien was hurtling fast toward his own climax. There was no stopping it, not when her innocent movements were coaxing it from him. Gripping her hips tighter, he helped her keep the pace, moving her back and forth until pinpoints of light sparked his vision. His groan was guttural and deep as he thrust faster and faster until she cried out below him, her body shaking as a third orgasm shattered her.

He quickly pushed her forward, simultaneously leaning away so that his cock rested in the cleft of her round bottom. Gripping himself tight, he rubbed his hand up and down his shaft in a rapid fashion, an incoherent curse escaping him when his seed erupted across her backside in scalding hot, cascading ribbons. Keeping a tight grip on his cock, he stroked and squeezed until every inch was expressed and the euphoria subsided in lazy waves that rippled through his entire body.

Lucien sagged, his weight pushing Charlotte until she was once again flat on her stomach, the marble bench pressing into her breasts and stomach. They were both breathing heavily and for a moment, he wished he could stay there forever, lost in the pleasant cocoon of satisfaction. But practicality rushed in and swearing softly, he moved away from her, whipping out a silk handkerchief from the pocket of his coat.

"Be still, siren. Let me tend to you right now. You've been such a good girl so far… let me do this," he muttered when she tried rising off the bench. Placing a hand between her shoulder blades, he held her down while cleaning his seed off the pale skin of her buttocks.

Charlotte silently obeyed, her only movement the trembling of her body as she receded from the heights of her orgasm. When he was done, Lucien helped her sit upright, noticing how she avoided his gaze. Together, they tugged her skirts down and straightened the bodice of her gown. The soiled piece of cloth was rolled up tight and shoved into an interior pocket of Lucien's suit coat. Its disposal would be dealt with later. Right now, he realized Charlotte was struggling with the reality of what they'd done.

"Charlotte, look at me." Sliding his hand along her jaw, Lucien turned Charlotte's face until their gazes collided. "If you are feeling shame over what we just did, I will not allow it." He hesitated, drowning in the brilliant blue sparkle of her eyes then admitted softly, "I've never done anything like that with another woman. And I've never cared enough about their feelings to give them a second thought in the aftermath of lovemaking. But this… it's different with you." Raking a hand through his tousled hair, he swore again. "Do you understand what I'm saying, siren? *You* are different."

Charlotte stared at him, still not saying a word although she frowned while he spoke. Finally, she cocked her head as if truly puzzled by his abrupt admission. "Am I really that different, Lucien? I don't think I'm very different at all. Like the other women you've been with, I surrendered for a few moments of pleasure. I enjoyed it. God knows I did, and I won't deny that I wanted you to do those things to me. But it is very foolish of us both to think this brief interlude changes anything. I am still just a vicar's daughter. You're still an earl. You will soon leave Ashcroft and return to London." Standing up from the bench, Charlotte smoothed the stubborn wrinkles from the yellow silk of her gown. Her smile was so sad that Lucien's heart swelled with misery for what he'd done to her. "And I must still do what is necessary to survive this world and provide for my sister," she continued softly. "Please do not follow me back into the house. I'd rather no one know we were in the garden together. After all, we don't wish for any hint of scandal, do we?"

LUCIEN TOSSED BACK the whisky, then splashed another helping into the crystal tumbler.

After Charlotte fled the garden, he remained behind for a while, contemplating the path his relationship with her had taken. Struggling with the knowledge that soon, he would lose her. Fighting the internal suggestion that there was a simple solution to this quandary, if he possessed the fortitude required to take those steps.

I could marry her. Make her my wife and bind her to me forever. It's not that far-fetched of an idea. We share mutual affection. Even better, we desire one another. Charlotte is kind. Sweet. And absolutely gorgeous. She's not a member of the ton but still, she is quality and would be a fine asset to the Westley family. My parents will adore her and be grateful I chose so wisely. There are many things to recommend her for marriage, but topmost is the fact I am completely obsessed with her.

"You are muttering under your breath again," Simon dryly remarked, lining up the cue ball on the billiards table and taking his shot.

"Apologies." Lucien took a long swallow of his drink, rubbing the bridge of his nose to dispel the headache gathering there.

"I think it's patently obvious that country life does not agree with you, Lucien. You crave the bustle of the city. The gambling and clubs. The drinking and whoring. I'd say the best way to feel like yourself again is to return to London." Wylder came up beside him and reached for the decanter. After pouring himself a drink, he clinked it against Lucien's glass. "You've done your duty. Followed your father's orders and took a break from town life. You successfully hired a new vicar. There's nothing keeping you here now."

A twinge of irritation pricked Lucien. Normally, he would agree with his friend, but their combined insistence was beginning to bother him immensely. He recalled the accusation

Charlotte hurled at him in the garden. There was truth in what she'd said. His friends wanted him back in London, not just for himself but to bolster their own bachelorhood status.

"I'm not ready to leave just yet." He nearly snarled the words.

Simon grinned, holding up his hands in mock surrender. "Just suggestions, Ashcroft." The earl regarded Lucien for a moment then said, "Earlier this afternoon I decided I'd ride over to Lord Nichols's estate. Simply to pay my respects, you understand. Anyway, one thing led to another, and I wound up accepting an invitation to a soiree on your behalf."

Lucien glared at the man. "You did what?"

"What else could I do?" Simon asked, his tone steeped in innocence. He removed his spectacles and made a great show of cleaning the lenses with a bit of cloth before replacing them. "Lady Nichols brought it up, and I had no wish to be rude. Miss Joanna was beside herself with joy to learn that the three of us would be in attendance."

"I don't know what you hope to accomplish but I've no interest in socializing with the local gentry." Lucien's fingers tightened around the crystal tumbler. He had no interest in anything other than kissing Charlotte Windsor into submission and claiming her luscious little body for his own.

"Just thought you might enjoy a bit of frivolity. Maybe a round of hazard with the other gentlemen attending. Hell, maybe you'll even dance with a few of the ladies. God knows you need a distraction from the stress of your duties here."

"I do not suffer from stress," Lucien growled. "I cannot believe you did this, Simon."

"Oh, come on. It'll be a bit of entertainment, at least," Wylder offered with a shrug of his shoulders. "And I've heard from several sources that Miss Joanna is a good sport. Perhaps a bit desperate for a husband, but that's a condition many ladies of our acquaintances suffer with."

"I've no need for entertainment, but you've trapped me in a

corner where I cannot escape without appearing to be a complete wastrel," Lucien replied with a shake of his head. "And you know very well that I've no intention of being trapped into marriage by anyone."

"Good to know," Wylder laughed. "Remember that when the lady tries cornering you in a secluded corner of the garden."

Lucien tensed, wondering if Wylder knew of his interlude with Charlotte earlier that day. Was this a veiled reference or just a simple coincidence?

No one knew what he had done with her. No one could. Not unless Charlotte herself said something, and Lucien thought that was an impossibility. She would never voluntarily reveal their clandestine secret.

"And don't worry. The invitation included everyone currently a guest in your own house, so Miss Windsor is also welcome to attend. In fact, after I explained the circumstances of her extended stay here, Lady Nichols was quite insistent that she come too." Simon's mouth quirked upward in recognition of Lucien's ire.

"How considerate of you," Lucien said with a ring of sarcasm in his tone.

"It was the gentlemanly thing to do. Besides, there's no sense hiding the fact she's been your guest for more than a week now."

Lucien's stare would have withered a lesser man, but Simon simply grinned at him and continued, "I assure Lady Nichols it was all very innocent... and Miss Windsor has been strictly chaperoned during her stay. They are quite excited that she will be in attendance. With a few acquaintances making the trip from London just for this intimate gathering, it should be quite entertaining."

Lucien was not sure of Simon's motives, but the fact Charlotte had been a guest of his for a period of time was not something he wished bandied about. Especially since Charlotte had refused to play along as his love interest for his father's benefit. He wasn't even sure she would agree to attend this event but setting his jaw, he knew he must convince her of it.

Because there was only one way of stomaching a vapid, empty gathering that was identical to the events of London society. It would only be tolerable if Charlotte was there as well. This would be an excellent opportunity to introduce her to the *ton*, and there was still the hope she would choose him rather than take a governess position.

Tossing back the rest of his drink, Lucien vowed to change her mind over the rejection of his proposal. Once she realized the possibilities of an arrangement with him, saw the many doors it would open and the financial gains to be had, Charlotte would undoubtedly come to her senses.

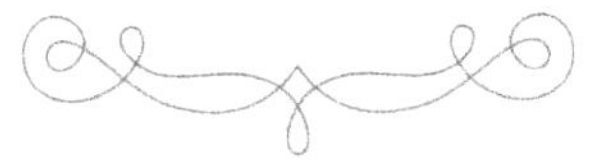

CHAPTER TWENTY-TWO

Charlotte

"I KNOW YOU are nervous, dear, but there's really no reason to be," Mrs. Phillips said cheerfully. "You will have a lovely time, I'm sure. Lord and Lady Nichols are very kind and I've no doubt you will just fit right in."

Charlotte weakly returned the housekeeper's smile from the opposite seat of the coach. The two of them rode separately from the second vehicle carrying Lucien, Simon, and Wylder. Separating her from the gentlemen and pressing Mrs. Phillips into service as chaperone provided a semblance of respectability.

A snort of disgust nearly escaped Charlotte at the ridiculousness of that concept. As if the presence of a chaperone now could ever change what had already occurred.

Charlotte could not believe she'd been coerced into attending this party. She had no business there… not when there was so much to do. She was still packing her and Faith's belongings for their return to Hollyhock Cottage the following morning. And she did not dwell on the future plans still needing to be set into motion. Those would soon require her full attention and this party was an unnecessary distraction from reality.

She certainly had not shared any of this with the pompous, overbearing earl who insisted she attend this gathering tonight. Smothering an exasperated sigh, Charlotte recalled how she'd been tricked into taking part in this evening's farce.

"I've sent out inquires as promised, but you may discover an acquaintance or friend of Lord Nichols is on the search for a governess," Lucien had murmured that morning over breakfast. "And if it should be a family from the area, how convenient would that prove for your situation? It would allow you to remain close to Ashcroft with no need to marry Earnest Russell. And with the money I have already set aside for you, you could live quite comfortably on that and your new wages."

Thankfully, the earl had not noticed the guilty tightening of Charlotte's lips upon his casual mention of Ashcroft's newly hired vicar. She decided it was best to abide by Lucien's wishes to avoid raising his suspicions. She must continue her search for a governess position, even if she considered it a contingency plan in the event that Earnest withdrew his offer of marriage.

So, she allowed Mrs. Phillips and an excited Faith to style her hair into a fashionable coiffure and dress her in the finest gown she owned. She even smiled and graciously accepted Lucien's assistance into the waiting coach as if attending society fetes were an everyday occurrence for her. She ran through every social grace and point of etiquette Mrs. Merriweather taught her over the years, ticking them off in her head so she wouldn't forget the many nuanced details of society's rules and guidelines.

But now, now as she was bumped and jostled on the road to Hickory Hall, she wished she possessed the nerve to command that the coach turn around as crippling doubt clouded her resolve. The reality of hiding her plans from Lucien and his reaction once he discovered the betrayal made her hands shake and damp with sweat.

He won't find out until it's too late to do a thing about it. He cannot stop me from doing what's best for myself and Faith.

"It may seem very daunting, but I have no doubt you'll do just fine, my dear." Mrs. Phillips leaned over, giving Charlotte's knee a motherly pat. "And you are an absolute vision in that gown. The color is so lovely on you. If every man there is not immediately entranced by you, then they have no business calling themselves men, I can tell you that! I'm sure they will all be fighting for the chance to make your acquaintance and to dance with you."

Charlotte wiped her hands down the front of the turquoise dress, glad for the elbow length, white gloves that kept the gown's fabric in a pristine state. "I'm not attending this event to find a husband, Mrs. Phillips," she gently reminded the elderly woman. "You know my hope is to locate a family in need of a governess for their small children. Lord Ashcroft assured me there would be guests there who can possibly help with that endeavor."

Mrs. Phillips harrumphed, shaking her head in exasperated dismay. "Lord Ashcroft should open his eyes to what's right in front of him. You and he are a perfect match. Anyone can see how you two look at one another."

Charlotte said nothing to that, worried the housekeeper might recognize the distress caused by her well-meaning attempt at matchmaking. The two women both fell silent then, with Charlotte's attention turning to the passing countryside. It was a lovely spring evening, and the landscape was bathed in the golden glow of a brilliant sunset. And as the miles between Ashcroft Manor and the small barony of Lord Nichols melted away, she wondered what the future held for her.

Mostly, she wondered how she would face it without Lucien Westley as part of it.

"So PLEASED TO meet you, Miss Windsor. Welcome to Hickory Hill. We were honored to have met with your father several times before his passing. The vicar was a fine, fine man," Lord Nichols said with a warm smile. His graciousness was echoed by Lady Nichols, who took Charlotte by the arm and tugged her along through the foyer and down a wide corridor.

"I understand that since your father's death you've been taking care of your younger sister on your own?" Lady Nichols asked, and when Charlotte simply nodded, she pressed a hand to her throat in sympathy. "Oh, you poor, poor thing. I'm sure you've done a fine job in his absence, and you are to be commended for your dedication." The lady gave Charlotte a gentle smile, guiding her along as Lucien trailed behind with Simon and Wylder close on their heels. "Now, let us put any sadness aside, at least for a while. You enjoy yourself tonight, and if you need anything at all, you only need ask." Turning to Mrs. Phillips, Lady Nichols motioned for the lady to catch up to them. "As Miss Windsor's chaperone, the same applies to you, Mrs. Phillips. We have several comfortable areas for seating in the ballroom and you are welcome to make use of them. There are refreshments there as well. And while I realize you must stay close to your charge here," the lady laughed, "I've a feeling she is going to be very popular with our gentlemen guests. You will certainly have a busy evening of it."

There was a strangled noise behind them and when Charlotte glanced back, she discovered Lucien's steady gaze upon her. His green eyes were lit with something that closely resembled jealousy but that in itself was not all that surprising. The earl behaved as though he owned every part of her. Charlotte's jaw tightened with a sudden, stubborn urge to show His Lordship that she belonged to no man.

Yet.

And especially not him.

Because belonging to Lucien Westley was like drowning in beautiful darkness. And if she did not steel her heart against him, she would only tumble deeper under his spell until there was no hope of coming back from it. And no hope of denying the man anything he wanted from her.

Lucien's intense stare was interrupted when Simon grinned, slapping him on the back. "I believe I can attest for all of us in regard to Miss Windsor's charm and pleasant nature. Lord Wyldewood and I have thoroughly enjoyed making the lady's acquaintance during our visit. I know the earl is in agreement that the lady has certainly been a much-needed bright spot in Ashcroft Manor's old halls."

Charlotte blinked, astounded by the unexpected graciousness of Simon's compliment. Even Lucien seemed surprised by it even as he stared at his friend as if trying to determine Simon's motives.

"Yes, I heard you had fallen ill, dear, and that Lord Ashcroft immediately took action to care for you," Lady Nichols flashed a smile at Lucien. "That was exceedingly kind of you, Lord Ashcroft."

"It certainly was," Wylder agreed, interjecting before Lucien could say a word. "And one must admit, quite out of the ordinary for a member of our particular circle to do something so blatantly selfless."

Lord Nichols chuckled at the blatant reference to the notorious reputation shared by the three men stalking the corridor. "I'm sure your father will be pleased to learn of your generosity, Ashcroft, and the way you've handled the various responsibilities of the estate. Now, as we all know, things are far tamer in the country and there are those who will seek to create excitement simply to dispel any hint of boredom. Do be good lads and refrain from encouraging the creation of any scandals tonight, especially since we've come home to Hickory Hill to escape the raucous nature of town for a spell."

"We have all enjoyed Miss Windsor's stay at Ashcroft Manor," Lucien said as they finally entered the ballroom. "It was an honor to be of assistance in her time of need. And rest assured, Lord Nichols, we shall all be on our best behavior."

Charlotte was saved from responding by a young woman who rushed up to the group. She was a lovely girl, wearing a soft-pink hued gown with matching ribbons in her auburn-colored hair, her eyes a bright hazel bordering on green. The wide smile plastered across her face was open and friendly.

She dipped a quick curtsey to the gentlemen, the excitement in her voice uncontainable as she turned to her mother. "Oh, I can hardly believe the Rakehells are standing in our ballroom, Mama! I shall be the envy of everyone when we finally return to town!"

"A bit more decorum, pet," Lord Nichols muttered good-naturedly while flashing the three men an amused grimace.

His daughter simply giggled, turning to Charlotte and linking an arm through hers. "I'm Joanna Nichols and you must be Miss Charlotte Windsor. Did you know the whole ballroom is buzzing about you? You are quite the topic!" Flashing a winsome smile at her parents, Joanna said, "Excuse us while I introduce Charlotte to our other guests. She doesn't know anyone, unlike the rest of us who know everyone here." With the skill of a wartime general, Joanna maneuvered Charlotte away from the group. The two girls walked the border of the ballroom, their conversation now private as Joanna exclaimed with delight, "You are so very pretty, Charlotte." Her hazel eyes widened almost comically. "May I call you Charlotte? I hope that is all right. You may call me Jo, if you like. All my friends call me Jo. Joanna is much too formal, and I prefer the shorter nickname. Do you have a nickname? I would think it would be Lottie, if you do have one. Although, not everyone likes nicknames. My mother says they are not dignified at all." The girl paused for a breath, then asked, "What do you think, Charlotte?"

Charlotte could not help the smile that curved her lips. Joanna Nichols was a bit of a flutter brain but it was easy to see she was a sweet, genuine soul. Charlotte liked her immediately. Her mannerisms and honesty reminded her very much of Faith. "I've never had a nickname, to be honest, but I do think yours is lovely."

Joanna giggled again, squeezing Charlotte's arm. "I'm so pleased you came tonight with the Rakehells, but it makes me very sad that we have lived so close and never even met one another. Your father visited mine quite a few times over the years, you know. Being the only vicar for miles around, he was called upon for the usual things required of a vicar and my parents liked him a great deal. I do wish you had come with him to Hickory Hill during those visits. We could have become friends that much sooner."

"I would like very much to be friends now," Charlotte murmured, although she was painfully aware that her and Joanna's lives were on completely different paths. They were both young, educated women but that was where the similarities died a quick a death. Joanna would continue enjoying a lifetime of social occasions with members of the *ton*. She would attend parties and balls and someday make a suitable match with a gentleman of quality and eventually bear his children, securing a comfortable, happy future.

Charlotte on the other hand, would become either a governess or the wife of a modest, unassuming vicar. Neither were very exciting possibilities. Her father, bless his soul, had been wise not to introduce his eldest daughter to a life she could only dream of. It had saved her from disappointment at an early age while also preparing her for the realities of life.

"Jo, I hope it is not too forward of me to ask a favor of you, considering we have only just met." Charlotte gave a quick glance over her shoulder to see Lucien strolling not too far behind. He appeared completely oblivious to the attention he and his friends garnered from those in the ballroom. The gathering of guests, the number of which Charlotte estimated to be no more than a hundred or so, watched the three men with avid interest while whispering behind raised hands. Her anxiety spiked when she realized that the same attention was also centered on herself.

"Of course! You may ask anything of me, and I will do my best to help," Joanna said, her brow furrowing. "Is this favor a secret? I hope not. I'm awful at keeping secrets. It's a horrible trait and I've tried everything to remedy it. But sometimes I just open my mouth, and things tumble right on out."

"Oh, no! It's not a secret at all. You see, I am hoping to find a position as a governess. I was told there may be guests in attendance tonight who might require those services. If you have any information on anyone who might be searching for a person to fill that position, will you let me know?"

Joanna tilted her head as they stopped at a long table loaded with glasses of raffia, lemonade, and water. "Would it not be easier to find a husband? I mean, you would have no problem with that." She motioned toward a small group of men making their way across the ballroom floor and headed in their direction. "See? Here come five potential husbands now. And don't think they will be the only ones expressing interest in you tonight. Those just happen to be the boldest of the group. Well, except for Rakehells, that is. There is no one else as bold and dashing as them." She paused, apparently noting Charlotte's dismayed expression. "Be that as it may, I will make discreet inquiries on your behalf but in the meantime, you can have a bit of fun. And since Mama has said there is no need for those silly dance cards like we do in town, we can dance all night, if we like."

There was no time to discuss the matter further as the two women were quickly surrounded by a group of Joanna's friends and several men. Joanna handled the introductions with surprising grace. And mere moments later, two gentlemen were whisking both Charlotte and Joanna onto the ballroom's parquet floor as the musicians struck up a lively tune for a cotillion.

From that moment on, it was an exciting whirl of quadrilles and Scottish reels as Charlotte danced until her feet began to ache. Despite her misgivings that she might not fit into this social setting, she found herself astonishingly at ease. In between dances, Joanna's group of friends gathered her in their midst. They were all so very nice, treating her kindly while also wide-eyed with respect upon learning Charlotte took care of herself and her sister with no assistance from parents or even family. Charlotte was included as the girls giggled and whispered over the men in attendance, discussing who might be dressed the finest for a country ball and who would make a perfect husband.

It was hardly surprising that the Rakehells of Mayfair occupied the center of those furtive conversations. Despite their notorious reputations, Charlotte recognized that the three men were considered to be top marriage prospects. One girl jokingly feigned a swoon upon learning Charlotte had been a temporary guest at Ashcroft Manor for the past three weeks.

"How have you managed to stop yourself from fainting with desire every time you see one of them? Each one is as handsome as the next." Lady Marie Downing laughed softly, her sparkling brown eyes seeking out the gentlemen in question. They currently stood in a group of men discussing the usual things men cared the most about. "I mean, just look at them. They are charming. Rakish. Rich. And so very dangerous to a girl's reputation."

Charlotte's cheeks pinkened. She had nearly fainted more than once because of one rakehell in particular but of course she could not possibly share those experiences with her new friends.

"I've been ill during most of my stay so my interactions with Lord Ashcroft and his friends have been quite limited. And my younger sister, Faith, who has been at Ashcroft Manor during my recuperation, takes up a great deal of my attention. I am solely responsible for her education and it is unacceptable if she should fall behind in her studies. His Lordship has been very accommodating. Indeed, he has been kindness itself in allowing the use of his library for the purposes of furthering Faith's education."

"Hmmm. Your situation has all the elements required for a runaway romance." Joanna sighed dramatically, clasping her hands to her chest. "The earl comes to your rescue, falls in love, and whisks you away after you agree to become his wife. Then he takes care of you for the rest of your lives and you both live happily ever after."

Charlotte said nothing to that, aware that such a fairy tale scenario was so far out of reach that it truly was a fantasy.

"Well, all I can say is if I were in your particular position, I would have been compromised several times over by whichever one of those three men I could manage to corner," Miss Deborah Davidson confessed in an amused whisper. The other girls erupted into gales of delighted laughter, smothering the outbursts behind gloved hands and ducked heads.

Charlotte spied Lucien occasionally during the evening. He paced, hovering on the ballroom floor's edge, as she was twirled past him while in the arms of several different partners. A look of resigned frustration stamped across his features; his hand was usually clenched about a glass of champagne while his emerald-green eyes tracked her every move. He watched, diligent and on alert, even while nonchalantly carrying on conversations with various people. He made no move to intervene until the beginning strains of the music indicated the next dance to be the first waltz of the evening. It was then that his entire demeanor changed. While his jaw clenched so tight it might have been granite, his gaze morphed into something glittery bright. Handing his empty champagne glass off to a mildly amused Simon, he immediately began to stalk Charlotte across the ballroom.

Before the gentleman Charlotte was currently dancing with could even muster up a request to partner her for the waltz, Lucien slid between them. With his large muscular body blocking Lord Abernathy's view of Charlotte as he smoothly said, "Pardon the interruption, Abernathy," Lucien flashed the man a glance over his shoulder while sliding his arm around Charlotte's waist and taking her hand in his much larger one. "Miss Windsor previously promised me the first waltz of the evening. You understand, I'm sure."

And as the other man sputtered with indignation, Lucien swept Charlotte away.

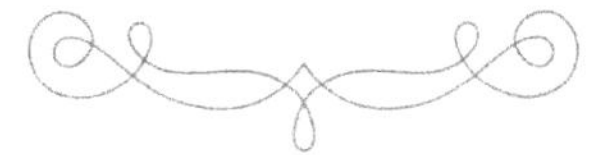

CHAPTER TWENTY-THREE

Lucien

IT WAS GENERALLY understood that country social events did not adhere to the same rigorous rules as those that took place in town. So, the fact Lucien basically stole Charlotte away from a fellow gentleman would most certainly be overlooked by others in attendance.

However, it remained to be seen if Charlotte would be as forgiving. Even now as he twirled her around the ballroom to the lilting music of the waltz, she glared up at him, her eyes glittering dangerously even while a pleasant smile was plastered across her face.

"You, Lord Ashcroft, are an exceedingly rude and ill-mannered scoundrel," she said in a low, accusing voice.

"True. But if you thought I'd let another man have you in his arms like this, you don't know me very well. And I especially would be remiss if I allowed you to dance with Lord Abernathy in such a manner."

"And why is that? He cannot possibly possess a reputation as notorious as your own." Her tone was lofty as she flashed a pretty smile in the other lord's direction.

"He's a well-known spendthrift," Lucien retorted, his jaw tightening until it felt like a chunk of stone. If Charlotte's intent was to rouse his jealous nature, she had skillfully accomplished that goal. "Worse, he's a terrible womanizer."

"A disciple of yours, is he?" Charlotte shot back. "Don't answer that, my lord. I would not be surprised if you said yes. But what does it matter to you if I waltz with a known womanizer? You do not control my actions, Lord Ashcroft."

"Damnit, Charlotte. Stop referring to me by my blasted title," Lucien ground out. "And it would be wise if you exercised caution when issuing challenges like that to someone like me."

It was adorable when Charlotte nearly stomped her foot atop his boot in the middle of a turn. "It's not a challenge! It's reality." Her gorgeous blue eyes flashed at him, twin spots of scarlet outrage staining her cheeks. "If you were not so pompous and stubborn, you would realize there is no hope of your plan ever coming to fruition. I've repeatedly told you I will not engage in any sort of illicit relationship with you. Fake or otherwise."

"Careful, siren. Anyone could overhear you and conclude that we are engaged in a lover's spat. Even now, we are garnering attention from others. Not that I mind, of course." He nodded toward the edges of the room where guests had apparently halted their own conversations in order to watch Lucien and Charlotte as they danced. "I rather hope they all come to the conclusion that we are courting."

"Enjoy that delusion while you can, my lord," Charlotte said icily. "Now seems the perfect time to inform you I am moving back to Hollyhock Cottage first thing in the morning. Once this night is at its end, there will be no reason for the two of us to have any association with one another."

Lucien's grip tightened around her waist, but he purposefully kept his features neutral. "I am aware of your plans, Charlotte. Don't you know I have knowledge of your every move?"

"How can you possibly know—"

"Your sister tattled on you earlier this afternoon," he calmly interrupted. "It was accidental, of course, but she's quite upset over the thought of leaving Ashcroft Manor. It appears she's quite enamored with my kitchen and the staff. Regardless of where you go, this does not change things between us."

Charlotte huffed at the news Faith had betrayed her. "You are the most annoying, aggravating, irritating man I've ever met."

He couldn't help but smile at the sullen tone of her voice, and her deliberate choice to use basically the same adjectives to describe his nature. "And you are the most desirable woman I've ever known, little siren. Letting you go would be one of the worst mistakes of my life. I am determined to keep that from happening."

"You have no option, my lord," she said firmly, sapphire-blue eyes narrowing on him. "You have no hold over me. No right to dictate or run my life. Now, please let me go before I scream this ballroom down around your ears. And if you are foolish enough to believe I would not dare something so scandalous, please remember I have no social standing and therefore I've nothing to lose."

"Such a little firebrand," Lucien murmured in admiration. "But truly, there is little need for such dramatics. The dance is coming to an end, and you may escape my clutches without threat to your reputation or ruining your chances to find a governess position."

Charlotte bit her bottom lip in sheer frustration, obviously recognizing the truth of Lucien's statement. She managed to contain her temper as the dance did indeed draw to a close but before she could yank away from Lucien's grasp, he leaned forward to whisper a warning in her delicate ear.

"It is very tempting to throw you over my knee and spank that gorgeous bottom of yours right now, Charlotte. I stop myself only because no one else has the right to hear your little cries for mercy or the privilege of seeing how prettily you come undone for me. Now, I expect you to behave yourself and mind my words. You may dance the waltz with me. Only me. No one else. Do we understand one another?"

For a moment, Charlotte appeared both stunned and defiant, but the sternness of Lucien's tone softened her just as he suspected it would. She melted against him, her body giving in before her spine straightened into a rigid line. His little siren was inherently submissive, and that knowledge only sharpened his resolve to bend her to his will.

Her chin jerked in silent acquiescence, a quiver shaking her body as Lucien finally released her from his grasp.

"That's a good girl," he said in a low, rough voice and it was enough to make Charlotte spin on her heel. She fled from him without so much as a glance backward.

Lucien ambled off the ballroom floor, confident his warning would be heeded as he watched Charlotte head in Mrs. Phillips's direction. The lady sat in a chair toward the back of the room, and she smiled widely up at Charlotte as she plopped down into a chair beside her. For a few moments the two women had a hushed conversation before Lady Downing approached them. She sat on Charlotte's opposite side, taking her hands in hers in a friendly manner. Lucien wondered what their conversation consisted of as Charlotte's surprised expression melted into intense interest. She nodded several times while Marie spoke, then leaned forward to give the woman a small hug. Mrs. Phillips, on the other hand, was obviously disturbed by the conversation between the two young women. Her lips were pressed tight in a familiar expression of disapproval, and she had her arms crossed over her chest.

His curiosity peaked, Lucien began making his way toward that corner of the ballroom but quickly found his path blocked by Simon.

"The satisfaction on your face and the anger on Miss Windsor's can only mean one thing. You issued an ultimatum of some sort and Miss Windsor has reacted accordingly." Simon laughed, his hand landing in the middle of Lucien's back. "Come have a drink with me, my friend. Something much stronger than champagne is likely appropriate in this moment."

"I could use a whisky," Lucien murmured in agreement, casting another glance in Charlotte's direction. She noticed him at once, but immediately turned her head, dismissing him as she continued speaking with Marie. He was still curious about the content of the conversation, but consoled himself with the knowledge she wouldn't dare defy him during his brief absence.

"Follow me then. I had no idea until this evening that Lord Nichols keeps such an impressive stock of spirits. And I'll take any opportunity to escape the clutches of the young ladies determined to trap me in a dark corner."

Outside the ballroom and down the corridor was a large parlor which had been set up to accommodate games of whist, faro, and hazard. A sideboard along one wall held an array of brandy, whisky, port, and wine. There were several gentlemen in the room engaged in hands of chance. Cigar smoke swirled and hung in the air and every so often a curse would rise above the din.

"Ashcroft. Camden," one lord called out upon seeing them enter the parlor. "Come join us in a game or two of faro."

Lucien inwardly groaned. He was in no mood for gambling tonight. A glass of whisky, yes, but he understood taking a turn at one of the card games or even throwing the dice at hazard could become a time-consuming distraction. Already he was anxious to return to the ballroom where he could easily keep an eye on Charlotte's activities.

Simon nodded at the man before stepping to the sideboard and pouring two tumblers of whisky. He handed one to Lucien then perused the selection of cigars in an ornately carved wooden box before choosing one.

"I'm sorely tempted to join that hand," Simon said in an aside to Lucien. "Lord Jenson lost heavily at the tables the last time I saw him at White's. His pockets are deep enough but I doubt his luck is on the rebound. Might be worth it to relieve the man's purse of a few pounds." He shot Lucien a grin. "Are you in?"

Lucien shook his head. "I haven't the concentration required for gambling right now."

Simon's gaze turned contemplative as he stared at Lucien. "I imagine that would be the fault of one Miss Windsor, would it not?"

"You know it is. If I play, then I cannot also keep an eye on her." He sighed heavily, taking a healthy gulp of whisky. "Fuck, but she's a vexing creature."

"And what do you intend to do about that, Lucien? Do you even know what you want from her? If it's just to bed her, then do so and get it out of your system."

Lucien's hand tightened around the glass. "That is not an option. For one thing, she refuses to enter any form of illicit relationship. For another, I don't think I would want her to."

"That hardly makes sense. Since when do we care about a woman's morals when it comes to bedding her?" Simon drew on the cigar, blowing the smoke high into the air. His laughter was sharply cynical. "We do what we do because it is what we wish to do. It's the unofficial motto of our brotherhood. Are you saying you wish to change things?"

"I don't know what I want," Lucien said in a low voice. "Only that I know I want her, and I cannot have her in the manner to which I am accustomed. It's a tangle I cannot seem to unwind."

"Do you care for her?"

The question caught Lucien off-guard. He tossed back the whisky then immediately poured another until it nearly over-flowed the glass. He said nothing for a long moment, then answered with fierce honesty, "Yes. I do. I don't know how it happened, or for what purpose fate has decided to play its cruel tricks on me, but it's true. I want Charlotte more than anything I've ever wanted in my life. And I worry that she is going to disappear from my life and I'm left forever regretting the moment I allowed her to slip through my fingers. She fires my blood like no other woman before her and I find myself alternating between protecting her from the harshness of this world or turning her over my knee when she does foolish things such as dancing with fools like Abernathy."

Simon's smile was sad as he clinked his glass with Lucien's.

"Then there's only one thing to do, my friend."

"And what is that?"

"Why, marry her, of course. The girl has caught you in a trap without utilizing the normal standards of her kind. Her refusal to succumb has only enhanced your desire to claim her. It's a brilliant strategy on her part, really. God help the rest of us if other women discover this secret weapon and actually use it."

"Are you saying I only want her because I cannot have her?" Lucien asked in a tight voice. He wasn't sure if his friend was insulting him or simply pointing out the obvious.

"I'm saying she's done a fine job of crystalizing your intentions. She's a smart girl. I actually think she is the perfect woman for you, and if you convince her to marry you, I daresay you will not be sorry she's the reason you ended your state of bachelorhood forever. However," and here Simon paused, a frown creasing his brow, "if you only wish to bed her for the sake of bedding her... if you cannot imagine yourself being with this woman and this woman only many years from now, then you should sit down for a game of faro and forget about her. Let Miss Charlotte Windsor's future play out without you having a say in the matter. The choice is a simple one, don't you think? Remain a rakehell and enjoy a different woman every night or become one of those lovesick fools who bore others with simpering tales of how wonderful their wives are and how fortunate they are to have married them."

Lucien chewed the inside of his cheek to keep from punching his friend square in his jaw. Simon's pragmatic words of advice struck him at his very core, and he despised the way they made him question his own intentions. Was that the only reason he pursued Charlotte with such vigor? Because she would not submit to his advances? Or was it because he truly cared for her and wanted her by his side forever?

Was Charlotte worth giving up his beloved bachelorhood and the camaraderie of his two closest friends?

He turned his back to Simon, stalking toward the table where

Lord Jenson sat with two other gentlemen. Setting his glass down, he pulled up a chair and withdrew a stash of notes from the inner pocket of his waistcoat. Ignoring Simon's sardonic laugh as he too took a seat, Lucien threw the bills down onto the table.

"Deal me in, gentlemen."

CHAPTER TWENTY-FOUR

Charlotte

CHARLOTTE STEPPED OUT on the balcony terrace, breathing deep of the spring air. She hoped the cool breeze would clear her mind but as the muted sounds of the ball faded into the background, she realized that even the tranquility of the evening had little effect on her racing heart.

Lucien's words… his actions… his blatant possessiveness… all of it had worked her emotions into a veritable whirlwind. Her fists curled against the smooth railing of the balustrade, her nails digging into the stone, and considered the predicament she had been thrown into. The earl had done what she was sure could never be accomplished. He made her question her own decisions and the path of her life moving forward. He made her think the impossible was possible. That happy endings might exist. And that a man like him, drenched in power and wealth and privilege could actually fall for the daughter of an impoverished vicar.

But even those sparks of hope could not stand against the realities of her situation. Lucien desired her, that much was certain. But would he disappoint his friends, his family, his acquaintances by offering something other than a warm spot in his bed? Was he capable of giving more of himself rather than receiving? And could he truly fall in love with her?

Sighing heavily, Charlotte recognized the truth as it battered its way around her mind. It was even more difficult for her heart to see what was real and what had begun as nothing more than passionate moments shared between two people. And she hated herself for the stubborn way her heart refused to let go of the illusion that the earl cared more than she rationally knew he did.

Oh, how she hated the way her body melted against his, how her eyes tracked his mouth while she dreamed of those firmly carved lips claiming her own. It was unfortunate that she dissolved into an absolute scatterbrain every time his heated, emerald eyes traced her features. Tragic that the feel of his large, warm hands on her trembling body had every rational thought in her head melting away like snow caught in a circle of warm sunshine.

Worse, she hated that she even cared.

Taking another deep breath, she leaned over the terrace wall, watching as the trees below swayed in the gentle wind. While her body reveled in the reminder of the waltz she'd shared with the earl, her practical nature reminded her that coming here tonight was far more of a success than she could have imagined it to be.

Lady Downing, or Marie as she'd insisted that Charlotte call her, had eagerly relayed information that her own dear cousin was on the search for a suitable governess for her two small children. And if Charlotte was truly serious in seeking out such a position, Marie would happily pass along her information for the position and help arrange an interview.

While Marie talked of her cousin and her husband, and the ages and mannerisms of the little girls Charlotte would be responsible for, Charlotte could not help but feel a twinge of pride. She had possibly found a position without needing Lucien's assistance or even his approval. She felt both empowered while at the same time apprehensive to even consider taking the job if it were offered to her. After all, Marie's cousin resided far away from London. Indeed, the lady related that Lord and Lady Stratham's family home was located in Hexham in the county of Northumberland. Still within the boundaries of England, but it might as well be a million miles from London and the school Charlotte hoped to send Faith.

Was she brave enough to consider going so far from home? So far from the graves of her parents and to be so many miles away from Faith? It would mean visits with her sister would be few and far between. She wasn't sure if she could take such drastic steps. Wasn't sure if she was strong enough to bear it… at least not while Faith was so young and totally reliant upon her.

But you can stay in Ashcroft Village, if you can give yourself to a man you don't love. You can remain here and live in your beloved cottage. Continue to enjoy the friendship and caring of Lady Merriweather and the friends you've made at Ashcroft Manor. You can perhaps even keep up the budding friendship with Joanna as you would most certainly accompany Earnest as he ministers to the residents of Hickory Hill. It would mean keeping Faith close by for another two years before sending her off to school. You would be home. In the place you grew up and have grown to love so dearly. Close to the final resting place of your dear mother and father. Are such things valuable at all? Or do you move past this stage of your life and forge new memories?

There were two drawbacks to the idea of remaining in Ashcroft. One, the requirement that she marry Earnest and two, the presence of Lord Lucien Westley. The hold he had over her volatile emotions seemed nearly impossible to break. Could she bear seeing the man on occasion? Remembering the passion they'd shared while also ignoring the fact they'd occurred? Could she look at him as the wife of another man and not wish for his kiss? Or his touch?

Charlotte's head swam at the possibility of that sort of nightmare scenario. Even as she swallowed back a surge of anxiety-provoking nausea, she realized she would face a lifetime of something much worse. When Lucien eventually married, how would she ever bear the overwhelming heartache and pain? Seeing the man she loved wed to another woman would utterly destroy her.

Love?

Yes. Love. Charlotte sagged against the balustrade with that staggering realization, her eyes welling with scalding tears. She had fallen in love with the arrogant earl and in her viewpoint, there were few things more tragic than that.

"He's different with you."

Charlotte whirled around, gasping in surprise to see Lord Wyldewood standing in one of the open doorways leading onto the terrace. He carried two glasses of champagne and as he came closer, he silently offered her one.

Dashing the tears off her cheeks, she accepted the offering with a shaking hand. "Lord Wyldewood." Her voice trembled and without a second thought, she drained the glass in one quick gulp. She closed her eyes against the burn of the alcohol and when she opened them, she discovered Wylder standing even closer than before. Seeing the concern that creased his brow, she composed herself enough to let loose with a self-deprecating laugh. "Thank you for the beverage. I did not realize how parched I was from all the dancing." She nervously shifted her feet at his continued silence then asked, "Did you wish to speak with me about something, my lord?"

"Yes. Maybe. I'm not sure, to be honest. I don't think anything I say to you will change things." His dark head cocked to the side as if trying to work out a puzzle. "I commented that he is different with you. It surprises me."

"Who are we speaking of, Lord Wyldewood?" Charlotte asked innocently, although she knew full well the subject of their conversation. She just wasn't sure why Lord Wyldewood was intent on pursuing this discussion with her.

Wylder huffed in frustrated amusement. "As if there is anyone other than Ashcroft that I would discuss with you, Miss Windsor." The man moved with the graceful strength of a panther as he leaned against the balustrade beside her, staring off into the darkness of the grounds below the elevated terrace. "The damn fool is utterly enamored of you, you know. And unfortunately for you, he is also stubborn enough to steadfastly ignore it. He proved that tonight in the most contradictory of ways. He has thus far ignored every woman here clamoring for his attention. Instead, he watches from a distance while you dance with other men. He does this rather than amuse himself with the choices readily available to him." Wylder wagged his index finger at her in admonishment. "You are more dangerous than Simon or I could have ever realized. Bravo, Miss Windsor, for succeeding where the most sophisticated and determined debutantes of London have previously failed."

Charlotte stared at Wylder, remembering the conversation she'd overheard just days before between this man and Simon. "I refuse to believe I pose a viable threat to Lucien's chosen status as a confirmed bachelor. And certainly not to yours and Lord Camden's."

Wylder's mouth quirked upward at the bitterness in her voice. "Maybe there are those of us who truly do not relish wearing the title of bachelor, Miss Windsor. Some of us may actually long for someone beyond our reach and we have no option but to cope with disappointment in different ways."

"I don't understand what you mean, my lord." Charlotte's hands twisted with one another in her confusion. What a strange conversation to be having. It was as though the earl shared his own disappointment with an unrequited romance in a mystifying effort of explaining Lucien's behavior. It didn't make sense. "The three of you enjoy your reputation. The Mayfair Rakehells are infamous, so much so that even those of us hopelessly ambling about here in the countryside have heard of your exploits."

Wylder's head swiveled toward her. Even in the dim lighting of the terrace, she could see his smoky gray eyes harden until they resembled pieces of flint. "If there was a chance of being with the one woman I truly want, I would be the first man to say to hell with the Rakehells. But what I want is not possible. And it never will be. I've resigned myself to that fact and learned how to live with it. But there is nothing holding Lucien back other than his own arrogance and sense of loyalty to his friends. And while he will not marry you, there is always the opportunity of experiencing a bit of happiness together while you can. In doing so, you will help him with his dilemma, and I shall put it as plainly as possible. You, Miss Windsor, are driving our friend insane with desire. To the point of obsession. Do both yourselves a favor and get it out of your systems. Then you can both move on with no regrets." His tone softened as if suddenly realizing the harshness of his words. "I am begging you, Miss Windsor. Either give Lucien what he desires or cut yourself from his life for good."

Charlotte's anger grew higher and higher until her hands shook with the force of it. Tears welled in her eyes again but this time, she hardened her heart and refused to allow them to fall. "If this is your way of proposing that I become Lord Ashcroft's mistress, you should know I already refused that offer more than once. But I will impart this bit of knowledge, for you to use as you will. In very short order, I will be completely unattainable to Lucien and this conversation will have served no purpose other than to illuminate the depravities of your souls. I feel very sorry for all of you. Sorry that the thought of love and happiness is so abhorrent that you would deliberately sabotage your chances to feel it for yourself. I hope the three of you realize one day how very wrong you all were, but I'm afraid by then it will be too late."

Wylder's jaw clenched and unclenched with unspoken emotion. Finally, he said in a low voice, "If there was any hope for a rakehell's redemption, it would be Lucien's. And if it could be with anyone, it would be with you, Miss Windsor. Simon and I... we were wrong about you." The look he gave her was rife with sympathy and dawning understanding. "I know you love him. Anyone can see that. But I fear that's not enough for men like us. Men like Lucien. I can't explain why we are the way we are, but if it means anything at all, you should know that I am sorry. And that's the truth."

Charlotte handed the empty champagne glass back to him. Scalding hot, fresh tears streamed down her cheeks but she did not brush them away as she had before. She wore them now as if they were a badge of honor. A symbol of her right to happiness and the freedom to remain true to her morals. She did not care if Wylder saw how upset she was. She would not hide it and she wondered if he would share with Lucien the depths of her emotions in this moment. This moment when the love she carried for Lucien Westley became nothing but an aching, hurtful memory. "If you would be so kind as to inform Mrs. Phillips I am returning to the coach and wish to go home, I would be grateful for your assistance. I-I am unwell and have no desire to impose my current state on other guests. Good night, Lord Wyldewood."

"Good night, Miss Windsor. You may find it astonishing that I hope Lucien realizes what is slipping from his grasp but we both know he won't." Then in a surprising move, Wylder lifted Charlotte's hand to his lips and pressed a respectful kiss to the back of it, his eyes sad with regret. "I wish you happiness, Charlotte. Truly, I do."

CHAPTER TWENTY-FIVE

Lucien

LUCIEN THREW HIS cards on the table in disgust. He'd recklessly lost most of his money, playing foolishly and without a care. Beside him, Simon gathered up his winnings and had the gall to smile at him.

"Better luck next time, Ashcroft."

"Go to hell, Camden," Lucien growled back.

"So damned hostile." Simon laughed. Pouring a drink for himself, he did the same for the other men at the table, including Lucien. "Drink up. It makes you a much happier loser when playing faro."

"How long have we been playing?" Lucien barked impatiently. He would have checked his own pocket watch for the time, however he'd wagered it in the second round and promptly lost it to the earl.

Simon made a great show of checking the timepiece before tossing it back to his friend. "Nearly three hours. But don't worry. Lord Nichols assured me that even when the dancing draws to a close, gentlemen are invited to continue with their activities at least until dawn." He took a sip of whisky, eyes intently trained on Lucien when he stood up with such haste that his chair tumbled over. "I'm hungry. Let's go find something to eat here besides this paltry offering of slices of ham and cheese."

"Three hours?" Lucien asked incredulously, raking a hand through his tousled hair. He had intended on playing just a hand or two, if for no other reason than to wipe that smug smile from Simon's face. That all changed when he lost the first two rounds of cards, and his own stubborn nature demanded he recoup those losses. Obviously, he'd lost track of time and now, he didn't dare think about Charlotte's activities during his absence. How many partners had she danced with? How many waltzes? How many times had one of those men attempted to sneak a kiss from those luscious, strawberry sweet lips of hers after leading her to a darkened corner of the ballroom?

His hand clenched around the timepiece Simon had returned as gesture of friendship. They did that quite frequently with one another. It was a game they'd played for many years. Winning and losing valuables only to turn them back over to their previous owner.

"Excuse me, gentlemen," Lucien said, replacing the watch in his inner coat pocket before stepping back from the table and resetting the chair in place. "I should make an effort to check on my houseguest's welfare. It was not my intention to abandon her."

"Are you referring to Miss Windsor?" Sir Carey asked over the low din of conversations. "It is my understanding that the lady departed some time ago. A shame, too. I intended on snagging at least one waltz with her myself. Alas, it seems I missed my chance this time. How on earth has that one been allowed to hide out here in the country? She's an absolute delight. Although, I suppose her situation can be somewhat explained by the lack of family connections and a sizable dowry."

Gone? She left? Lucien was momentarily stunned by the news but as Sir Carey blithely continued speaking, worry crept in mingled with a healthy dose of absolute rage.

"But still, even with those drawbacks, one could see her easily becoming a companion if she proved agreeable to such an arrangement. I find it fantastical that she's not already been claimed by one of—"

There was a nearly silent whoosh of air as Lucien launched himself at the man. Within seconds, he had the startled, middle-aged lord smashed against the wall, his fists clutching huge handfuls of the man's suitcoat.

"Say one more derogatory word about Miss Charlotte Windsor and I shall enjoy ripping your heart out through your throat," Lucien snarled, shaking him with such force that the man's teeth rattled. When he tried speaking, the tightness of Lucien's hands at the base of his neck only allowed garbled gasps for air.

"Goddamnit, Ashcroft!" Simon jumped in, doing his best to insert himself between the two men. It was a struggle but eventually he succeeded in convincing Lucien to release his grip on Sir Carey. "What the hell has gotten into you?"

Sir Carey stumbled away from Lucien, his features pale with fear. "I meant no offense to Miss Wi..."

"Say her name and lose your tongue," Lucien growled, his fists clenched tight. God, he ached with the need to smash the other man's face in. Cripple him for daring to insinuate Charlotte was only worthy of being a man's mistress. Annihilate him for voicing aloud the suggestion that he might be interested in her for himself.

But isn't that exactly what you have done? Reduced her worth while deciding she would make for a fine whore for your pleasure?

Lucien swore under his breath, whirling away from the men who watched the exchange in stunned astonishment. The rakehells were renowned for their cool and detached manner and the enviable way they avoided conflict by simple employment of detachment. To witness one break down in an explosion of hot-blooded temper was unheard of.

Pulling himself back under control, Lucien glared at Simon. "Were you aware she had left the ball?"

Simon nodded. His expression remained neutral even as Lucien clenched his fist again in preparation of rearranging his friend's aristocratic nose.

"And you allowed it."

"What is the reason for your anger, Lucien? You made your choice when you sat down and were dealt a hand of cards," Simon said calmly, placing a hand in the middle of Lucien's back and guiding him into the corridor where they could discuss matter privately. "No one forced you to sit at that table and gamble for the past three hours."

"She was left alone." Lucien raked a hand through his hair in his agitation, stumbling a bit. He'd drank more than he intended, the whisky potent enough to make his head swim now. "God only knows how many men took advantage of that fact. You know how mercenary men can be. Especially supposed gentlemen like us."

Simon waved a hand in dismissal of Lucien's concerns. "She wasn't alone. Wylder was watching over her the entire time along with Mrs. Phillips. And although he's certainly a reprobate, he would never dare behave inappropriately with Miss Windsor. Christ, if I have enough faith in the man to allow him around my own dear sister, then I'm certain you can trust him when it comes to the woman you want."

Lucien scowled, brushing past his friend. "I'm returning to Ashcroft. With or without you. If she's not here, then I've no wish to be here either."

"If we leave now or later, it does not matter. Miss Windsor has made it back to the manor by now and is probably abed dreaming of new ways to vex you," Simon called out to Lucien's retreating back. "But if you insist, Wylder and I shall come along as well."

⁕⤜⤛⤜

ONCE LUCIEN GRILLED Wylder over every move Charlotte had made during his absence, the coach ride back to Ashcroft was a silent one.

Lucien stared ahead, stonily ignoring his two friends. Although they'd not done anything overtly seditious, he could not help the feeling of betrayal he was experiencing. And he could not shake the feeling that the two men conspired to separate him and Charlotte from one another at the ball. For what purposes, he did not know. But it stung to think they'd acted in a deliberate manner to sabotage the evening.

They were nearly to the manor when Wylder cleared his throat, drawing Lucien's glowering stare.

"I-*we* owe you an apology, Lucien," Wylder finally said in the cutting stillness. Letting out a heavy sigh, he glanced at Simon to gauge his reaction to the confession. Simon simply nodded, turning his head to watch the dark scenery of the countryside fly by, shrouded by the night and illuminated occasionally by the light of a pale, full moon.

"Why is that?" Lucien replied. He was angry enough to tell the two of them to go to hell but stopped short of doing so. These men were more than brothers and although he wanted to punch them both, he could not bring himself to discard their friendship over a woman he hadn't even claimed for his own.

"Our hope was that your infatuation with Miss Windsor was a temporary thing. That your interest in her was so damnably intense due to the lack of female companionship during your time at Ashcroft. We thought that by ensuring you attended this ball, you would discover that your pursuit of the lady was simply a fleeting obsession. You would snap out of it once you found yourself once again enjoying the familiarity of our normal activities." Wylder had the grace to appear ashamed, his face a dull red easily seen in the dim light of the coach's interior lanterns. "But I believe we were wrong. Wrong in our handling this attempt to help you, although not wrong to have done it."

Lucien rubbed his jaw with his hand. He understood the reason but could not condone it. His friends had deliberately misled him and that was unforgiveable. "Charlotte said she overheard the two of you plotting. She did not tell me specifically what that consisted of, but she was upset when she accused me of going along with whatever the two of you had concocted. I did not understand then, but I do now. And while I know you believed you were acting in my best interests; I cannot dismiss my anger for it. But then again, it doesn't matter now. She's leaving tomorrow and my life will resume as it was before I came to Ashcroft."

Simon's bright-blue eyes darkened. "Do not allow her to leave if you want her that badly, Lucien. If she is what you want, then hold onto her with all your might."

"I cannot and will not force Charlotte into something she does not want. It should be her choice. I've already bribed and coerced her into things an innocent, naive girl like here should never have been a part of. So, if she leaves, she does so because she wants to go. I will not take that decision from her," Lucien said softly and with firm resoluteness.

"We made a damnable mistake, Lucien. You don't have to make it worse with one of your own making." Wylder's voice was gruff with regret.

Lucien simply sighed, seeing the lights of Ashcroft Manor burning brightly in the near distance. They were almost home, the hour late, and most of the servants would be in their beds by now. Charlotte had arrived hours before and he knew her bedchamber would be locked to him even if he wanted to breach her room and explain things to her. He rubbed both hands through his hair, cradling his head as if that would ease the pounding in his temples. He was suddenly, inexplicably exhausted, the evening's events and the alcohol wearing him down. "There's nothing to be done for it. I must let her go."

CHAPTER TWENTY-SIX

Charlotte

THE TALL CASE clock on the landing outside her room chimed the hour as Charlotte shut her chamber door softly behind her.

Three o' clock.

Lucien had returned only an hour before. She'd stood inside her room, ear pressed to smooth oak of the door as she listened to the sounds of him making his way down the corridor toward the wing housing his suite of rooms. Mr. Phillips spoke with him as they walked, and Lucien responded to the steward's questions with short, impatient answers. Charlotte could not make out what either man said but the overall impression was that the earl was certainly aggravated and more likely than not, inebriated at well.

Now, with a dressing robe wrapped tightly around her body, she made her way down the corridor, headed for Lucien's room. She prayed she would not encounter any of the servants during her journey. Surely, the entire house was asleep by now. If someone actually caught her, she would surely die of mortification before ever needing to explain why she crept down the corridor outside his room, wearing only a nightgown and a dressing robe. She hadn't even bothered with her slippers, reasoning that her bare feet would enable her to move without making too much noise.

Thankfully, she reached Lucien's room without seeing a single soul. Pausing outside the door, she paused, wondering if she was doing the right thing. With her hand on the ornate doorknob, she took a deep breath, steeling herself for the courage to follow through with her plan. But even as her resolve swelled, her heart pounded so hard it was making her light-headed, and apprehension twisted her stomach until it was little more than a ball of nerves. Taking another deep breath and blowing it out softly, Charlotte closed her eyes, said another prayer, then quietly turned the knob.

She slipped inside the room, her gaze immediately going to the huge bed. It was so expansive; it took up nearly an entire wall toward the back of the enormous chamber. It was possibly the largest piece of furniture she'd ever seen. For a long moment, she just stood and marveled over its size. What would it feel to sleep in such a luxurious space? Heavily carved dark wood posts stretch toward the ceiling and lush, thick bed drapes of a dark hunter green shade hung from the canopy on all four corners, but they were tied back, allowing her to see past them.

Lucien was hardly visible in the mound of pristinely white bedclothes but as her eyes accustomed themselves to the dimly lit room, she made out his arms and the tousled mass of his dark hair. He slept on his stomach, one arm half hidden beneath the pillow he clutched, the other flung over and outstretched on the thick mattress. His biceps gleamed like slabs of oak in the flickering light of a single lamp burning low and Charlotte swallowed down a tide of emotions. She was unused to seeing him in such a vulnerable state and the butterflies in her stomach refused to settle down as she approached the bed.

Charlotte stared at him for several long seconds, fighting with her decision to come to him. But there was little choice, she sadly reminded herself. She was leaving at daybreak and soon enough she would either become the wife of another man, or she would be at the other end of England and far removed. No matter what choice she eventually made there would be no opportunities for one more kiss. One more embrace. One more smile flashed at her from across the room, sparkling green eyes brimming with promises of what he would do to her. That would all be over once she departed this room. She would go on with her life and the earl would go on with his. They would swirl around with the daily mundane of existence, trapped in opposite corners of the universe.

That's how it must be.

When she reached her hand out, it was trembling, but it did not stop her from gently sinking her fingers into the thick mass of his dark hair. That a man so hard and so charmingly arrogant could possess hair so soft and silky always surprised her.

Lucien groaned, stirring slightly as she caressed him. "Christ, that feels good," he muttered into the fluffy pillow, moving his head so that she could easily reach him. His hand that lay stretched out across the mattress clenched and unclenched as though he dreamed of gripping her flesh in his fingers.

Afraid of saying anything aloud that might startle him, Charlotte continued stroking his hair in silence, her lips parting with the pleasure of touching him while he slept. This was a different side to him. One that she'd only caught a glimpse of the first time he kissed her. There had been a flash of uncertainty in his gaze that day. An unguarded question and fear of her rejection of his advances. Seeing his vulnerability now softened her insides, and she smiled tenderly when he arched his neck to allow her better access. Her own breathing grew more shallow as she imagined slipping off her robe and climbing up into the bed beside him. What would he do if she was brave enough to act on her wishes? Would he embrace her? Or push her away?

"Charlotte, Charlotte, Charlotte. Dear God, you are driving me mad," he muttered and when he rolled onto his back, a forearm resting across his eyes, Charlotte realized he was only half-conscious. Perhaps he believed her to be a dream. An apparition, maybe, sent to haunt him in the middle of the night while all the world slept on around them.

Her eyes fixated on his bare chest, and it was with sudden awareness that she realized his state of undress. He was nude beneath the fine, cambric sheets which had become bunched in a tangle around his waist and narrow hips. Fascinated by the width of the smooth expanse of his chest and shoulders as well as the lean muscles that marked his ribcage and abdomen, Charlotte unabashedly drank in the sight of him.

Lord, he was so finely made that it made her ache with desire. He could have stood as a model for the classical Greek sculptures depicted in her father's books on ancient societies. In fact, his form was so exquisitely carved, he did not appear to be flesh and blood.

Lucien's lips parted, his mouth moving as half-muttered words and moans escaped his throat. The words made little sense, but Charlotte did not care. She was completely entranced by him and the glory of his body splayed out before her. Her fingers tingled with the need to trace every part of his body. She wanted to commit it all to memory. It would be a treasure she could draw upon during the bleak, dismal years of her future. A memory of the night she boldly took what she wanted for a moment of pleasure and happiness. Like that stormy day in the woodcutter's cottage and the sun-dappled afternoon in the secluded garden alcove, this night would be something she would remember forever.

Reluctantly easing her fingers from his hair, she carefully slipped the dressing robe off her shoulders. It landed in a pool of fabric at her feet. Now wearing only her nightdress, she knew if Lucien opened his eyes at that very moment, he would see how flimsy the material was. He could easily look past it to her naked form and drink her in in the same way she stared at him now.

Her breath caught in her throat at that thought. Of him see-ing every inch of her and she seeing every inch of him. She'd felt that part of his body against her own in those moments of passion they'd shared but she'd not actually seen the male part of him unfettered by clothing. Her body responded to that idea in the most primitive way. Her breasts tingled, her nipples tightening into hard buds that wanted his mouth and teeth upon them. Her core ached for him, needing him to fill her until she exploded with ecstasy and he swallowed her wanton cries with ruthless savagery. There would be pain, of course, but it was such an insignificant price to pay for a longer glimpse of heaven.

Charlotte closed her eyes, swaying as memory of the climaxes he'd given her overwhelmed her with frightening emotion. A little whimper of frustration escaped her, her body heating until she felt like she might burst at the seams with longing.

"What the fuck are you doing here in my room, siren?"

Her eyes flew open at the sound of Lucien's husky voice, her gaze searching his face. She found him watching her with burning, dark-green eyes, a glint of surprise in their depths.

He'd moved his one arm so that it was now propped behind his head. Charlotte shifted her feet, ready to flee when his free hand whipped out, snatching hold of her wrist with the quickness of a striking snake.

"Ah-ah," he *tsked* with a rough laugh. "No retreating now until I get the answers I want." His gaze raked her form, tiny fires lighting the darkness of his eyes. "What are you doing here?"

"I-I want you to kiss me," Charlotte whispered haltingly, twisting her hand within his grip while she wondered if he would let her go. She desperately hoped he wouldn't.

Dark head tilting, Lucien regarded her with such suspicion that it was evident he believed her words were a trap. "Is that all, little siren? Or did you sneak into my room hoping I would fuck you?"

Yes. Please, yes.

Charlotte's chin jerked high at his crude words, but she remained stubbornly silent. Lucien tugged her close then abruptly yanked harder until she tumbled into the bed and on top of him with a little cry of alarm. His arms wrapped around her waist, keeping her trapped along the length of his body as she gasped in shock. The spicy scent of whisky lingered on his breath, mingling with the crushed mint powder he used to clean his teeth. She wondered how inebriated he'd become after abandoning her at the ball.

"I wake up from what I think is a goddamn dream and find you standing here, Charlotte. The natural assumption is that you decided to become mine. That you are ready to accept the position as my mistress and you've come to give yourself over to me." His voice was low and husky, his gaze boring into hers. She could feel his shaft pressing into the junction of her thighs and she shuddered in shameful, helpless response. "Is that it? Answer me, damn you."

When she simply stared at him, he snaked a hand around her throat, squeezing until she swallowed hard against the force of his fingers and gasped out a response.

"I-I want to pleasure you. Like you did to me before." Her cheeks burned with embarrassment with the admission but once uttered aloud, she could not keep the rest of it from spilling out. "With my m-mouth. If that's something you would want... I want to do that for you. Just that... nothing else," she finished in an agonized whisper of shame. Maybe women did not do that to men. Maybe men didn't like that sort of thing... or maybe the act itself was too depraved to even consider among decent men and women. She reasoned to herself that if something felt that wonderful and magical for a woman, then it should certainly have the same effect on a man.

His fingers tightened as he glared up at her. He said nothing for what seemed an eternity then briefly closed his eyes. When he opened them again, the depths were so dark and so green they were almost black with desire. "Charlotte... I cannot... fuck, I *will* not take you as a mistress. It's too goddamn late for that." A shuddering breath escaped him, his tone guttural as if he were in excruciating pain. "Go back to your room, damn you. Go back to your room so I can wake up in the morning and tell myself this was nothing but a dream."

Charlotte shook her head as much as he would allow. For some reason, her body always reacted to his as though the two of them were infused with bolts of lightning striking against each other. A moan rose in her chest as her lower half helplessly rotated against him. Her eyes fluttered shut at how good it felt. His shaft was erect and even through the tangle of bedclothes separating their bodies, she felt every glorious inch of him. She faltered with uncertainty. He was so big. Massive and straining toward her soft center. How would he fit…? How exactly would that work?

"Fuck. Stop fucking moving, Charlotte. For the love of God…" he pleaded, his eyes flashing with warning.

"I can't…" she admitted softly, and it was true. It was as though her body had decided independent of her head with no thought to the consequences. She pressed harder against him and the sensation was so intense she nearly saw stars.

Lucien groaned as if those two words were unbearably painful, then his hand left her throat only to embed itself in her loose hair. He gripped it tightly, wrapping a chunk of the blonde waves around his fist as he also curled his fingers around the nape of her neck Then he jerked her down, finally claiming her mouth. He devoured her, plunging his tongue deep and sucking on hers until she innocently mimicked his actions. For a long moment he kissed her with such savageness that Charlotte could not catch her breath.

"You want to please me, siren?" he asked hoarsely when he finally tore her away from his mouth. He glared at her. "You think you want to wrap those plump, lush lips around my cock and swallow me down that tight throat of yours?"

Charlotte's eyes glazed over. Pure, unadulterated lust shot through her veins like liquid fire. She felt delirious. Unhinged. Desirable and… powerful. So damn powerful that at that moment, nothing would stop her from taking what she wanted and giving him pleasure in return.

She nodded slowly.

Lucien again squeezed his eyes shut as if trying to gather his strength before he released her hair. His hands grabbed the hem of her gown where it had ridden up to her thighs. Before she could even think twice, he whipped it over her head and tossed the garment to the floor. Shoving her upright so that she straddled his hips, his eyes devoured her body that was now completely bare. He caressed her bare breasts with both hands, his palms hot and burning as they smoothed the underside of each globe in turn. Watching her with narrowed eyes, he pinched her nipples, plucking at them until she moaned and writhed over his midsection. And his hands dropped away from her waist, leaving her free to escape if she wanted to.

"You are a goddamn goddess, Charlotte. And if you don't remove yourself from my bed in the next two seconds, I will oblige your wishes and fuck that pouty, sweet, sassy mouth until you choke on me."

Indecision froze Charlotte in place while her pulse pounded like thunder in her veins. For a moment, she considered fleeing him but then, she placed her hand on his chest, her fingers lightly gliding over the smooth, iron-like muscles there in gentle exploration. When her fingernails raked experimentally over his flat, round copper-colored nipples, he hissed in immediate response, his shaft jerking beneath the covers. Emboldened by his low curse, she shifted her hips so that she could reach down with her free hand and shoved the bedclothes out of way.

"Charlotte..." he growled in warning, his cock twitching impatiently against her backside. "Don't..."

"Shhh..." Leaning forward she pressed a soft kiss to his hard mouth. "I won't let you do anything we both regret later." When he choked in surprise at her vow, she took the opportunity to slide down his body, her breasts rubbing against his rock-hard physique. Knowing he was breathless and desperate for her made Charlotte feel more alive and far more powerful than she had ever felt in her entire life.

She ended up between his spread legs with his shaft rising

before her. She stared at it in awe. It was so beautiful. Like a gorgeous slab of marble waiting to be molded into whatever she desired. The wide, mushroom-shaped head had her licking her lips. Before she could second guess her actions, she swiped the head of his penis with the tip of her tongue. He was so much larger than she thought he would be, and her mouth watered at the thought of this part of him filling her until she could not breathe without his permission.

"Jesus Christ." Lucien's curse was a strangled moan. Both of his hands wrapped in her hair, thick lengths of it wrapped about his fists as he held her in place. "I cannot restrain myself, siren. I need you. Need you now. *Now*. For the love of all that is holy…"

Charlotte responded by taking him into her mouth, swirling her tongue around the head of his cock, experimenting with the taste of him, the feel of him. It was so strange and yet, she was aroused to a fever pitch by her actions and the guttural groans flowing from his throat as his hips rose so he could thrust deeper.

"Goddamn… yes, love. Just like that. Open your mouth a little wider so I can slide in…" His instructions came in stuttered moans as he showed her how to move her head, when to suck, when to let him control her actions. He murmured words of desperation, of lust, of need as he plunged slowly in and out of the recesses of her mouth. He was careful not to give her the entire length and breadth of him, as if deliberately holding back from hurting her, but sometimes, he inadvertently went so deep that his cock touched the back of her throat and she instinctively gagged around him before continuing, determined to please him. She wrapped her hand around the base of him, stroking the part of him that would not fit inside her mouth.

He groaned at the feel of her fingers, throwing his head back as his cock twitched and throbbed.

"I'm going to come… Charlotte… do you understand what that means?"

Charlotte moaned, nodding yes when she actually had no idea what he was talking about. She only knew that this brand of lovemaking was something she wanted to do with Lucien again. That she was the one making him gasp and curse was intoxicating. She was the one whose hair his fists clenched so tightly. And she was the one taking him to the heights of ecstasy.

"I'm going to spill my seed in your mouth, siren. Unless you stop, unless you move away, I'm going to fill your mouth. And if that happens, you will swallow every drop I give you." Lucien sounded like a crazy man, his hands tightening in her hair to the point it was almost painful, his hips rising and falling as he thrust into her mouth with abandon. Charlotte opened her mouth wider, giving him permission to do whatever he wished, as hard as he wished for as long as he wished.

Suddenly, a groan escaped him. It was a sound like nothing she'd ever heard him utter before.

"Charlotte… siren… bloody hell what have you done to me? Goddamn it, swallow me now… now… *now*."

Lucien's body stiffened, his head thrown back against the pillows, his rough hands holding Charlotte's head immobile. Then warm salty fluid flooded her mouth, sliding down her throat as she sputtered while trying desperately to swallow.

"Don't fucking move," he growled, his cock still thrusting its way deep into her mouth. "Take it all. Every inch. Every drop." And Charlotte obeyed, her body melting with need for him as she whimpered in supplication. She let him fill her mouth with his release and she swallowed it down until his cock pulsed in slow satisfaction. She did not move even when his hands loosened their grip on her hair and became softly caressing instead.

"Fuck… what a good girl you are, Charlotte. Such a good girl…"

His voice was rough with sleep and contentment, and it poured over Charlotte like warm honey, washing away any regret she might have felt in the aftermath of the intense experience. Her throat ached when she tried to swallow but even that did not bother her. She had relished the entire act… every lustful, heart-pounding moment of it. She would not allow shame to sink into her consciousness… not after witnessing the amount of pleasure Lucien experienced. She hoped he reflected on this night with the same heated flush of enjoyment washing over him now. She knew she would.

It surprised her when his hands hooked under her armpits, dragging her upward until she sprawled across him. He tenderly kissed her, nibbling her lips, her jawline, her chin while humming his gratification.

"Little siren, I've no idea what to do about you," he murmured, settling her until her head rested in the crook of his neck and shoulder, her face turned toward his. He continued kissing her with languid, sleepy affection with his arms wrapped around her waist. "You've turned my entire world upside down and I've no idea how to cope with that."

Charlotte did not answer. She simply lay quietly, enjoying how carefully he held her. If she closed her eyes, she could almost pretend he loved her. And as his breath deepened and his grip grew weaker, she basked in the warmth of his embrace until it was evident he had drifted off to sleep.

Only then did she allow her tears to fall. She held him as long as she dared, his heart thumping rhythmically beneath the hand she rested on his chest. Choking back her sobs, she pressed a soft kiss to his firm lips, then carefully lifted herself from his body. She pulled on her nightclothes with shaky hands, watching as he sleepily mumbled and turned onto his side away from her.

At the door to Lucien's bedroom, she turned for one last look at the maddening earl she'd foolishly fallen in love with. She would cherish every memory. Every smile. Every kiss and every caress. She would even cherish the tears because their presence made everything that much more real.

"Goodbye," she whispered, touching her lips with her fingers, tracing their plumpness and savoring the lingering sweetness of his mouth upon hers. Then she slipped out of his room, wiping her face clear of any traces of her sorrow. Squaring her shoulders, she reminded herself of one important fact.

It was pathetic to cry over someone who was never truly hers.

CHAPTER TWENTY-SEVEN

Lucien

W HEN LUCIEN WOKE sometime around noon the following morning, he knew immediately.

Charlotte was no longer there.

There was a heaviness to the house. A heaviness that permeated every room and every corner with the unmistakable truth that she was really gone. Pulling himself up with his back against the headboard, Lucien raked both hands through his hair. He closed his eyes as his heart clenched with reality.

She was gone and he'd let her go. She'd come to his room, nearly broke him apart with pleasure, then disappeared after gifting him with one of the most erotic experiences of his life. Stupid fool that he was, he had promptly drifted off to sleep and let her slip away from him. He should have gotten up from the bed, tied her to it, and made love to her until the sun crept in at dawn.

But it's for the best, isn't it? I mean, did I really believe there was a way to mentally bind her to me?

After all, Charlotte was determined to make her own way in life. She certainly did not need him or any man to pave her way or cushion the path. She was the most headstrong, stubborn, vexing creature he had ever encountered, and he had let her go.

His hands clenched into fists. Rubbing his chest, he hoped it would erase some of the awful ache there. God, he never knew it could hurt this badly to let the woman he loved more than anything on this earth slip away from him.

And he realized at that moment that he did love her. With a rush of exhilarating joy and the heart crushing knowledge that a man like himself would never deserve someone as good and kind as Charlotte Windsor. He existed on a plane so far beneath her, he should be eternally grateful for the times she allowed him to kneel before her.

Kicking the covers away, Lucien rolled from the bed and stood on unsteady feet. His head pounded relentlessly with the lingering effects of the whisky he'd drank the night before. God only knew how badly he wanted to crawl back beneath the covers, to wail and gnash his teeth while wallowing in regret but he wouldn't. He couldn't. There wasn't much sense in it. The only thing he could do at this juncture was try to make things better. He couldn't have her, but there was no reason why he couldn't make her life more comfortable.

TWO WEEKS PASSED before Lucien gave himself permission to seek Charlotte out. Alone in the manor, he found himself wandering from room to empty room now that Wylder and Simon had returned to town ahead of him. The three men did not speak about the night of the Nichols ball, nor of Lucien's desire to provide for Charlotte's future. His friends simply nodded in agreement, imparted a few words of advice, and offered brotherly embraces when they departed just three days before.

The day was bright, sunny, and quite warm for late spring as Lucien rode away from Ashcroft Manor on one of his favorite geldings. His first stop was Hollyhock Cottage.

The cottage was unoccupied, other than a few workers who were finishing up the repairs Lucien had promised would be made. Two days, they told him. Two more days and they would be done. Satisfied with the progress there, he continued on to the location of the new vicar's home.

The plot of land where it was being built was much closer to the village than Hollyhock Cottage. Lucien decided during the planning process that the new vicar should be near his flock. He doubted Mr. Russell would mind but Lucien hadn't yet advised the man of his new address. He wanted to be sure the home would be close to completion before he shared the news. Relief washed over him when the carpenters assured him the home would be ready in less than two weeks. The men had been working practically non-stop, spurred by the promise of hefty bonuses but the rapid progress was still nothing less than amazing.

From there, Lucien continued to Mrs. Merriweather's home. He could wait no longer to share with Charlotte what he had done. Hope that she would accept his gift saw him clenching his hands tighter on the reins, sending the gelding prancing along the path as he fought the bit.

Riding up to Mrs. Merriweather's modest home, Lucien slowed his pace and allowed the horse to delicately pick its way along the small dirt pathway. From the road, he saw the elderly lady where she stood in her elaborate garden. Faith was beside her, watching as the woman leaned on her cane and called out instructions to Mr. Mackie. The gardener used a pair of shears, clipping the rhododendron bushes into pretty, mounded bushes.

"May I ask you to trim the jasmine vines as well, Mr. Mackie?" Mrs. Merriweather asked the older man, her tone warm and more friendly than Lucien could have ever imagined. "The ones over the garden arbor have grown so heavy, I fear the structure might collapse.

"Of course, Mrs. Merriweather," Mr. Mackie responded. "Aye, those vines have a way of overpowering things, they do."

The jingling of the gelding's bridle caught Faith's attention first. Shielding her eyes in the morning sun, she watched as

Lucien approached and squealed with excitement when she recognized him.

"Lord Ashcroft!" Faith called out, waving a hand in greeting. Her pretty face was wreathed in smiles and Lucien felt his heart tighten with affection for the young girl. Surprisingly, he had missed her and her bright, cheerful manner. He even missed the curious and inane questions she asked him about a variety of subjects. His household staff missed her and Charlotte as well. He had come across Mrs. Phillips sniffling over her tea more than once and had overheard Cook lamenting the fact Faith had not come to the manor once since Charlotte moved them back to their cottage.

Lucien prayed his actions would change that. He wanted the two girls to come visit the estate as often as they liked in the future.

Before Faith could run to greet him, however, Mrs. Merriweather tugged her close. Whatever the lady whispered in her ear made Faith laugh in outright delight. Nodding in agreement, Faith restrained herself and solicitously offered her arm as the woman shuffled toward him. She used her cane for balance, but Lucien bit his lip in amusement, remembering she also used it as an instrument to whack a fellow's shins.

Swinging down from the gelding's back, he met them just outside the front steps to the widow's home.

"Good morning, Mrs. Merriweather. Faith." Lucien bowed at the waist. "You both look as pretty as a bouquet of tulips on this beautiful morning."

"Bah," Mrs. Merriweather scoffed. "You may turn the heads of young women, but I know better than that."

"Thank you, Lord Ashcroft." Faith grinned, dipping a pretty curtsey that was ruined by the thick mud on her slippers. "I'm young enough to enjoy my head being turned." Cocking her head, she mused, "Do you think we might grow tulips at Hollyhock Cottage? How pretty it would be… rows upon rows of all colors of tulips."

"We should investigate that possibility. I shall ask Mr. Mackie to look into it. I've just come from the cottage. I'm pleased to see the numerous repairs have moved along much quicker than I anticipated. Indeed, they tell me they will be completely done two days from now."

Faith's features fell and Lucien felt a twinge of shame. He'd kept it a secret that he would be gifting the cottage to Charlotte. He wanted to surprise her. To see her beautiful, bright blue eyes light up with relief and happiness when she realized there was no reason to leave Ashcroft Village. She and Faith could live in Hollyhock Cottage for the rest of their lives if they wanted to.

"Oh," Faith said, her tone curiously downtrodden. "That's good news, I suppose. Charlotte was afraid she and Mr. Russell would have to stay at the inn when they return from their trip."

Lucien's fists tightened on the bridle's reins. "What the devil are you talking about, Faith? What trip?"

Mrs. Merriweather peered up at him from beneath the brim of her overly large bonnet. "Don't you know she's set to marry the new vicar? No other choice, really. Not if she wants to remain in Ashcroft Village. She does love this place dearly, so it certainly makes sense."

Lucien wondered if he was the only one who felt the world was swirling about too fast. Dizziness assailed him and to counter it, he leaned his shoulder against the solid mass of the gelding. His blood was freezing cold in his veins as comprehension slammed him.

Charlotte had agreed to marry Earnest Russell? This could only be a terrible joke. Charlotte could not marry the vicar. She couldn't. Especially now that there was no need for such drastic measures. Not after he'd taken necessary steps of ensuring his little siren could live her life just as she pleased. There was no reason she must give herself to a man she did not love simply to remain in the home she adored.

When he could finally speak, the words came out in a hoarse croak. "May I see her, please? There is so much I must explain to her." Something hot and uncomfortable was spreading through his body. Regret. Shame. Anger at himself for not following his heart and making her his own. He'd fought an internal battle for weeks now, resisting the urge to go to her. He'd been so sure he could prove himself to be selfless and considerate but it had backfired. Not only had he lost her, but she would wed another unless he explained what he had done and why. "Please, tell her I'm here and must speak with her privately."

He had never experienced real terror before, but it swamped him now, closing his throat until he was breathless.

Mrs. Merriweather shrugged while Faith dipped her head and scuffed the dirt with the toe of her slipper.

"She's not here, Your Lordship. The vicar picked her up some time ago," the widow said nonchalantly. "Driving a rented carriage from the village, he was."

"Wh-where were they going?" Lucien's voice cracked and at the sound, Mrs. Merriweather shot him a sharp look before nodding to herself.

"I overheard them saying something about eloping, Your Lordship, but you know, my old ears don't pick up on things as well as they used to. Charlotte did ask that Faith stay here while they were gone, however."

Faith piped up then, her voice high and excited. "Yes, I so wanted to go but Charlotte said it was hardly something a young girl like me should be involved with." Giving him a bright smile, she added, "I know they were headed for Hickory Hill first. Charlotte said she wanted to speak to her friend."

"It's at least a four-day carriage ride to Gretna Green from here." Lucien scowled, swinging himself up into the saddle and gathering the reins. He had no doubt he could overtake them before they reached Hickory Hill but there was also no time to waste. He didn't even ask pertinent questions… things such as did Charlotte pack appropriately for the cooler temperature of Scotland? Was the rented carriage an open one or closed? Did they have any sort of provisions to make the trip easier? And did they have the money required for such travel? Perhaps those were the reasons for stopping at Hickory Hill… Charlotte could ask Joanna Nichols for those things and her new friend would certainly do all she could to assist.

And then there was the issue of robbers who preyed upon travelers when they ventured into the less populated areas of England. Did Earnest Russell have a gun? Did the man even know how to shoot a gun, and would he do so if necessary for Charlotte's protection?

"I cannot believe you allowed her to do something so very foolish, Mrs. Merriweather," Lucien said accusingly, his jaw clenching when the widow laughed and waved a hand in airy dismissal of his anger.

"I've no control over the girl, that's for sure. I told her before that she could live with me for as long as she likes. She and Faith are the daughters I never had, and I love them both dearly. But Charlotte refused my offer, stubborn, headstrong chit that she is." Mrs. Merriweather's silver head cocked to the side as she watched Lucien with amused, blue eyes. "Do you think you can catch them before they get very far, Your Lordship?"

"I know I will." Lucien whirled the horse about. "And Miss Windsor and I will definitely be working some issues out once I get my hands on her."

As he galloped down the lane, he heard Faith shouting behind him.

"Good luck, Lord Ashcroft! Good luck! And give Charlotte a kiss from me when you catch her!"

CHAPTER TWENTY-EIGHT

Charlotte

"Do you suppose the poor creature has rested long enough?" Earnest asked, his voice high with concern.

Charlotte rubbed the horse's muzzle and crooned softly to it. "I think she'll be all right now." She glanced at Earnest and found him standing a bit closer than she would like. Sidling away, she gave him a friendly smile. "Perhaps Lord Nichols would be inclined to loan us a horse when we are ready to return to Ashcroft. We could tie this one to the back of the carriage rather than expect him to pull us both."

"That's an excellent idea, Charlotte. How clever you are."

Charlotte stroked the horse's mane, ruffling the thick, auburn mass with her fingers. It sighed and leaned toward her, its head dipping low and its bottom lip protruding as it proceeded to take an impromptu nap. The poor thing. It was one of the oldest horses Charlotte had ever witnessed pulling a carriage. It was despicable that the stables in town still rented the mare out for that purpose. She determined that she would have a stern talk with the stable owner. "Then we agree that we walk the rest of the way to Hickory Hill?"

"I suppose we should. My apologies for this mishap, Charlotte," Earnest said, his manner sheepish. "Mr. Lander assured me she was quite sound. I guess he was wrong."

"Oh, she's sound. She's just not suitable for pulling a carriage with two riders." Charlotte waved her hand and glanced at her slippers. They were unsuitable for walking but there was no other choice open now. "Don't worry. I don't mind walking. I'm quite fond of it, actually. Besides, it's such a beautiful morning and the weather is quite pleasant. We shall be there in no time."

"I, for one, am looking forward to a tall glass of lemonade once we arrive. Perhaps we will be offered a bit of lunch as well," Earnest mused absently, squinting at something in the distance. Whatever it was raced across an open, rolling meadow which lay diagonal to their location in the middle of the road. "I say, that's rather odd."

"What is it?" Charlotte stood on her tiptoes, watching the figure as it drew closer. A few seconds passed and it became apparent it was a man on horseback. He was bent over and nearly parallel with his mount's neck, the horse's thick mane whipping in the rider's face. Their speed was evident in the clumps of dirt and grass that flew up from under its flying hooves and when the pair encountered a low, stacked stone wall, they sailed over as if it were no higher than a dandelion. The sound of the horse's hard gallop thundered in the quiet stillness of the morning and Charlotte's skin prickled with awareness.

It can't possibly be…

"Dear heavens… I do believe Lord Ashcroft is riding that horse at breakneck speed. Whatever could be the reason for such haste?" Earnest asked, his eyebrows shooting up so high they nearly disappeared into his hairline. "I pray there has not been an emergency of some sort."

"I hope not as well," Charlotte said, abruptly anxious. Fear that something might have happened to Faith squashed any fanciful idea that the earl was coming for her. There was surely a practical reason for his actions… all of which would be explained within a matter of seconds since Lord Ashcroft rode his horse as though the very devils of hell nipped at his heels.

Upon reaching them, Lucien pulled the gelding up short at

the last minute. A fine shower of dust settled over Earnest while Charlotte wisely shielded herself from the worst of it by ducking behind the carriage and the mare.

Lucien slid from the back of his horse before it even came to a stop. The gelding neighed with excitement at seeing another horse but the mare simply heaved out a sigh, cocked her back hoof, and continued dozing in the warm, morning sun.

"My dear Lord Ashcroft, whatever is the matter?" Earnest asked while slapping at the layer of dust now covering his suit coat.

"Is it Faith?" Charlotte asked the wild-eyed earl. His gaze had not left her form and beneath his sense of urgency, Charlotte recognized his fear. It sent her own spiking higher. "Please tell me she is all right."

Lucien clenched the reins of his horse tight in one hand. "Faith is fine. She's not the reason I've come…" A strange look crossed his face as he shook his head in denial of his own words. "I mean, she's part of the reason but not the reason you must think."

Charlotte's head tilted as she stared at Lucien. "I don't understand what that means. Why are you here, Lord Ashcroft, if not to inform us of some manner of emergency?"

"Why are you here?" Lucien shot back and Charlotte blinked at the fury in his voice. Confusion made her eyebrows knit together as she studied the earl. Perhaps he was inebriated. It wouldn't be the first time she'd encountered this man in a state of drunkenness in the middle of the road.

"If you must know, Lord Ashcroft, we are on our way to Hickory Hill. Mr. Russell thought it would be a nice gesture to—"

"Don't marry him, Charlotte. There's no need for it… for the love of God, I'm begging you not to go through with it," Lucien interrupted in a fierce hiss, raking a hand through his dark hair as he glared at them both.

When he abruptly dropped his hands to his sides and clenched them into fists, Charlotte was instantly reminded of the night she'd snuck into his room. She remembered how his gently rough hands explored her body and how hers had explored him until he had clutched at the bed sheets. It made her remember how much she had loved being in control of this man… even if that control was a simple illusion never to repeat itself. When she blushed at the memory, Lucien's gaze ignited. He pinned her to the spot with blazing green eyes, his jaw clenching tight, and she knew he was remembering that night as well.

"Marry *me*…?" Earnest repeated in confusion, his tranquil brown eyes lighting up with hope. "Well, that is the hope, of course. Unfortunately, Charlotte's decision depends on what happens at Hickory Hill."

Charlotte's chin tilted, wishing that the vicar would be quiet. "This is something that does not concern you, Lord Ashcroft."

"The hell it doesn't," Lucien cried out. "At the very least, you should be better prepared for an elopement to Gretna Green. An open carriage and a nag that looks as though it cannot take another step without collapsing is hardly a good plan."

"Elopement?" Charlotte sucked in a breath of shock. "I… we… this is not an elopement, my lord."

"Mrs. Merriweather informed me of your plans… that you were headed for Hickory Hill then eloping from there. Are you saying that's not true?" He began pacing like a wild man, the gelding taking a few steps in time with the earl until finally the creature gave up and stood in one place.

"Of course it's not true. I don't know why Mrs. Merriweather would deceive you in such a manner. She is obviously con-fused…" Charlotte began but Lucien abruptly cut her off.

"Faith confirmed it. Was she confused as well?"

"Then obviously they were having a bit of fun at your ex-pense," Charlotte said calmly although her stomach clenched with nervousness. She gave Earnest an unsteady smile of regret and continued. "I've not yet accepted Earnest's proposal of marriage so there is no immediate need to travel to Scotland. We are headed for Hickory Hill so that Earnest may meet some of his new congregation outside of Ashcroft's immediate vicinity… as my father did when he was vicar. He asked if I would accompany him, and I agreed since I have business to discuss with Lady Joanna Nichols regarding a governess position her friend's cousin may have."

"Where is this position? London? Or somewhere close to Ashcroft?" Lucien's expression was suddenly hopeful only to apparently have his hopes dashed by Charlotte's reply.

"No, it is a position through a cousin of Lady Downing that resides in Hexham. The position is there. If it's still available, I most likely will take it. If not, then…" Charlotte shrugged, glancing at Earnest who immediately puffed out his chest, proud that he was still being considered as a viable option.

"Hexham in Northumberland?" Lucien appeared beside himself with agitation as he gaped at her in disbelief. "*That* Hexham?

"Is there another Hexham?" Charlotte frowned in confusion. What on earth was going on here? Why was Lucien so distraught that she was considering a move to Hexham? And why was he roaming about the countryside weeks after hiring Earnest for the vicar's position? Shouldn't he have returned to London by now and gleefully resumed his degenerate activities with his fellow Rakehells?

"Damnit, Charlotte, you don't have to marry the vicar, and you don't have to move to the wilderness of England for a governess position," Lucien cursed, coming forward to lightly grip her shoulders in his hands. "You don't have to do anything you don't wish to do. I am giving you Hollyhock Cottage. Yes, giving it to you. You may use it as long as you like and dispose of it how you like. It's yours."

"And where shall I live, my lord?" Earnest chimed in with a perplexed scowl. "That is to say, where shall I live if Charlotte rejects my proposal? Which she hasn't yet done, if I may be so bold as to point out the obvious."

"That's true. I've not committed one way or the other, although there are many reasons I should marry Earnest," Charlotte said softly. "And only one to say no."

Lucien did not even look at the man. His gaze burned Charlotte's as he answered. "Under my direction, a separate cottage for Mr. Russell has been under construction for the last two weeks and will be completed shortly. Hollyhock Cottage is yours, Charlotte, if you want it. Yours and Faith's. No ties. No obligations. No strings. It is yours."

Charlotte gasped in surprise at Lucien's unexpected generosity, her heart expanding with the possibilities of remaining in the cottage she loved, in the village she called home without the need to shackle herself to Earnest. It seemed too good to be true.

"You don't have to marry him, Charlotte… please do not marry this man." Lucien's voice lowered, his emotions crystalizing in a display of anguish, desperation and adoration as he took Charlotte's hands in his. He kissed the tips of her gloved fingers, then pulled the articles away. He pressed her hands to his chest, ensuring that she could feel how rapidly his heart pounded. His eyes softened even as an internal battle appeared to take place within him. His jaw tightened as the war escalated until finally, he glanced heavenward for guidance then settled his gaze on Charlotte once more. His emerald eyes sparkled with resolve. "I can no longer fight this or even myself and there can be only one outcome to this situation." He sucked in a breath, held it, then said in rush, "Marry me instead, Charlotte."

"That's impossible, Lucien. Impossible. Ridiculous. Absurd." Charlotte could not bring herself to pull her hands away. She wanted more than anything to melt against him. She had missed this man with a pain and anguish that had no words and expressed itself in a jumble of emotions that left her careening from one feeling to the next. "I've no family connections… no dowry…" A self-deprecating laugh escaped her. "I've not even been presented at court. You cannot possibly be serious about this…"

"I don't care about any of that." Lucien dropped his forehead to hers, sighing with heavy contentment at having her so close once more. "I have lived in absolute misery for the last two weeks without you, little siren. I have missed you to the point of madness. I have spent my nights roaming the halls of Ashcroft Manor as if I were a ghost, remembering the time you were there. And I have looked for your face in every cloud, every ray of sunshine, every flower that blooms, and in the raindrops of an evening shower. I want you to be my wife; however, I also love you enough to give you freedom to make your own decision. But I'm also selfish enough to hope you choose me. And if you do, my family will become your family. My parents will adore you and you don't need a damn dowry to become my wife. I'm rich as Midas and don't need a woman's money to add to my fortune. Everything that is mine will also be yours. All I want… all I *need* is the chance to make you happy for the rest of your life. To keep you safe and to grant your every wish. Your every desire." He paused, kissing the tip of her nose and swiping the tears away from her cheeks with the pad of his thumb. "Choose me, Charlotte. End my endless misery of being without you and marry me. I love you so much, and I swear before God, that you will not be sorry."

Charlotte wavered, searching the depths of his green eyes for the truth of his words. What she saw there burst the walls around her heart. She slowly nodded, a helpless laugh ringing out. "You are a scoundrel and a rake and hopelessly, terribly arrogant, but I love you as well, Lucien. Yes. Yes, I will marry you."

The moment her words registered, Lucien swore beneath his breath and claimed her mouth in a bruising kiss that left no doubt as to how much he had missed her. Then he swept her up off her feet, his arms wrapped tight about her waist. He swung her around in a dizzying circle in the middle of the dusty road until Charlotte squealed in delight.

Earnest watched in silent astonishment, mouth agape at this unexpected turn of events. Then a wry smile twisted his pleasant features as he addressed the couple frantically kissing one another without a care to their surroundings. "As the newly appointed vicar of Ashcroft Village, my lord, it would be my honor to perform the marriage ceremony. In fact, I insist upon it as my first official duty."

CHAPTER TWENTY-NINE

Lady Charlotte Kathleen Windsor Westley, Countess of Ashcroft and too many titles to humbly list

One month and one week later
Ashcroft Manor, Lincolnshire

"I CANNOT WAIT to get this gown off you, Lady Ashcroft," Lucien whispered in her ear as the first course of the wedding breakfast was served. "If only you had allowed me to obtain a special license rather than following the inane practice of posting the banns, I'd be buried inside you right now in the privacy of our room." He paused, glancing around the room, then continued under his breath, "Instead of sitting at this table with people I have no desire to see unclothed."

Charlotte blushed, squeezing her husband's hand beneath the edge of the table. Her gaze flitted down the length of the table to where the Duchess of Westley, Lucien's mother and now her new mother-in-law, smiled indulgently at the bridal couple. Truth be told, she had second guessed her own insistence that the brief engagement should follow society's rules. Based on her own wishes, the banns were posted for three weeks at the church and then there were two weeks of preparation for the intimate ceremony today. "Please behave yourself, dear husband."

"How can I when I want to kiss every inch of your body and worship it in the way it should be worshipped?" He grinned with unapologetic desire, his hand escaping her grip to slide over the material of her gown. His fingers closed over her knee. "I want to see my beautiful bride naked and ready for me to show her pleasures she's only dreamed of."

"And I would like to see my husband exercise just a bit of patience." She giggled softly then quietly shushed him, sitting up straighter as Lucien's father rose from his chair at the opposite end of the table. Lucien's hand would not budge however, so Charlotte gave up and accepted that he would touch her if that's what he wished.

The duke clinked his glass with a knife and cleared his throat as the small gathering of guests grew quiet.

"The duchess and I are ecstatic to welcome our new daughter-in-law to the Westley family. We are blessed that such an intelligent, beautiful, graceful young woman said yes to our son's proposal of marriage. She is truly a gift." His Grace laughed softly, giving Lucien and Charlotte a wide smile. "Indeed, she is a gift to our entire family. So, I lift my glass and say with heartfelt emotions, congratulations to the new couple. Lady Westley and I wish you many years of happiness together."

The entire table burst out into salutations of best wishes and long life. Even Simon and Wylder, who once were firmly opposed to Lucien's ever taking a wife, cheered loudly with exuberance. Faith, unable to contain her excitement, jumped up from her chair beside Mrs. Merriweather and ran to Charlotte. Throwing her arms around her sister's neck, she said, "I'm so very happy His Lordship's moral turpitude could be fixed, and you were able to marry him, Charlotte."

Lucien cocked his head as he regarded his young sister-in-law. "What does that even mean, Faith?"

The guests who had arrived for the ceremony that morning and the subsequent breakfast all began to rise from the table, chattering amongst themselves. The celebration would continue in the ballroom with dancing and games, but Charlotte knew Lucien had no intention of their attending that portion of the wedding festivities. Indeed, he'd already whispered some of his plans for her and they made her cheeks flush red and certain parts of her body tingle with anticipation.

Charlotte squeezed her sister hard. She was overcome with love at this moment, surrounded by all those who had become so dear to her. Catching sight of Mr. and Mrs. Phillips standing near the double doors of the dining room, she smiled in return when the housekeeper gave her a wink.

Then she kissed her new husband on the cheek and murmured, "I'll explain Faith's inappropriate comment later."

Lucien's smile glowed with promises of pleasure. "I look forward to it, wife. Now, let us make our exit."

Faith leaned back in Charlotte's embrace, frowning with confusion as she glanced at Lucien. "But, my lord, you and Charlotte aren't leaving for London until the day after tomorrow. That's when the honeymoon begins. Right, Charlotte?"

"That is true. But the earl and I would like a bit of quiet time with one another before then, dearest," Charlotte said as Lucien stood and drew her up beside him in preparation for their departure. "You may stay at the dance this morning as long as you like, but no more than two pieces of cake, agreed? Now, go on. Mrs. Phillips will look after you." She pressed an affectionate kiss to the top of her sister's golden head and shook a finger in mock admonishment. "And Faith? I expect you to be an absolute angel while we are gone."

Faith scampered away, pausing to say something to Mrs. Merriweather who was being escorted from the dining room by Simon. The elderly lady blew a kiss to Charlotte and gave the earl a beaming smile. "I shall expect a note expressing your gratitude in ensuring this wedding took place, Lord Ashcroft. All it took was a little push in the right direction to get things moving."

"I THOUGHT WE would never get away from them all," Lucien said, pulling Charlotte back against his hard body. Nuzzling her nape which was exposed by the elegant coiffure, he pressed a series of warm kisses to the skin there. His arms wrapped around her slender waist, holding her tight. "God, this past month has been torture. Seeing you and not being able to touch you like I want to… it's been hell."

"It has been the same for me, Lucien." She sighed in contentment as he nibbled the back of her neck. "I thought about sneaking into your room so many times but worried I would get caught."

Lucien's laughter was softly dangerous. It made Charlotte shiver. "I owe you for the little stunt you pulled that night. A punishment for driving me half out of my mind."

"What kind of punishment?" Charlotte asked, her interest piqued by his words. She wasn't frightened. No, not all. Lucien had already spoken of the things he wanted to do with her, the many ways he would give her pleasure while gaining pleasure himself. His explanations and descriptions excited her, leaving her feeling as though she might explode with lustful thoughts. She knew he would not harm her, although he had assured her there were moments when it would certainly be uncomfortable.

"Hmmm… I believe a spanking to be an excellent start. What do you think?" He hummed in her ear then gently bit the lobe, tugging at the drop pearl earrings he'd given her as a wedding gift with his teeth.

"Yes, my lord." Charlotte smiled. Moving quickly, she removed the pins from the upsweep of her hair, allowing it to fall in golden waves over her shoulders and down her back.

"Call me by my name, Charlotte. Remember?" His fingers began working on the pearl buttons of her pale-blue gown. Once they were undone, he helped her push the dress down until it landed in a pool at her feet. A moment later, his warm hands were skimming over the flare of her hips, caressing her bottom beneath the hem of her chemise. He squeezed one rounded cheek then stepped back. "Unlace your stays, little siren."

Glancing over her shoulder, she saw Lucien quickly unwinding his ascot and throwing off his coat. When Charlotte's fingers fumbled at the sight of his broad chest, his upper body now without his tailored shirt, he gave her an encouraging smile and turned her to face him. He kissed her hands, drawing her attention to the sparkling sapphire ring he had slipped onto her finger as they exchanged their vows. The large stone was set in a halo of diamonds, and its brilliant fire caught every ray of light and reflected it.

"The exact color of your eyes, little siren," he'd murmured as Earnest Russell read scripture and began blessing their union. "I look forward to seeing you wearing nothing but this ring and my kisses when I truly make you my wife." And Charlotte had blushed such a fiery shade of scarlet, she was sure her cheeks must be permanently stained.

The beautiful ring was worth a fortune, she was sure, and just one of the many gifts Lucien had given her over the last few weeks of their engagement. Even Hollyhock Cottage was hers although she still had not decided what its future use should be. A library for the village, maybe. Or a tea house. She decided she would discuss those possibilities at a later date with her new husband.

"Do not be afraid, my sweet, little wife. I shall be so gentle with you this first time when we make love," he murmured, regaining her full attention while taking over with the removal of her half-stays and the silk chemise she wore beneath it.

Charlotte shivered as she stood naked before him, wearing only gossamer thin stockings tied with pale-blue ribbons and her wedding ring while Lucien still wore trousers and shoes.

"And what if I cannot be gentle with you?" she asked with a sly smile.

Lucien laughed in delight. "You don't have to be." Taking her by the hand, he pulled her toward the bed. The room was softly lit with golden sunshine that streamed in filtered swaths through the window's half-opened drapes. It was a sumptuously appointed space, the furnishings luxurious and richly carved. Charlotte took it all in now. The night she'd sneaked inside to pleasure him, she been so focused on Lucien that she'd not noticed much of anything else.

Sitting on the bed, he pulled her into his lap and cradled her face in his hands. "Do you trust me, Charlotte? You promised to love me. To obey me. To honor me. But I want to know if you trust me."

"With my life," she answered simply.

"Then bend over my lap, siren. Let me show you how a punishment can also be pleasurable." When she was arranged to his liking, Lucien smoothed a hand over the globes of her buttocks. "You are so smooth. So goddamn soft. And soon, this pretty white skin will be pink from the palm of my hand. Are you ready to begin, wife? You will count out the strikes as I administer them."

"Yes, Lucien," Charlotte said in a husky voice. She couldn't help but squirm in this position, anticipating the strike of his hand on her tender skin. And she still was not afraid. She was aroused by the primal aspect of Lucien's intentions. Curious and eager to become part of his world in a way no other woman ever would. She was his wife. His. And as much as she belonged to him, he belonged to her as well.

"I love you, Charlotte. You are my very life. You know that, right?" His voice contained a note of hesitation. As if he worried her devotion was a fleeting thing and unable to withstand the darkness of his desires.

Charlotte wiggled on his lap, deliberately letting her body rub against his massive erection. "I know. I love you more, Lucien."

"Not possible." He huffed out a laugh then his palm connected with her bottom, causing her to gasp in shock at the thrilling sting. "That's for sneaking into my room that night… and I do not hear you counting."

"One," she murmured obediently.

He struck again and she practically melted into his lap. "That's for driving me half mad while you sucked my cock."

"Two," she said, trying to analyze how it was possible that the slight pain morphed into a glow that settled between her legs and made her ache.

Another resounding strike and Charlotte found her arms and legs were limp and as useless as a ragdoll even while her body roared for more.

"That's for leaving me the next morning and making me believe you hated me."

"Three." Her voice wavered. Experimentally, she rolled her hips, the motion causing the tips of her breasts to rub against the material of his trousers. They began to throb in the same manner as her bottom. "Oh, God."

"I think my little siren likes her spanking," Lucien crooned, smoothing his hand across the fiery flesh of her bottom. When his hand slipped between her legs and teased her for several long moments, she wondered if her bones were melting. Fingers pinched the tiny bundle of nerves there before one long forefinger sank into her opening, plunging slowly until Charlotte thought she might lose her mind from how wonderful it felt. "I think she wants more than my hand on her bare arse. She wants my fingers exploring her body. My tongue sweeping over her sweet nipples. My cock deep inside her tight little cunny as I fuck her for the first time. Is that what my wife wants?"

"Yes, Lucien. Please." Charlotte knew how she sounded. Breathless and desperate. Willing to give herself to him completely.

He spanked her again, this one harder than the others, his finger still embedded and plunging inside her with devious purpose. Charlotte squeezed her eyes tight as the euphoria swelled like a tidal wave. "Four!" The word came out in a plaintive wail of desire.

"That was for making me so goddamn greedy for you that I cannot even properly dole out a simple punishment," Lucien growled in a husky voice as he lifted her up from his lap and laid her across the bed. Within seconds he had stripped off the rest of his clothes and settled between her thighs. "We'll do this in many different positions over the coming hours, Charlotte, but for this first time, I want to see your face as I make love to you. I want to share the moment you reach your climax with my cock buried inside you." Taking his shaft in his hand, he guided it to her wet folds and rubbed himself there, coating his member with the silkiness of her arousal. "You are so wet already. That pleases me, wife. *You* please me." Bending his head, he gently took one of her nipples inside the heat of his mouth, rolling the tight bud around with his teeth before nipping her.

Charlotte moaned in blissful agony, arching toward him as he guided himself inside her. She looped her arms around his neck, closing her eyes. The pain was distracting, her body rejecting the inevitable invasion, but Lucien was patient. He withdrew a fraction, then pressed forward a little more each time, groaning when she tightened around him.

"You feel so good, little wife. So tight and snug around me. Let me in just a bit more, my darling love. Open your legs a bit wider. Yes, that's it. Good girl," he whispered in his rough voice, his hands anchoring her hips and holding her steady. Then he was surging inside her and while the sharp pain took her breath away for a moment, Charlotte knew pleasure would soon follow.

"Steady, love. Steady." Lucien's breath expelled in short, panting bursts, and his eyes closed as if sharing Charlotte's pain. "That's it, be still for a moment so you can adjust to me. I'm sorry… I know it hurts. But this is the only time it will feel like this. I promise you."

Charlotte did as Lucien instructed. She lay motionless, listening and feeling his heart pounding against hers, his skin warm and damp with a fine sheen of sweat, his breathing harsh as he restrained his own movements until she was ready. And after a few moments, her body felt as though it had come alive. Her skin tingled, her nerve endings lighting up and her breathing increasing as she trembled. She wanted to flex her hips, to move, but she remained perfectly still, exhilarating in this new experience. It was so beautiful that she wanted to weep for some unknown reason. Her tongue darted out, moistening her lips and that was the invitation Lucien was waiting for.

"There she is. There's my good girl," Lucien muttered, kissing her with such fierceness that her heart pounded in her chest until she was lightheaded. "I can feel your body coming alive around me, Charlotte. God, it's almost more than I can bear." His cock twitched inside her but other than that, he still did not move. He was waiting on her to say yes.

"Lucien?" Her head tilted back, exposing her throat to him and Lucien groaned again, his hand coming up to lightly encircle it. "Show me what paradise looks like. Show me what it means to be yours for eternity."

"Anything for you, little siren." He began moving then, sliding in and out of her with ease, going deeper with each thrust. "Hold on to me while I take you to the stars."

Charlotte kissed him, her arms tightening around him, refusing to let go. And when the world exploded and the pleasure was almost more than she could take, Lucien was there to guide her back down to earth. She held on as he rocked against her, driving harder and faster, his movement less precise than before and more erratic.

"Fuck, I'm going to come, Charlotte," he rasped, his fingers tightening around her throat. "I wanted this to last, but you are too beautiful. Too warm and soft. God, you are perfect. My little siren. My little wife. My love." His admission immediately threw Charlotte's body into a tailspin, a second orgasm taking her by surprise as he slammed into her with almost animalistic grunts of pleasure. Then, his body stiffened, his beautiful face contorted with the throes of desire. Warmth flooded her as his release coated her insides.

Charlotte's body shook as Lucien gathered her close, his hips now rocking lazily against hers as he helped her ride out her climax while his own subsided.

"I had no idea it would be like that," Charlotte whispered,

tears wetting her cheeks as emotions overwhelmed her. "It was amazing. Is it always like that, Lucien?"

"It's only like that with someone you love, Charlotte. And when the other rakehells figure this out, they will be just as hopelessly entranced as I am," Lucien breathed, his warm breath stirring her hair.

"Will you miss being a rakehell?" Charlotte asked the question that had nagged her since agreeing to marry Lucien. "Your friendships with Lord Camden and Lord Wyldewood will change now. I worry you will discover you resent that."

"They are my closest friends, but I will never choose them or anyone else over you, Charlotte. Never." He kissed her forehead, then rolled to his back so that she ended up sprawled on top of him. His cock was still embedded in her channel, and it stirred with renewed vigor. "Once you have somewhat recovered, I think we should take a bath. I want to see you with your legs spread on either side of the tub so I can lick every inch of you clean. Then I have a few different positions to show you that I'm pretty sure you will love. One involves placing you on your hands and knees so I can fuck you from behind."

Charlotte sucked in a breath, scandalized by the images Lucien painted but her body responded even as her veins throbbed with shameful eagerness. "Lucien!"

He laughed because he knew he'd shocked her and curled his hand around the nape of her neck. "I cannot wait to spend the rest of my life shocking you, corrupting you, and loving you, Lady Ashcroft. You are my everything. Mine forever if you let me keep you."

She stared down into his brilliant green eyes, overcome with love for this redeemed rakehell. "I won't allow you to let me go, Lucien. I will love you to the end of my days."

Lucien's eyes softened. "I love you more."

"Imposs—" Charlotte's protest was cut off as Lucien claimed her mouth.

"Don't argue with your husband, little siren," he said sternly when he finally let her breathe. Charlotte smiled and nodded, tangling her fingers in his hair and leaning down so their mouths could melt together in another heated kiss.

"Fine. I'll let you win this time, Your Lordship."

EPILOGUE

One month later
London

SIMON SIGHED HEAVILY, rubbing his forehead in frustration. Wylder sat opposite of him in a matching club chair. White's, the premier gentlemen's club in London, was packed with other men like the two of them. Men searching for distractions from the endless round of balls, parties, and musicales of London society.

"It's not the same without him, Wylder, and you know it." Simon's voice vibrated with the aggravation young, spoiled lords like himself experienced when matters took an unexpected turn. "We're like a statue that's suddenly missing a leg. It still stands, but it's just not the same."

"I've never seen someone so in love as Lucien is with Charlotte. He fucking adores her," Wylder said glumly. "It's quite depressing."

"I know. But this only means we must stay diligent if we are serious when it comes to retaining our rakehell status. The women coming out of the woodwork, thinking we will fall like Lucien, is astounding. It's becoming a hazardous activity just attending a simple ball lately. Even my own sister has stars in her eyes when it comes to seeing me married off. She's convinced it's her duty to pair me with one of her simpering, vapid friends."

Wylder studied the brandy in his glass, his eyes darkening at the mention of Simon's younger sister. "Maybe we should—" He began only to have Simon cut him off.

"Don't even think it, Wylder. There may only be two of us, but the Rakehells of Mayfair will not go down in flames. We owe it to ourselves and to Lucien to continue doing the things we enjoy." Simon's eyes hardened, thinking of the fiery lecture his father bombasted him with that very morning. There was even a half-hearted but foolish threat to banish Simon to the country if it meant he would end up marrying a wonderful woman like Charlotte Windsor.

"I was only about to suggest a new gambling den I thought we might try. We could go tonight." Wylder shrugged his shoulders. "They have comfort women there as well. Perhaps a new place, new experiences, will bring us out of the doldrums we find ourselves in since Lucien and Charlotte married."

"That's an excellent idea," Simon replied enthusiastically. Raising his glass, he leaned toward his friend. "So, are you ready to show our fathers and all of London that the Rakehells will not be controlled or ruled?"

Wylder clinked his glass to Simon's and tossed back the drink with a slight grimace. "I cannot wait. Let's do our worst."

The End

About the Author

April enjoys writing both historical and contemporary/dark romance with a generous splash of heat. When not penning tales of passion, she enjoys traveling with her husband, attending rock concerts with friends, and time spent with family. Brainstorming new storylines is best done while riding her horse or during long walks with her German Shepherd. A tumbler of good whiskey helps tie all the details together and brings her characters to life.

VISIT APRIL'S WEBSITE
www.aprilmoranbooks.com

SIGN UP FOR NEWSLETTER AND UPDATES
http://bit.ly/AprilMoran_BookUpdates
April Moran Book Updates

STALK APRIL EVERYWHERE
facebook.com/AuthorAprilMoran
facebook.com/groups/aprilshoneybees/
bookbub.com/profile/april-moran
instagram.com/aprilmoranbooks
goodreads.com/Author-AprilMoran
pinterest.com/aprilmoranbooks
tiktok.com/@authoraprilmoran

www.ingramcontent.com/pod-product-compliance
Lightning Source LLC
Chambersburg PA
CBHW072115300726
48975CB00003B/815